RULE MASTER

Also by Sienna Snow

Rule Breaker

RULE MASTER

SIENNA SNOW

FOREVER
YOURS

New York Boston

Copyright © 2017 by Sienna Snow
Excerpt from *Rule Changer* copyright © 2017 by Sienna Snow
Cover copyright © 2017 by Hachette Book Group, Inc.

Forever Yours
Hachette Book Group
1290 Avenue of the Americas
New York, NY 10104
forever-romance.com
twitter.com/foreverromance

First published as an ebook and as a print on demand: March 2017

Forever Yours is an imprint of Grand Central Publishing. The Forever Yours name and logo are trademarks of Hachette Book Group, Inc.

The publisher is not responsible for websites (or their content) that are not owned by the publisher.

The Hachette Speakers Bureau provides a wide range of authors for speaking events. To find out more, go to www.hachettespeakersbureau.com or call (866) 376-6591.

ISBN 978-1-4555-6877-2 (print on demand edition)
ISBN 978-1-4555-6878-9 (ebook)

E3-20170124_DANF

To Nishi, for being one of my biggest fans even before I published anything.
To Leah, Lauren, and Iris. You three are what everyone wishes for in best friends.
Last but not least, to Hitesh. Thank you for always supporting me and pushing me to achieve my dreams.

RULE MASTER

CHAPTER ONE

Ms. Castra, once you sign, I can file all the necessary documents."

My fingers gripped my pen as I scanned the forms. The moment I wrote my name on the papers, I'd begin the process of making up for all my mistakes.

The mistakes I'd never have admitted to if I hadn't gone through the terror of the last six months.

But could I do it? Could I end something that started more than ten years ago, something that meant the world to me?

I set my pen down, took a deep breath, and looked up at my assistant, Rachel. Her face told me she wasn't happy with my decision, but would do what I asked.

"You don't have to execute this now. You can wait until you get home, and then decide."

Swallowing the lump in my throat, I pushed back from the patio table and walked to the balcony railing of my family's Italian villa.

Church bells rang in the distance, signaling the end of mass at the *duomo*, the cathedral marking the center of the town's square.

I clutched the balcony railing overlooking the busy streets of the city of my birth, Milan. The summer heat dampened my skin with a light sheen and made me long for the cooler weather in the city of my heart.

Boston.

There I wasn't the rebel daughter of one of Italy's most renowned families, who got into more trouble than necessary. In Boston, I was a well-respected, successful entrepreneur who ran two multinational corporations and had friends who loved me more than my own mother.

I also had…

Lex.

A painful ache clenched my heart. He'd made so many sacrifices for me over the past years; now it was my turn.

He deserves a fresh start, Milla.

Six months ago, the only thing I took seriously in my life was my work. I lived by the motto "work hard, play harder."

My perspective completely changed after I was kidnapped as part of a plot to steal security software my company had developed for the US government. I'd left Boston hoping to forget the pain and devastation in my life, only to learn I couldn't run from my problems. The longer I waited to face them, the more I hurt the one person who meant the world to me.

"Ms. Castra. I need you to tell me what our next steps are."

I released the railing, pushed a strand of hair behind my ear, and turned toward Rachel. Without another word and before I lost my nerve, I walked over to the table, picked up the pen, and signed my name.

"It's done," I whispered, trying to keep the tremor out of my voice.

"I'll take care of contacting your attorney." Rachel gathered the papers and left the terrace.

I let my head and shoulders drop as I settled my hands on the back of my chair.

My fingers went to the collar of my shirt and rested on the necklace underneath. I closed my eyes, and a vision of Lex's piercing blue ones staring back at me appeared. The eyes I'd spent hours looking into. The ones that used to know all my secrets and saw deep inside me to the real Milla. To the girl who was nothing like she appeared in the press.

How was I going to live without him? Without the long talks and laughter or the heated arguments or the feel of his body against mine?

Or the orgasms he pulls from you with the slightest graze of his whip.

I shivered, pushing the last image back. I couldn't go there right now.

The hardest part would be the day when he had someone else by his side. A woman who could give him the pleasure and satisfaction I once had and couldn't anymore.

I wiped a stray tear from my cheek when my phone buzzed in the back pocket of my jeans. I pulled it out and answered.

"Hello."

"Hey there, *mera behna*. I miss you." My heart lightened at the sound of my best friend's voice and the standard Hindi greeting she gave me.

Arya Rey Dane was my sister in everything but blood. We were two girls from completely different backgrounds who became best friends and created the world's first female-founded, billion-dollar technology development firm. Ditching high school was the only thing on our agendas the day we met, and now we couldn't imagine a life without each other.

After an incident during my fifteenth birthday, where a few of my friends and I got drunk and ran half naked through the streets of Milan, my parents decided to teach me a lesson and send me to boarding school. Their biggest mistake was believing that by sending me to a school run by nuns halfway across the globe, I would miss home and start behaving. They should've kept me in Italy, where the nuns are much more hard-core. I got into more trouble in California than I could ever have at any of the convents in Italy.

"I missed you, too," I said, trying to add a cheery tone to my response. I hadn't told Arya of my plans for the future, and I wasn't sure she'd let me go through with them if she knew.

"What's wrong?"

How would she know that I was feeling sad?

"Huh? What makes you think something is up?"

"Well, for one, you responded to my question with a question. Second, your voice gave it away. Third, you didn't answer me with your haughty Italian heiress greeting of '*Pronto*.' You said 'hello.'"

I never used that phrase, and she knew it. It was a running joke between us from when a friend of ours vacationed in Rome and came back educating us on proper Italian etiquette.

"Yes, yes, Miss Genius IQ. I forgot my Italian protocol. I've been hanging out with your half-Indian ass too long."

"My ass is huge right now, and you would know that if you were home. And don't say we video chat, because it isn't the same. I need the deliverer of my chocolate croissants here in Boston with me.

Max doesn't go to the same bakery as you do."

I couldn't help but smile at the joy I heard hidden around the whining. She was finally going to have the family she'd wanted all her life.

Arya had spent five years building herself up following the deterioration of her relationship and devastating loss of her babies. Finally, she had her fairy tale. After reuniting with the love of her life, she was expecting twins again.

"I know, *bella*. I'll be home soon to see the giant whale you've become with those boys."

"I miss you. He misses you."

My breath hitched.

"Why would Max miss me? Isn't he your husband?"

"Don't be a smart-ass." Her voice grew stern.

"I know, Ari. I'll talk to him when I get back." I hesitated for a second. "How is he?"

"How do you expect? He's been with the same woman for a decade, and she left him. Something we still haven't discussed, by the way."

I cringed. I'd avoided any conversation regarding my relationship with Lex, especially the part where I'd kept it a secret and never told her he was the Dom I'd been with for years. Or that he was even more than my Dom.

"Is he…is he…"

Do I want to ask this question or get an answer? It would make my plan easier, but it won't lessen the pain.

"No, he isn't seeing anyone, you moron. For some reason, he loves you and takes the commitment he made to you seriously."

Relief flooded me. "Pregnancy is making you bitchy."

"Yeah, well let me count the ways I am pissed off at the whole lot of you. First, my two best friends lied to me for years, pretending to see different people when they were together the whole time. Surrounding me with overwhelming sexual tension and making me think it was love unfulfilled."

I cringed. "Well there were personal reasons for all of that."

"Second, when I found out they were a couple, they left out a tiny detail that they were more than Dominant and submissive."

"Well, you see…"

"Shut up. I'm not done."

"Sorry, I'll zip it." I motioned with my fingers on my lips and laughed at myself when I realized she couldn't see me.

"Third, my other best friend and sister-in-law, Carmen, has become a complete workaholic and has no time for me. Fourth, I don't have you here to keep me sane while on bed rest and prevent me from killing my overprotective husband. And fifth…" Arya sniffed, and her voice cracked. "I'm scared out of my mind that I'll lose these babies too."

My heart ached for her. She'd been through so much and by some miracle, she was pregnant again. "Don't cry, *mia sorella*. I'll be home soon."

"I'm sorry. I'm just a big, pregnant, hormonal fucking mess."

I shook my head and adjusted my phone to the other ear. "Language! Max is going to kill you if the first word those kids utter is 'fuck' or 'shit.' I thought you were working on your sailor's mouth."

"Whatever," she grumbled. "Try being ten thousand months pregnant and confined to a stupid bed."

I laughed. "You know you love every minute of it."

"I do, but I don't have you to share it with," she whined.

The weight of the previous conversation shifted. Thank goodness, no more talk about Lex or me.

"I'll be home soon and come massage your fat feet and keep you company until my nephews come into the world."

"I'll hold you to it. Okay, I better go before Max finds out I snuck out of the house."

"Why are you sneaking out of the house to call me?"

"Um, you see…"

"Ari," I admonished with a grin.

"I wanted to go baby shopping."

The girl thought she could pull one over me, but I was onto her tactics.

"Not buying that. You hate shopping. What is going on, *bella*?"

"Fine," she muttered. "I snuck out to get chocolate from that shop you took me to in Little Italy. Max said I had to limit my sweets since the doc was worried about my sugar levels. But, Mil, he should know better than to keep a pregnant woman away from her cravings. Oh hell, I think I see his car."

"Don't blame me if you get caught. I'm not the one who ditched her security detail to get a chocolate fix. I was the innocent recipient of your call." I shook my head.

The girl never gave Max a moment of peace, always getting into something or the other.

I grunted to myself. I was one to talk.

"I'll keep you out of it. You're in enough shit with Lex."

"Ari," I exclaimed and then glanced at my watch. "*Merda.* Gotta go. I have to get ready for the ball tonight."

Arya sighed. "Such is the life of an Italian socialite."

"Bite me, Dane."

"Back at you, *Duncan*."

I winced and opened my mouth to respond, but she'd hung up.

Well, that was nice of her to leave it like that. I tucked my phone back into my jeans pocket. I knew the moment she had me alone I was in so much trouble with her. I couldn't blame her for wanting answers.

I stepped away from the balcony area and walked toward the terrace stairs. A second before I crossed the threshold, my sister-in-law Leena reached the top, nearly slamming into me. She was windblown and out of breath.

I grabbed hold of her arms, keeping her steady on her feet. "Whoa, there, pregnant lady. What's going on?"

She put a hand against her chest and then sat down on the nearest chair.

"Milla, you have to be ready." Leena rubbed her temples and tried to steady her breath. "I ran up here as soon as I heard."

This probably had something to do with Mamma; it always had something to do with Mamma.

"Okay, you're scaring me. Please tell me what's going on." I glanced at my watch again. "I'm going to be late if I don't get ready for the gala soon."

Leena grasped my hand and tugged me toward her. "He's here."

Okay, that's a bit dramatic.

"Who's here?" I crouched in front of Leena.

She glanced behind me as a deep voice spoke.

"Your husband. And I'm here to take my wife home."

CHAPTER TWO

My skin prickled as Lex's deep Irish brogue washed over me. I closed my eyes for a moment and then opened them, staring at Leena's shocked face.

"You're married?" she asked me.

"Yes." I nodded.

"For how long?"

"Ten years," Lex answered, drawing Leena's attention to him.

"You kept it from us all these years?" She looked back at me, shaking her head. "I don't understand. Why would you keep this from us? Didn't we deserve to know? Especially Marcello and Dominic?"

I grimaced, hearing the underlying hurt in Leena's question.

"It's complicated," I whispered, not knowing what else to say.

She watched me for a moment, not saying anything, then stood, bringing me up with her.

"Mil, we can't help you with this if you don't let us in." She gave Lex a wary smile over my shoulder. "I'll leave you two alone to talk."

She kissed my forehead and then glared at me, telling me without words that I was in deep shit.

At this moment, thinking about what I was going to tell my family was the least of my worries. All my attention was focused on the man behind me. How would I face him, knowing what I'd signed only fifteen minutes earlier?

This wasn't how it was supposed to happen. I wanted to wait until I was back in Boston. Until I'd found a way to explain why I was breaking both of our hearts.

I stared at the vines growing along the terrace walls.

"Mil. Look at me," Lex ordered, in the liquid-smooth way that made anyone listen, in or out of the courtroom.

A shiver crept up my spine, and I pushed back the urge his mere presence brought forth, the desire to kneel and wait for direction. Six months apart and I still couldn't resist his pull.

I had to remain strong, or I wouldn't be able to go through with my plans. This wasn't about me anymore; it was about Lex and giving him a better life without me.

"Why are you here, Lex?"

"Can't you even turn around and look at me, Mil?"

I couldn't. If I turned around, I'd want to touch him. My skin burned with the desire.

At that moment, fingers glided along my bare arms, causing a desperate ache deep inside me. I held in a deep moan that tried to escape.

"Look at me, baby," he crooned.

I willed my body to remain where it stood, but it betrayed me, and I turned to face him.

His beautiful, almost piercing cobalt eyes burned into me, searching for answers to questions I couldn't respond to or at least didn't know how to.

A golden tan shaded his skin, and sun streaks highlighted his blond hair, telling me he'd spent a few days at the beach. Who was he spending his time with? The only vacations he'd ever taken were with me.

Don't go there, Milla. It is none of your business. Especially after what you've started.

The wind picked up, blowing my own locks into my face. Lex lifted his hand to tuck the stray strands back, but I flinched away.

His eyes narrowed, but he didn't say anything.

"Why are you here?" I asked. Good, my voice didn't quiver. "I know Rachel sent the office my itinerary. The plane will be here in a few hours."

"I canceled it."

I tilted my head to the side and cocked my hand on my hip. "Lex, you don't have the authority to cancel my flight. My company owns the plane."

"But I do, you see." He stepped forward as I moved back, stopping as my legs hit the patio table. "I had a chat will your business partner, and she agreed that I'd be the best person to bring you back."

My temper flared, and I pinched the bridge of my nose. I couldn't believe Arya would do this to me. We'd just talked on the phone; why didn't she tell me Lex was coming? Oh, she was so dead when I got home. She couldn't fix what's wrong with my relationship with Lex by sending him to me. It wouldn't work. Plus, even if I wanted it to, I wasn't the same, react-then-regret girl anymore.

I reined in my anger—getting mad wasn't going to solve anything—and took a deep breath. First, find out why Lex needed to bring me home and then call my meddling best friend and tell her to mind her own business.

"What could you have said to her to convince her that I needed you to bring me home?"

The corner of Lex's mouth turned up. "That was impressive. I thought you were going to explode, but you held back. Who are you and what have you done with my wife?"

"A lot has changed in the last few months." I closed my eyes and pushed the sadness my words brought forth and focused back on Lex, who was no longer smiling.

"What's going on, Mil? You used to tell me everything."

I shook my head. "I can't talk about it right now." I leaned against the table. "Please just tell me why it was so important for you to bring me home. I'm a big girl. I can manage to get back to Boston without a chaperone. What's the worst that can happen to me? I'm surrounded by security twenty-four seven, isn't that enough?"

I glanced to my right at Tony, a member of my security detail. He leaned against one of the high walls of the terrace, giving off a re-laxed aura, but I knew he was aware of everything going on around him.

He inclined his head toward me and then said "Sir" to Lex and returned to scanning the area around us.

I looked at Lex. "He's with me everywhere I go. Tony can protect me for the next few hours until I get on the plane."

"This is non-negotiable. I'm bringing you home. Besides, the only plane available for you is our plane."

His words awakened images of the escapades we'd engaged in during our many flights together. My skin tingled, reminding me of how long it had been since we'd touched.

I wiped sweat from my brow. "Does making these high-handed decisions without discussing them with me get you off?"

"You're the one who knows what gets me off. Why don't you tell me?" His eyes bored into mine.

"You are insufferable." I ground my teeth and held back the urge to tell him I'd book a commercial flight, just to spite him. Since my kidnapping, I wasn't stupid enough to risk my safety simply to make a point with Lex.

"I'm your husband. I have a right to bring you home."

"Why now? Why not a few months ago or, for a matter of fact, yesterday?" I turned my back to him, closing my eyes and clenching my fists open and shut. "Please, Lex. Tell me why you're here."

If he'd come sooner, I might not have signed those stupid papers. I might have waited to see if we still had a chance. No, I couldn't second-guess my decisions anymore. He deserved someone who wasn't selfish.

"You want to know why I waited? I wanted you to heal. You wouldn't talk to me. You needed something I couldn't give you. And in my ever-loving stupidity, I believed you'd get that here. When I realized you were hiding from me, I decided I'd come get you. I've spent the last month clearing my schedule so I could spend time with you here until we figured things out. That was until a few days ago."

"What changed?"

Lex sighed. "I don't know how to tell you this." He moved behind me but didn't touch me. "I got this in my private e-mail."

He reached around me and gave me a printout. It had a picture of me bound against a pole, bleeding from whiplashes, and my head hanging down. There was a message underneath that read, *Although she suffered, she still owes me a debt that I plan to collect.*

My feet buckled, but before I fell to the floor, Lex grabbed me. The hours of my torture and captivity flashed before my eyes, and nausea invaded my stomach. I'd worked so hard to push all the memories back, and now everything seemed fresh once again.

"Easy, baby. I've got you." Lex lifted me into his arms and sat with me in the nearby chair.

I couldn't breathe. A heaviness settled on my chest. I had to get clean. I rubbed my arms, trying to cleanse the feel of dirty hands on my body.

"I'm not going to let anyone hurt you again," Lex whispered into my hair.

His scent enveloped me, soap and light cologne. I leaned into his comfort, letting the security of his body drive my fears back. I was protected here, more than I'd felt with the ten bodyguards who'd watched over me during my entire stay in Italy. I buried my face into his chest and clutched his shirt.

I was safe if I was with him.

No, Mil, you can't do this. You're leading him on.

I tried to push out of Lex's hold, but he held me tighter. "Please let me go. I'm not good for you. I'll only cause you more pain."

"You're my wife. Your being a pain in my ass comes with the package. Plus, I've had ten years to build up an immunity," Lex said with a hint of humor and a smile.

I tilted my head back and glared at him. "This isn't a joke."

His face lost the glint of amusement. "I know, Mil. Has Christof made any contact with you?"

"N-no." I shook my head and bit my lip for a moment. "This is the first I've heard of him wanting to get my attention."

"He didn't send the message to you. He sent it to me. He wants me to think I can't protect you." Lex cupped my face. "I can't bear anything happening to you."

I wanted to lean into his touch but held myself stiff.

"Please, Lex. Let me get up. I can't depend on you like this. I'll fall apart."

He opened his lips to argue, but then conceded, loosening his arms and allowing me to stand. He remained in the chair, staring at me, in the way that made me want to kneel and give him anything he asked.

I knew this would be hard, but how was I going to make it if only a few minutes in his presence gave me the urge to call Rachel and cancel the plans I'd set in motion?

"Talk to me, Mil."

Ignoring his command, I asked, "Did you tell anyone else that we're married?"

Hurt flashed across his face and then disappeared just as fast. "No, but I'm sure Leena has spread the news by now."

Relief and disappointment hit my gut. I wasn't ready for the fallout from keeping our relationship a secret, but at the same time, I wanted the world to know he was mine.

Shit, I'd done it again. He wasn't mine, not with the divorce papers I'd signed.

"I'm taking you home, Mil. I'll throw you over my shoulder and carry you onto the plane. Just know you won't get back to Boston without me."

I took a deep breath trying to keep my anger in check. The old Milla would have given him a piece of her mind, but I couldn't let him get me riled up. My safety was the most important thing, and no matter how much my gut wanted to play the brat, it wasn't smart.

"Fine," I conceded. "We'll go back together."

He gaped at me in surprise. "What's the catch?"

"Nothing. Until I can wrap my head around what's going on, it's better for you to take me home than for me to travel on my own."

Lex frowned at me, looking a little confused. "Milla, I don't know what's going on with you. Why aren't you fighting with me?" He stood, stepping forward, as I moved back.

I had to tell him what I'd done. He deserved to know.

"Lex, I'm not the same. Things are going to change, once we're back home."

"Whatever it is, we'll work through it. That's what marriage is about."

"There's something you should know before we get on the plane." I paused. *Here goes.* Pain stabbed my heart. What I was about to say would hurt no matter how I told him.

I had to get it out before I lost my nerve.

"Lex. Today, I started…"

A loud commotion sounded from the terrace doors.

"Why is he in my house? He is not welcome here. He is not good for you."

I cringed as my mother stepped onto the balcony, followed by my exasperated sister-in-law a few paces behind her.

"He does not belong here."

"Mamma. Not now." I stared at Lex, pleading with my eyes not to mention what we were discussing.

He nodded and mouthed, *This discussion isn't over.*

CHAPTER THREE

Lex stared at me for a few seconds, telling me I wasn't getting out of our discussion. Then he touched my fingers and walked past my mother without acknowledging her.

This was his standard response to being in my mother's presence. Something I think he did because it kept him from giving her a piece of his mind and the fact it annoyed her more than if he engaged her.

I counted down from ten in my mind, waiting for the explosion about to erupt from Mamma. Her flushed face told me she was ready for an argument, but I didn't have it in me to give her what she wanted and what I'd avoided for months.

When I'd first come back to Italy, we fought about one thing or another on a daily basis. It all revolved around my being a spoiled, rebellious daughter who engaged in a sinful lifestyle. She believed the way I lived was the reason for my kidnapping and assault.

Her views were set in stone. I couldn't defend myself, and trying was a moot point. I'd relished giving my parents a hard time over the years, but my lifestyle was anything but sinful. Enjoying kink didn't mean I had issues. It just meant I was a bit more sexually adventurous than what my mother wanted.

Over the past two months, I'd spent more time ignoring her than responding to any of her accusations. Which, I believed, pissed her off more than my talking back.

I shook my head inside. I sounded a bit pathetic to myself. An almost thirty-year-old with mommy issues. Oh well, I was working on it.

"Milla, you must get over him. He is no good for you." Mamma walked up to me, inspecting me as if Lex's presence harmed me in some way.

"You don't understand, Mamma. He's here to take me home, nothing more."

"I don't like it. He led you down a path full of sin. Without him in your life, there is hope for your redemption. I should have put a stop to your relationship years ago. At least you never married him."

I grimaced but kept my mouth shut, then looked at Leena, who grimaced, too.

I wrapped my arms around myself and rubbed them. "Mamma, please. No more lectures. Be happy knowing what I had with Lex is over. I can't give you anything else. I'm going back home, to Boston. I have a business to run, and I've neglected it long enough. I don't want to spend my last day here fighting."

I waited for a sharp retort, but none came. "Fine. It looks like there is no point in arguing with you. Go get ready for the gala. You are representing our family, and I want you put together properly."

"Thank you, Mamma," I said, as I walked inside the villa.

* * *

Thirty minutes later, I came out of the shower and examined my reflection in the vanity mirror. Hazel eyes speckled with green stared back at me. Good genes gave me a more youthful appearance than most twenty-nine-year-olds, but the last few months had taken their toll on my body.

I shifted my hips from side to side and frowned. The sexy curves I'd become famous for were a thing of the past. I'd lost so much weight that I no longer resembled the bombshell, wild-child heiress the world knew me as. The outspoken and independent woman the tabloids loved to report on had disappeared.

The fire is still in there, Milla. You just need to find it.

Who was I kidding? I had never been the girl everyone believed I was. My forthright manner was the only true part of all the reports. What would the world think if they knew I'd had only one lover my entire life and not the numerous suitors everyone assumed, or that I hadn't participated in any of the scandalous things I allowed the press to print? Well, maybe I had engaged in a few.

I played the part as a way to upset my parents. In the end, I was the one who had to deal with the consequences.

The only people who knew the real me were my best friends, Arya and Carmen and even they didn't know me as well as…I closed my eyes and inhaled.

Lex.

He understood who I was and accepted me, flaws and all.

My phone beeped, reminding me I was already late and had spent too much time reflecting. I hurried to the closet, pulled out the couture gown the tailor had refitted earlier in the morning, and dressed. I moved to the oversized vanity in the bathroom and sat down to apply my makeup.

"A little concealer will hide those depressing circles, Mil. Let's sex it up for our last gala in Italy," I mumbled to myself.

Ever since I was a little girl, I loved playing with cosmetics and clothes. Thanks to the teachings of one of my aunts, I learned the difference between glamorous and overdone. Tonight, I'd use my products to cover the sadness and pretend the past six months never happened. Tomorrow, I'd deal with Lex and the consequences of Christof's renewed interest in me.

A shiver crept up my spine, and I pushed the lingering fear down. I had to put on my big-girl panties and represent my family as well as the firm Arya and I'd worked our asses off to build from scratch.

I finished the last touches to my face, when I realized I hadn't slipped on the one piece of jewelry I always wore somewhere on my body.

I walked toward the far wall of my bedroom, where a childhood picture of me with my siblings hung. The image captured our identical, mischievous smirks, reminding me of all the pranks we'd played on our family members.

I tapped the side of the portrait, and it shifted to the side, revealing a safe tucked into the wall. I disengaged the lock with my fingerprint and opened the door. Slowly I pulled out a purple velvet pouch. I loosened the string and tipped the contents into my palm. A banded platinum ring with marquise and round, brilliant-cut diamonds fell out.

I sighed, clutching the ring in my fist, and held it to my heart.

What we have is special, Milla. I won't touch you until you wear my ring and belong to me completely.

At nineteen, I'd had no comprehension of the importance of those words. Now at twenty-nine, and with six months of reflection and healing, I understood the depth of what our vows meant to him and how much hurt I'd caused him over the years by withholding what we'd shared from everyone.

I shuddered as a hiccup escaped my lips. I had finally agreed to wear the ring at all times when my world fell apart.

He deserved better than me, someone who'd put him first.

I shook the thought from my head. I had to stay focused tonight. I'd deal with Lex and my future tomorrow.

I strung the ring on a thin platinum chain, slid it around my neck, and then tucked it under the high collar of the gown.

I looked around my room. The last thing to do was find my clutch.

At that moment, Leena and my other sister-in-law, Simona, walked into my room, looking very serious. Well, as serious as two pregnant women in fancy ball gowns could look.

"*Salve, signore*. Come right in without knocking," I said as they both sat on my bed and crossed their arms.

"Come over here, Mil. You have some explaining to do," Simona ordered.

I smirked as I had a brief flash of Ricky Ricardo's voice saying the same thing to Lucy.

"What's so funny?" Simona raised a brow at me.

"Um, nothing." I moved to the bed and followed her command.

I knew what this was about and mentally prepared myself for the inquisition about to take place. No matter how much I'd hoped they would leave me alone, my family was going to want answers. Hell, I'd want answers if my baby sister kept her marriage from me for ten years.

I slid onto the bed and released a deep breath. "Okay, I'm ready. Give it to me."

It took less than a second before the questions came in rapid fire.

"How could you keep this from us?"

"Do you know how upset Marcello and Dominic are?"

"You are so dead when your brothers get you alone."

"Do you know how hard it was to keep them downstairs?"

"You better tell Papa and Mamma before they find out from someone else."

I waited until they finished their inquisition. "Well, if you want answers, I'd suggest letting me speak."

"How long, Milla?" Leena asked as she leaned back on a pillow and set her hand over her belly and closed her eyes.

I got up from the bed, walked over to the fridge in my room, pulled out two bottles of water, tossed one to Simona, and brought the other to Leena. "Drink this before you pass out. Pregnancy, high blood pressure, and family drama don't mix."

After following my directions, Leena closed the cap to the bottle and rolled her shoulder.

Uh-oh, she was about to let me have it. I took a deep breath and waited. Of my two sisters-in-law, she was the scary one. The quiet, no-nonsense doctor rarely lost her temper, but when she did, people took cover.

"How could you keep something like this from us? We're your family. We always knew you were together, but not as husband and wife. What's wrong with you? How could you keep your husband away from you for all these months?"

I winced at her reprimand, but she was right. Soon, I would make up for my mistakes.

"Leena, it's complicated. I…" I fidgeted with the clasp of my bracelets.

"So uncomplicate it for us," Simona interjected. "If you don't tell us, how are we going to be able to help you when Mamma finds out?"

At least I had a short reprieve until my parents found out. With any luck, they wouldn't know until I was halfway across the Atlantic.

"I know, I know." I pinched the bridge of my nose. "You remember those rumors about me seeing other people? Well they weren't true. I've been with Lex for the last ten years."

Simona frowned at me. "Duh. We know this, *bella*. Your brothers would have stepped in if they believed half the shit the tabloids printed."

"I guess," I mumbled.

Simona took my hand. "I want to know when you were married and why we weren't there to stand with you."

I scrunched my shoulders and bit my lips. "Well, you see…I kind of got married…before you two married my brothers."

"What!" they both shouted.

"Oh, you are so dead when Dominic finds out." Simona released my hand, rubbed her belly, and then tucked her blond hair behind her ear.

My two sisters-in-law shared a look that could only mean they were going to call my brothers upstairs. If Dominic or Marcello got involved, none of us would ever make it to the gala. Moreover, tonight's event was important, not only for my business, but for the family's shipping conglomerate, as well.

I had better defuse these two before they blow.

"Lex and I were married ten years ago, when I traveled to Ireland to visit Aunt Isabella and the cousins the summer after my freshman year at Harvard."

"Stop." Simona lifted her hand. "You mean when you were nineteen?"

I cringed and continued. "Well, I was...I'd had a crush on Lex since I was seventeen. But at the time I was dating Alberto." I scrunched up my nose. Alberto was someone I took no pleasure in thinking of at all. Dating him was a bad idea from the beginning, and to this day, I still didn't know why I'd agreed to go out with him.

"So when did it start? Did you break up with Alberto for Lex?" Leena asked.

"Really? Both of you were there when that happened. Remember that fun day, right after my graduation from the boarding school when Mamma announced I was going to marry Alberto?"

Simona covered her face. "How could I forget? You got on a table and announced that you weren't a mare for auction and you were moving to the US for the rest of your life."

"Not one of my better moments." I cringed.

"When did Lex come into the picture?" asked Leena.

"The first time I met Lex was my senior year of high school, after I came home for spring break. At that time, he only saw me as the annoying sister of his friends, but even then, I sensed there was something special between us."

"Now it makes sense. The reason your mamma hates Alexander. She thinks he did the same thing that his father and your uncle did to your aunt."

My temper piqued. "Lex did not seduce me! I don't care what Mamma thinks. I tried to get him to see me as a woman and he rejected me. So, I went after him."

Shit, I sounded desperate. Hell, when it comes to Lex I always am.

I glanced at the bedside clock and pointed. "Let's table this discussion for later. If we don't leave soon, we'll be late, and you know how pissed Mamma gets if we're late."

"Can we say 'understatement'? She's pissed at you for breathing," Leena said, then pushed me down on the bed as I motioned to get up. "Sit your ass down and tell us the rest."

No getting out of this. Well, they do deserve the whole story.

I blew out an exaggerated breath and smoothed my gown in my lap. *Here goes.* "I can admit I had a thing for him from the beginning, but it wasn't until I started at Harvard that I realized he was interested in me but thought I was too young for him."

I remembered walking into the international law class he taught as a teaching assistant. The moment he caught sight of me, a look flashed in his eyes telling me he no longer considered me a child. At the end of the class, he pulled me aside and ordered me to withdraw.

"Milla, if your brothers find out you're in my class, they're going to think we're seeing each other. I won't have them believing something that isn't true."

I folded my arms around myself. "I'm just meeting a course requirement for my international business degree."

Lex smiled his devilish Irish grin. "We both know that's not true. I'm too old for you."

"You're the same age as Dominic. You sound like I'm some silly girl attracted to someone twenty years older than her instead of just four."

"Milla, I've done things and want things you can't understand."

"You can teach me."

He closed his eyes, as if I'd offered him something he couldn't bear. "You have no idea what you're saying."

I peered at him until he stared back at me. "Then explain it to me.

I'm not as naïve as you believe. I know about Papa's club. I grew up running through its hallways."

"But you are. Knowing about things isn't anywhere close to experiencing them. You have to complete your degree and grow up a little more."

My breath hitched, and I scowled at him. "What difference will that make?"

"Because one day, I will come for you. When that day comes, I won't only fuck you, but I'll possess you. And you're not ready for what I want to do."

"Oh."

He kissed my forehead and walked away.

"You can't just leave us hanging," Simona complained, snapping me out of my thoughts.

At that moment, our family's butler knocked on my open door.

We all looked in his direction.

"Signor Dominic sent me to get you. The car is ready to take you to the gala."

I released a sigh of relief and Simona grunted in response. "Don't think for one moment that you're off the hook."

"Just do me a favor. Don't discuss this in front of Marcello or Dominic. I'll talk to them myself."

"Whatever you say." Leena shook her head and slid off the bed. "Don't wait too long, or they'll follow you to Boston to get their answers."

I grabbed my clutch and walked toward my door.

"I wouldn't expect anything less."

* * *

Approximately an hour later, my family and I arrived at the Salvatori gala. My hope to table the discussion about my marriage never materialized. The second the limousine doors closed, my brothers laid into me. After I admitted to the stupidity of my youth, I explained my plan for the future. They, like Rachel, disapproved but accepted my decision.

I took a deep breath to settle my nerves as we pulled up to the mansion. I couldn't have asked for a better reaction from my brothers and their wives. Their unconditional love and support meant so much to me.

Now I had to talk to my parents. Papa would probably react the same way Dominic and Marcello had. That left Mamma.

How would Mamma take the news when she found out? With anger and crazy demands, no doubt.

I shrugged. *No point in worrying about that right now.* Talking to Mamma and Papa could wait until morning.

The door to the car opened, and my brothers and their wives exited first.

"Want me to escort you in?" Marcello asked, leaning in to take my hand and help me out of the limo.

"No. You go on ahead. I have to do a few PR interviews for ArMil. I'll meet you inside before we go to dinner."

He nodded, then turned to Simona, slipping his arm around her and guiding her up the stairs of the castle.

Fifteen minutes later, I entered the majestic palace and gave my wrap to the approaching attendant.

I surveyed the beautiful foyer of the sixteenth-century palace. The soft glow of a car-sized chandelier added a regal appearance to the room.

The Salvatoris were a fixture in Italian culture for over a thousand years. They epitomized the image of wealthy aristocrats. Their prominence remained over centuries and through wars and changes in political climate.

The Castras shared the same social status. My family was to set the example for others to follow, but, of course, my antics over the years not only scandalized my mother but most of her social circle, too

Well, at least she wouldn't have to worry about my behavior anymore. I didn't have the energy or inclination to act out.

I crossed the threshold of the ballroom and paused, squaring my shoulders and preparing to pretend. The confidence that negotiated the phenomenal merger, which turned Arya and me into billionaires, lingered inside me, and I was determined to use it.

"Milla, my sweet girl. It is good to see you."

I turned in the direction of the soothing voice.

"*Buona sera*, Signora Salvatori. I'm happy to see you as well." We kissed each other's cheeks. "One day you will have to share your secrets for staying timeless."

"Oh, posh. None of that, *bella*. You are a shameless flatterer like your papa." She glanced behind me. "Where is your escort?"

I'd rarely attended the gala with a date. Well, with the exception of last year. Lex had flown in, and we'd spent an entertaining night meeting potential business clients and making fun of the stuffy women who hadn't gotten over my dramatic breakup with Alberto.

My heart clenched. There wouldn't be any more nights like that in my future.

"I'm solo tonight." I tried to hide the slight tremor of my lips and glanced over her shoulder, pretending to see someone. "Please excuse me, signora. I have to say hello to Admiral Mosima."

She kissed me again. "Go, go. Remember to step away from work and enjoy yourself. No matter what the tabloids print, I know you are a good girl."

My smile wavered again. It baffled me how a complete stranger saw through the antics, while my mother remained blind. "I'll try. I'll leave you to your other guests."

Slipping past Signora Salvatori, I approached the attendant, handed him my invitation, and waited for his announcement.

"Signorina Milla Amalea Castra."

I descended the stairs and gave my best Hollywood actress smile. Halfway down, I caught a glimpse of blond hair that I'd recognize anywhere. My heartbeat accelerated.

Lex.

I continued to the bottom of the steps and paused at the edge of the dance floor. Lex moved out from behind the crowd and held my gaze, dead-on.

My breath hitched, and a shiver slid up my spine. He'd peered at me in the same way ten years before from across this very ballroom. It was the summer after my first year at Harvard. I had just turned nineteen, and nothing or no one was going to stop me from getting Alexander Jameson Duncan.

Back then, he'd captivated me with his confidence and piercing blue gaze. He called to a part of me I'd never known existed. The same held true today. A quiver glided into my stomach.

He sipped his champagne, and the corners of his mouth turned up. He knew exactly what he was doing to me. I'd felt it when he was at the villa, and I felt it now.

God, he was gorgeous. At six foot three, he stood taller than most men around him. The tuxedo he wore tonight accentuated his form perfected from years of intense martial arts and Tai Chi.

My core clenched; that body had brought me so much pleasure. I licked my lips and waited.

His blond hair was slicked back, projecting the image of an international playboy.

He tilted his glass in my direction, and I lifted my chin in response.

"You love playing the brat, Mil. Always finding some way to defy me."

His statement rang true. He allowed me room to play the rebel even at his expense. However, he reined me in whenever he decided I'd gone too far. Like when I danced on a table during a party in the Hamptons. I cringed at the memory.

Lex chuckled, as if reading my thoughts, and continued staring at me. I remained fixed to the same spot. He lifted his glass again, and the light from the chandelier reflected off the ring he wore on his left hand.

To the naked eye, it resembled a standard family crest ring, but it was much more.

"I had this made for you, Lex. It has your family seal and something special on the inside. Our wedding date."

The ring never left his finger. I sighed. Another reminder of how he refused to hide who he was to me.

Lex followed my gaze to his hand, and then he raised his eyebrow. Without thought, I touched the necklace hidden under my gown.

With slow, precise steps, Lex moved toward me through the crowd. I held my breath. He was a predator and I was his prey. My Master was calling to me. The urge to kneel pushed at my senses.

What would he do when he reached me?

My pulse accelerated, heating my body, and a slight hint of arousal tingled my skin.

All of a sudden, a scowl crossed his face.

"Hello, *cara mia*. How about a drink with your old love?"

CHAPTER FOUR

I closed my eyes for a second. The same irritation I'd glimpsed in Lex's eyes prickled my temper.

Why, oh why, now?

I glanced back toward Lex, but he was gone.

This wouldn't end well.

"Hello, Alberto. I doubt I've ever been your love."

He smiled at me in the same *you are so stupid* condescending way he had when I was a teenager. "Oh, don't be like that. We were friends before…" His brow creased and he gestured to where Lex stood a few minutes ago.

"Don't go there, Alberto. We broke up. I did not leave you for him."

"We view events differently." He handed me a champagne flute. "Here. I remember you always had a taste for the finer things in life."

That was why I never saw a future with him. The high-handed ass only listened to what he wanted and believed his version of the truth. If it weren't for my momentary lapse in thinking that I could please Mamma, I wouldn't have ever dated him.

Alberto placed his hand on my lower back, and I flinched, shaking his hold.

Don't touch me. No one touches me but Lex.

I gulped down half my drink, inhaled deep, and settled the uneasiness coursing through my body.

"Alberto, excuse me, but I must speak with a few business partners."

Please let me leave.

"I only need a few minutes of your time. I am sure your keeper can handle the wait."

My emotions moved from irritated to pissed. *What does he gain by bringing Lex into every conversation?*

"Fine, but don't touch me. You felt no desire to do so when we were together, so don't start now."

"As you wish, *cara*. Let's talk on the balcony." He extended his arm.

I ignored his gesture and stomped two paces ahead of him onto the ballroom terrace. Lucky for me, because of the antics of my youth, no one would take notice of my stalking through the ballroom.

I approached the stone railing and surveyed the beautifully manicured gardens. When Alberto approached my side, I turned to him. "Okay, what do you need to say?"

"How are you coping after your attack?"

"Excuse me?" *Where had that come from? Why would I talk to him about this?*

"The press made such a big deal about your condition. It is only natural to ask."

I supposed he was right. Wait a second, why was he concerned now? The attack happened more than six months ago. "I'm fine, doing better every day."

A chime rang, informing the guests that dinner would start in thirty minutes.

"Alberto, my brothers are expecting me for the table seating. What do you need to speak with me about?"

"I did not bring up your situation to upset you. It was a mere inquiry about your health."

Here we went, round and round, with no point to any conversation. If I didn't push him, he'd never get to the point. "Alberto, it's time for me to go inside." I moved to return to the ballroom.

"You were always so standoffish. With Duncan's tastes, it is a wonder he comprehends how to handle you."

I stopped midstep, turned, and glared at Alberto, who leaned against the railing. "His tastes are none of your concern."

Milla, calm down. He is just trying to get under your skin.

Alberto strolled toward me and traced a finger down the side of my cheek.

I jerked my head back.

"Alberto, you've wasted ten minutes of my life that I will never get back. When you have something substantial to discuss, let me know."

"*Bella*, your mamma indicated you were open to suitors and that you'd welcome my interest."

Mamma's interference held no bounds. Telling her my relationship with Lex was over never meant I was ready to start dating. If I was honest with myself, I'd never be open to it again. Lex was my one chance at happiness.

"You're misinformed. I have no interest in a suitor now or in the future. Is there anything else you'd like to discuss?"

"We do have things to talk over, but I'll leave it for another time." He leaned down and kissed my cheek.

I held my breath in hopes of hiding the disgust crawling on my skin at his touch.

"I'll see you soon, *cara mia*." He smirked at someone over my shoulder. "I believe Duncan would like a word with you."

What?

I glanced behind me, and Lex stood in the entryway of the terrace. Aside from the angry burn in his blue eyes, his face gave away no emotion.

Alberto passed Lex with no greeting from either man.

"Lex. I was just getting some fresh air."

Why was I explaining myself?

"Save the bullshit." The Irish brogue that sent me to erotic places now simmered with cold anger. He stalked toward me, and I instinctively stepped back. "Either hand me divorce papers or stay faithful. I will not have you cheat on me."

"What?" Was he kidding? The thought of anyone else touching me made me want to vomit.

"Did I stutter? Don't play innocent, Milla. I saw Alberto kiss you."

"It was completely innocent. I have never wanted him and never will."

"Let's drop it."

I admitted to playing the spoiled heiress, but I had never lied to him or cheated on him. God, this was a mess. If he didn't trust me, than maybe the decision I'd made earlier today was for the best.

"We'll go home tomorrow. We can figure out where this relationship is headed there."

My lips trembled and then my annoyance bubbled over.

I shoved at his chest with my finger. "Alexander Jameson Duncan, you do not control me."

He ran a frustrated hand through his hair and caught my wrist with the other. "Don't you think I know this? If I'd had any say, you'd never have left Boston. I'm sick of the games."

So am I.

"You don't trust me. You think I'm a cheater. It's obvious I can't give you what you need. Why do you want me?" I pulled free of his grasp. "You should find someone else."

There, I said it.

Nausea filled me.

A startled expression crossed his face. "Mil, you don't mean that. I shouldn't have reacted that way. I just wish you'd talk to me like you used to."

"I can't. I'm not the girl you fell in love with. She no longer exists. Besides, she wasn't good for you."

"Mi—" He stepped toward me.

I lifted my hand. "Lex, I can't do this." I took a deep breath. "I've made my decision."

Hurt flashed in his eyes, and then they grew cold. "If that's how you see it. I'll heed your choice. I suppose it won't bother you when I take Marcello up on his offer to join him at the club tonight."

My brother wouldn't do that, would he? No matter what I told him in the car, I never expected Marcello to help Lex move on.

"But you just—"

Lex cut me off. "Since my wife doesn't want my company, I'll find my own."

He turned without a backward glance and exited the terrace.

I stood frozen in one spot as Lex left me on the balcony. He wouldn't go to someone else. Would he?

He disappeared into the crowd, and a wave of sadness washed over me. I'd set this chain of events in motion, and now I had to live with the consequences.

He deserves happiness, Milla.

My hand shook as I wiped a tear from my cheek.

"Milla, it's time for dinner." Marcello approached with a smile, but then his grin lost its happiness.

I rubbed my arms around myself and turned away so any lingering tears would dry.

He placed a hand on my shoulder. "Tell me what's wrong."

"How could you?" I turned into his arms and buried my face against his shoulder.

"What have I done? One minute you're on the balcony with Alberto, then I see Lex stride through the ballroom and out the door."

I glimpsed and another tear slid down my face. "Why are you helping him leave me?"

Marcello squeezed me tight. "You can't have it both ways. You're either with him or not. I can't imagine what it is like to deal with all that you've been through, but you're only going to hurt more if you go through with your plan."

"But why did you invite him to the club?"

"*Bella*, I didn't invite him specifically to hurt you. He is a shareholder and I invited all the investors to a meeting tonight." He kissed the top of my head.

"I'm sorry. I shouldn't have assumed you would help him. My emotions are a wreck."

Marcello pulled back and scanned my face. He wiped away the stray wetness from my cheeks. "No apology necessary, baby sister. Love makes us all stupid at times. Maybe your reaction is a sign to hold off. Promise me you'll think about it."

I sighed, knowing he was right. "I promise."

With those last words, we moved into the castle and toward the dining room.

* * *

"No, please. Don't do this," I begged.

"Milla! Wake up. You're safe. You're home, in your bed."

Marcello? No, I need Lex.

"Lex, please help me."

"Lex is coming, *bella*. You have to wake up."

"We have to save Arya. Please." I shoved against the hands shaking me.

"Arya is safe. She's home with Max."

"Safe? No, he's going to hurt her, just like he did to me."

My body moved and warm arms gathered me close.

"No, baby, I won't let anyone hurt you or her again. He's dead. You have to wake up now."

Lex.

"Don't let him touch me again. He took what was ours and ruined it."

"I know, baby. I know."

My body rocked back and forth.

"I'm so scared."

"I'll protect you. Open your eyes, Milla. Wake yourself from this nightmare."

I'm dreaming? Oh, no. Not another one.

All of a sudden, a wave of relief and embarrassment rushed over me. Lex was here and he saw me. Tears rolled down my cheeks, releasing a flood of emotion I'd kept from him. I cried and cried without thought. Lex held me tight as I sobbed, crooning words of comfort. When I had no more tears left, I carefully opened my eyelids, blinking multiple times until my vision cleared.

Lex smiled at me and kissed the top of my head. "You're safe. It was just a bad dream."

Wait a second. Wasn't he getting his groove on with a new woman?

I clutched him tight. "Why are you here? You went to the…"

"Shhh." He held a finger to my lips. "We'll talk in a little bit."

Lex motioned his head toward the door, and I followed his gaze. My family stood by the bedroom door, my brothers, their wives, and my parents. Worry and concern were etched across their faces. With the exception of my mother, whose face radiated anger.

"I'll take care of her. Please, go back to bed."

"Are you sure?" Dominic asked.

"Yes," both Lex and I responded in unison.

"This is not appropriate. She shouldn't…"

"Maria, enough. Let's go." My father dragged my reluctant mother out of my room.

I remained silent, wrapped in the comfort of Lex's arms until the door closed.

"Why?" I asked, pulling back a little to look at his face.

He squinted his eyes and tilted his head. "Why what?"

"Why are you here with me?" I tried to push out of his arms, but he drew me back.

"Do you mean, why am I here with the only woman I have ever desired? The only person I've ever loved, over some random woman at the club?"

"Don't make fun of me. This isn't a joke, Lex."

"I'm not joking, Milla."

I can't give you what you need. Why won't you make it easier on me to let you go?

"Dammit, Lex. I'm broken." I struggled to get out of his hold so I could punch him, but to no avail. My arms remained locked tight within his.

"Are you finished?" He smirked as I continued to wrestle with his grip on me.

Pretending exhaustion, I released a deep breath. "Yes."

Lex flipped me out of his arms and onto my back, pinning my hands to the bed above my head. My breath quickened and my heart thumped out of control at the familiar feel of his body above mine.

Sky-blue eyes smiled down at me. "Tsk-tsk, naughty girl. I know all your little tricks. I've spent the last ten years studying them in detail."

His hand moved to my neck and the chain that hung around it. He pulled the platinum out from under my collar and sighed as the ring attached to the bottom came into view. He searched my eyes for something I couldn't give him.

"Please, don't. I have no defense when you look at me like that."

"Like what?"

Like I'm the only thing in the world that matters to you.

"Please."

The plea in my voice must have compelled him. Lex released the necklace, moved off me, and lay down at my side. "Milla, talk to me. Tell me how to fix this."

"How can I tell you something I don't know myself?"

He took my hand in his and kissed my fingers. Goose bumps prickled all over my body. His slightest touch could always awaken my senses.

"Tell me what happened."

"I…"

"I know how I found you." He shuddered. "I want to know what they did to you. I want to know the reason you're willing to break the vows we made to each other."

The pain in his voice shot straight to my gut. He deserved to know, but I couldn't relive the nightmare again. I wasn't strong enough.

"I can't tell you. I don't want to go there again. They damaged me…they…" My voice cracked. "He…"

"Shhh." Lex leaned over me. "It's okay, you don't have to talk about it. Let me get you to bed."

I nodded my agreement.

"Will you hold me until I fall asleep?"

"*A ghrá*, I'd do anything for you."

My love. It had been months since I'd heard those words.

He settled me under the sheets and joined me on the bed, pulling me to rest against his chest. I closed my eyes and listened to the steady drumming of his heart.

I had to clear up the scene on the balcony. "Lex, nothing ever happened with Alberto. We were just talking."

He sighed. "Let it go for now, baby. You're mine. No one can come between us."

His fingers glided up and down my back in a slow pattern, one he'd done numerous times over the years. Sleep crept up with the gentle rhythm of his hand.

He's so lonely. I have to let him go. This isn't fair to him.

"Go to sleep, baby. Whether I'm lonely or not, I won't let you go."

I jarred awake at his words.

Did I say that aloud?

"Yes, you did. When you're sleepy you verbalize every thought that crosses your mind."

Oh yeah, I forgot.

"Relax. We have all the time you need to figure this out."

"Okay." The exhaustion from crying and lack of sleep took over, and I drifted off.

CHAPTER FIVE

A stream of sunlight woke me from a deep sleep. I stretched, then rolled over, keeping my eyes closed.

How long had it been since I'd had a restful night's sleep? At least six months. It was all due to the man sleeping next to me. I smiled as his familiar scent of soap and light cologne comforted my senses.

I reached over to touch him and found empty sheets. I blinked, sat up, and searched around the room.

Empty.

No sign of Lex except the imprint of his head on the pillow next to me and a note tucked under one corner. I grabbed the pillow and hugged it close to my chest. Lifting the paper, I unfolded it and read.

Mil,

I have to take care of a few things. I'll meet you on the plane.

Lex

I moaned, thinking of in-flight escapades we'd engaged in over the years. I shook my head, trying to push the memories back.

Those are a thing of the past, Milla. Your decision, remember? Life moves forward not backward.

I took one last whiff of the pillow, set it aside, and trudged to take a shower.

I closed my eyes as the hot stream of water cascaded down my face and body. It was time to stop shielding myself and face the world, no more hiding and fearing everything around me. Jacob was dead, and he couldn't hurt me anymore. It was time to live a better life than the pitiful existence I'd had over the past few months.

I shrugged. Today, I had to face my parents and the fallout that would follow from Mamma.

Fifteen minutes later, I rushed down to the kitchen, hoping to grab some food in quiet before my mother found me and we had our daily verbal altercation. All her motherly concern for my sins and misquoted Bible scripture were too much to handle first thing in the morning.

What I wouldn't give to have her just once dote on and love me like Arya's Aunt Elana did on her. Arya may not have experienced the traditional mother and father, but Aunt Elana made up for it. That woman would slay any dragon for her baby.

I sighed. There was no point in wishing for something that would never happen.

Our family chef looked up from his vegetable chopping as I entered. He smiled and gestured to the covered tray under the warming light.

"*Pronto*, take the plate and go onto the terrace. I've already put your coffee out there. Signora ate earlier and is in the chapel. Eat before she returns."

"Thank you, Silvio. You're a lifesaver. I'll miss you when I'm back in Boston."

"Of course you will, signorina. I am the only person to keep your mamma in line. She is too scared I will leave and take my famous recipes with me."

"Or it could be that having a famous chef in-house gives her status, and without you, her stock would plummet," I muttered as I took my plate and entered the garden terrace.

I scanned the beautiful city that held an eclectic mix of residents. Some people were happy in their simple lives of work and family, while others enjoyed high fashion and all the joys of snobbery. This was the city of my birth but not the city of my heart.

That city is in America.

Moving to Boston had allowed me a sense of freedom I'd never experienced before. And it gave my family the prestige of having a daughter that was attending Harvard and then MIT.

Just as I lifted the newspaper sitting on the table, Mamma's voice screeched across the house. Covering my face with my hands, I prayed for calm.

I must not engage her. I must not engage her. Only a few more hours. You can get through this.

The French doors slammed open and Mamma threw papers at me. "Your papa received these documents this morning. What is the meaning of it? I will have it annulled if it is the last thing I do. I don't care if the date is over ten years old. How could I have allowed that horrible man into my house?" She rubbed a palm across her face.

I gathered the papers on the table and scanned them. "What's the big deal? It's a copy of my marriage certificate."

Good. That came out calm.

"Don't sit there acting smug. I will not have it. I will not allow another person from this family to become involved with more Irish trash."

The hatred radiating from my mother pricked my temper, but I couldn't let her get to me; no matter what I said, it wouldn't bring her acceptance. I took a deep breath and tried to calm my mind.

My mother paced. "If it wasn't for your father's lack of discipline with you, you wouldn't have become that man's whore."

Okay, that was it, fuck the not-engaging shit. Dammit, I was doing so well.

I shoved back from the table. "You will not. Let me repeat: You will not disrespect my husband. We chose each other even if you want to believe it isn't true. As for your issues with your sister, they're yours alone."

Mamma grabbed my arm and shook me. "You are a disgrace. I will have it annulled on the grounds it wasn't in a church. Don't think I won't."

"Mamma, marriages aren't ended that way anymore. Plus, you better read the date and location more clearly. Archbishop Peters married us in Saint Mary's Cathedral." I jerked my arm out of her grasp.

"You're a whore living a wicked life, just like your aunt."

"Mamma, I pray to God that one day you will see further than the tip of your nose and realize the mistakes you've made with your children. We deserved a mother who loved us unconditionally."

I walked toward the terrace doors, but before I passed the archway, I paused and glanced back. "This isn't how I wanted to leave things with us."

"If you leave this villa, you will never be welcomed back. Whatever I've provided for you will stop."

"Mamma, I don't need anything from you but your love." My voice cracked. "I'm sorry for what I put you though as a child, but I'm a grown woman now and I can't live my life looking for your approval. *Addio,* Mamma."

CHAPTER SIX

W e will miss you, Signorina Castra."

"No you won't," I said, then kissed Tony's cheeks. "I learned you've asked for a transfer."

"I wouldn't leave your protection to anyone but a fellow Italian. And since there aren't any Italians on your staff, I decided to change that." He grinned. "I also heard American woman the love the tall, dark, and handsome type."

"That they do." I glanced at my watch and realized our scheduled departure was in less than thirty minutes.

I adjusted my shoulder bag and then gave one last look behind me.

Time to leave the beautiful city of my youth, go home to Boston, and face life.

"I'll see you soon, Tony."

"*Sì*, signorina." He nodded as he took my hand to help me step onto the stairs of the Gulfstream G650.

The moment I entered the spacious cabin, all the memories of the last time I'd used the plane bombarded me. I dropped my bag on the nearest seat and braced my hand on the leather back of another.

It had been almost a year. Lex and I were leaving for a weekend getaway, and the only thing on our minds was to christen every surface of our new jet without scandalizing the pilot or the flight attendant. We'd succeeded for the most part.

"Lex," I said aloud and closed my eyes. I reached inside my sweater and pulled out the chain with my wedding ring. I rubbed the diamonds with my thumb.

"I control the scene; you control your pleasure, Milla."

My body heated, and I rubbed my thighs together. My body craved his touch, his voice, his body. Hell, I craved him, the man, the lover, everything.

The air conditioner kicked on, dousing the faint arousal in my body and snapping me out of my thoughts.

Merda! I had to stop thinking about the past. Lex deserved a fresh start and so did I. Focusing on what we shared would only hurt me more. I wasn't the old Milla who reacted first and then thought about the consequences later.

I released the back of the seat, tucked the necklace back under my clothes, and turned, slamming into Lex and losing my balance.

"I've got you."

His touch sent fire up my arms, and my skin prickled.

"Lex," I said breathlessly. "How long have you been standing there?"

He smiled, tucking a stray hair behind my ear. "Long enough. Going down memory lane, were you?"

I raised a brow, ignoring his question, and then stepped out of his hold. Moving to one of the reclining seats, I sat down.

"I figured you'd take that seat," Lex commented as he took the seat across from me.

I scrunched my brows at his statement, then it dawned on me, and I looked down.

There were scuff marks on the leather next to two sets of metal hooks hidden on the inside of the seat.

My cheeks heated and my core spasmed as the image of my naked, reclined body handcuffed to the D rings flashed before my eyes.

I glanced at Lex. His blue eyes darkened, telling me he was thinking of the same thing.

It was during our return to Boston after a weekend in the Caribbean. Lex had kept me on the cusp of orgasm for hours as punishment for trying to sneak in a few hours of work when I'd promised to unplug from the world.

I wasn't intentionally trying to be bratty. I had only wanted to get a head start on the week. Lex hadn't seen it that way and decided to hold my release until thirty minutes before landing. Which gave me enough time to freshen up, but without allowing me to come down from my orgasm.

I licked my now dry lips. "Why didn't you get it fixed?" I said, trying to keep the huskiness from voice.

He was doing this on purpose, and I was the stupid one for sitting in the seat.

"Because I wanted to remember my wife bound and open to my pleasure every time I traveled on the plane."

"Oh," was the only response I could say, without giving away too much of how my body responded to the memory and his answer. I shifted in my seat as the dampness between my legs increased.

I had to get myself under control.

I should change the subject. Yep, that's what I'll do.

"When do we leave?"

"As soon as Michael gets the all clear to take off."

I looked out the window as the sun started its descent over the city, giving Milan a beautiful glow.

I felt the weight of Lex studying me. He wanted answers, and after last night, I knew I had to talk about what happened to me. But I wasn't ready yet. I hadn't talked about the details of the kidnapping with anyone.

"Are you going to miss it?"

I answered without looking at him. "No. Italy doesn't have the hold on me that Boston does."

"Is it just the city you miss?"

"No. I miss my family. The one I chose."

Especially you.

I kept my gaze out the window as the jet's engine roared to life. I took a few deep breaths and clutched my armrests.

I will not throw up. I will not throw up.

No matter how many times I'd flown, I hated takeoff. I knew it was irrational, but my body went into panic until the plane reached cruising altitude. I despised the feeling of helplessness and not having any control of my mode of transportation. Maybe that was why I loved my fast cars.

The cabin vibrated with each turn of the wheel on the runway, increasing my anxiety. My stomach flipped in somersaults, and soon I'd be running to the toilet and losing the little lunch I'd eaten.

Leaning back against the headrest, I closed my eyes and practiced the calming techniques Arya insisted I learn after our first spring break trip, where I nearly scared her to death with my panic attack.

Breathe in. One. Two. Three. Breathe out. One. Two. Three.

I repeated the process over and over. Then the next thing I knew, Lex placed a glass of sparkling water in my hand, and I stared at him in confusion.

"Drink this and relax. I dissolved a Zofran in the liquid. It will settle your stomach and help you rest."

I nodded without saying anything, drank the concoction, and closed my eyes. His hand grazed my cheek, and then he placed a kiss on the top of my forehead.

No matter how I treated him, he always took care of me. With him, I was safe. I couldn't do this to him. I couldn't fall back into the same routine. I had to tell him my plans.

We hit a patch of turbulence as we lifted into the air, and I covered my stomach with my hand as it lurched again.

Well, I'd talk to him once we reached cruising altitude.

"Easy, baby. Only a few more minutes."

Nodding, I squeezed my eyelids tight and willed myself to sleep, at least for a half hour.

* * *

A cool breeze glided down my neck, and a chill rode up my spine. A moan escaped my lips, and a tingle ached between my legs. I shifted my body to the side, but couldn't move.

My eyes snapped open, and I peered into beautiful pools of blue.

"It's about time you woke up. I thought you were going to sleep through your orgasm."

"Lex," I whispered through a sleepy haze. "What are you—"

He silenced me with a kiss, deepening it until I couldn't process anything but the feel of his mouth, the way he tasted, the scent of his skin.

I tried lifting my arms, but realized he'd anchored them to the inside of the armrests.

Wrenching my lips away from his, I ordered, "Release me, Lex. We can't do this."

No matter how much I wanted him, this was only going to lead to more trouble for both of us.

He shook his head. "I'll never hurt you, Mil. And you should know by now, the only way to stop is to use your safe word."

Tarantula.

The word was on my lips. I couldn't say it no matter how hard I tried. But I couldn't let this go any further. It didn't matter how much I wanted or desired him, I still planned to leave him.

"Please, Lex. Don't make me do this," I begged. I'd never used my safe word in all of our ten years together. I'd hurt him by using it and I'd have to explain to him why I'd said it.

Merda. Why couldn't things be easier?

I gasped as he bit one of my nipples and pinched the other one.

Fuck. I was naked. He'd stripped me of all my clothes but underwear

The drink! What did he put in the water to make me sleep so hard?

"Lex. You need to release me and give me back my clothes." I glanced behind me toward the doors leading to the cockpit. "Chrystal will come back and see me."

"Nice try. She won't come in here unless I call her or it's time to land." He nuzzled my neck, and his five-o'clock shadow rubbed against my sensitive skin.

I held back a moan.

"Besides, if she doesn't know what we are up to during our flights, then she deserves a surprise." He slid lower, rubbing his face between my breasts and causing my heart to accelerate to an uncontrollable level.

I had to get him to stop. If he didn't stop touching me, I'd lose all willpower.

"Lex. Please, we can't do this." I gasped as he cupped my breast and took the other nipple into his mouth, sucking it hard. "It will complicate things."

I arched up, my body begging for a harder tug on my sensitive nub.

Lex paused, and a protest escaped my lips.

He face grew serious as he stared down at me. "I know, Mil. I don't expect it to change whatever is brewing in your mind. I just want to…I need to give my wife pleasure. Let me give you pleasure."

Well, when he put it that way, I could do this one last time. It would give me something to remember.

"Okay." I worried my lip, now second-guessing what I'd just agreed to.

He smiled, pressing a light kiss to my forehead, and my apprehension disappeared.

Reaching to the side, Lex picked up a glass of ice water. He drank deep, then leaned over me. Out of instinct, I opened my mouth, and cool liquid slid down my parched throat. I swallowed the last of the water from his lips until he dangled an ice cube above me.

He trailed it down my neck, over my shoulders, and then to each nipple, circling until they were tight, aching peaks.

"Please. I need…" I gasped and bowed, wanted more of the pleasure-pain of the cold sensation.

Lex pulled away, glaring at me.

My core contracted.

"Sorry. M-master."

His gaze grew more intense but softer at the same time. "Good girl."

He continued the trail with the ice, moving lower, teasing all over my arms, legs, stomach, and thighs. The wetness from the melting ice and the cool air on my skin sent a flood of anticipation to my throbbing pussy.

I lifted my hips, wanted his touch at the very heat of me.

"Soon, love. Soon," he crooned.

His exquisite torture ensued for I didn't know how long, but felt like centuries. My skin burned as if were on fire; I needed his touch. When he finally lowered the footrest of my seat and settled between my thighs, I held my breath waiting for the first swipe of his tongue.

But it never came. I looked down the length of my body and caught him watching me.

He smiled as he crunched up the remnants of the ice. "Is there something you want?"

Yes, your tongue in my pussy.

I wanted to say those words, but if I played the brat right now when he knew I was desperate for him, he'd hold off longer.

He shifted my thong to the side and blew out a breath against my weeping slit, making my clit swell and ache.

I thrashed my head back and forth. If he didn't do something other than torture me, I'd lose my mind.

"Say what I want to hear, Mil." He blew again.

"Please, Master. I need your mouth, please."

"Where, baby?" He nuzzled me, rubbing his nose along the sides of my labia. "God, you smell heavenly."

"My clit. My pussy. Everywhere. Anywhere," I answered.

"My pleasure."

His lips descended, sucking my clit into his mouth. At the same time, his fingers pressed into my pussy. He thrust in and out as my hips rose and fell to his rhythm. He ate at me until I was delirious. He held me on the cusp, tormenting me. I couldn't come unless he gave me permission, but I was out of practice. A few seconds before I couldn't hold back my release, he pulled away.

"No," I called out.

"Ask me." He wiped his mouth against his sleeve and stared at me with lust-filled eyes.

"Please…please, Master. Make me come."

He took my clit between his fingers and lightly pinched.

Yes. Finally.

"Master…"

The plane hit a patch of turbulence, jarring me awake.

CHAPTER SEVEN

My heartbeat continued to race as I looked around my seat, not understanding what was happening. My body was completely free.

Merda. I'd fallen asleep.

I ran a hand over my sweat-dampened face, then all of a sudden I froze.

Lex.

I couldn't bring myself to look at him. He had to know what I was dreaming about, especially if I was talking in my sleep as I often did.

Without thought, I glanced toward him and caught him shifting his legs and then adjusting the raging erection pushing against his pant leg.

My eyes flew to his face, and the heat and desire gazing back at me could have scorched me alive. I licked my lips.

"Milla, stop staring at me like that or I'm going to get up and fuck you like I've wanted to for the past six months."

Heat crept up my cheeks and body. "Sorry. Did I talk in my sleep?"

There was no need for him to say anything. I knew the answer.

"You could say that." His voice was thick and raspy with an edge of Dom. "The next time you ask me to make you come, I plan to be balls deep in your pussy."

I pressed my thighs together, willing away the image he painted. I bit my lips trying to gather my thoughts.

"Lex. It can't happen. I won't let it happen."

"Yes. It will," he stated with the arrogance I'd grown to love over the years.

"No, Lex."

"Your body says differently. Plus, your pussy is molded to the curve of my dick. You need it as much as I do."

He was being crude to get a rise out of me, and I refused to bite.

"Keep believing that. You'll be sorely disappointed."

"I'll win, *a ghrá*. I always do." He emphasized his Irish brogue, making my insides quiver.

Must steer the conversation in another direction. Must steer the conversation in another direction.

"Tell me about who you've assigned to my detail."

A slight grin hinted at the corners of his mouth, telling me he knew what I was doing. "James is lead for your security and once Tony gets his US clearance, he will take over. When they aren't with you, I'll be stuck to you like glue."

The old Milla would have retorted with something smart-alecky about where he could stick his glue. The only problem with that tactic was that I'd end up thoroughly and literally fucked, and I couldn't go there.

"Doesn't Arya need James? She's still in danger."

"No, Mil. She isn't." Lex's voice grew serious. "You're Christof's target now."

A shiver went up my spine, and the lingering arousal from my dream and previous conversation vanished.

I sighed. "I know. I just want her safe, too."

"Max has it under control. With her on bed rest at the estate, no one will be able to get to her without a small army."

My insides unclenched as a little fear eased. Arya and her babies were protected. First thing I planned to do after work tomorrow was drive down to see her.

"Mil."

I looked at Lex.

"Before you start arguing and getting your panties in a wad, let me give you the details of your protection."

I raised a brow at his words, but nodded my agreement. In the past, I'd argue if I ever felt anyone was trying to limit my freedom. Now, I would do what was necessary. The kidnapping and attack taught me a great lesson; my safety wasn't something to ignore.

"You will have James with you at all times, other than when you're at the penthouse. Arya has that place rigged tighter than Fort Knox. If you choose to drive, you will be followed." He paused. "I mean it, Mil. No trying to lose them in any of our sports cars."

"Okay," I whispered.

"No impromptu lunches out or shopping trips on the fly. No working late or alone at the office after five."

I frowned at that part. Late nights were a standard part of my day-to-day life, especially if I wanted to keep the finances for two companies up to date.

"Lex, I have to work, and some of our clients aren't in the same time zone."

"Then you can continue working after five and finish everything from your home office."

He made sense. I did have remote access to the secure server.

"Okay. I'm fine with that."

Something passed behind Lex's eyes, which I didn't understand. Was he upset I agreed with his demands?

"Lastly, and I know this will be the hardest with all your night-club ventures. No more late nights out. For all intents and purposes, you're done with the partying, table dancing, and your socialite life-style."

I wasn't going to have any problems following that particular directive. All the partying, drinking, and rebellion held no appeal. I was finished with trying to piss off Mamma. It was too much work and for what? For a childish need to stick it to her.

"No problem. I agree."

Lex growled, unbuckled his seat belt, and ran a frustrated hand through his hair.

"I don't believe this."

I scrunched my brows together and tilted my head. "I'm not following you. What are you talking about?"

Lex walked over to me, leaned down, and trapped me with his arms, giving me his Dom stare.

My breath hitched and, without thought, I lowered my gaze to my lap. A tinge of awareness prickled my skin.

His eyes burned into mine. "Why are you agreeing to everything? Why aren't you arguing with me? What the hell is going on, Mil?"

The edge in his voice cooled my desire, and I lifted my eyes to glare at him but kept my tone calm as I responded, "What do you want from me? I'm doing what's best for everyone. Give me a break."

"No. I don't buy it. This isn't you. You fight me tooth and nail until one of us gives in. I want the truth. You're never this accommodating or calm."

"Back off, Lex," I said through gritted teeth. He was pushing me to a point where I wouldn't be able to hold back the temper I was notorious for unleashing. I couldn't let him rile me up. I wasn't the same Milla anymore. "I don't want to say something I'll regret."

"Finally," he said. "I get a reaction out of you other than compliance."

I folded my arms around me. "What do you want from me? I'm doing the right thing. Why can't you leave it at that?"

"This isn't you, Mil." He touched my hand, but I flinched away, making his gaze narrow. "I want my wife back. The one who made love with as much passion as she fought me. I want the woman who I could talk to for hours about absolutely everything and anything. This"—he pointed to me—"is a stranger. I miss my wife, my Milla."

I turned my face to the window, unable to look him in the eyes anymore. Tears blurred my vision. He wanted a person who never put him first. I couldn't do that to him. He deserved better even if he didn't believe it.

"Please. I can't do this now."

"No, I deserve answers. Where did my take-no-prisoners girl go?"

I turned back to him. "She doesn't exist anymore. The girl you love, the one who hurt you continuously over the last ten years, had to grow up. I'm not good for you, Lex. Let me go."

He stood up and ran a frustrated hand across his face. "I made a promise in that church. Till death do us part. I won't let you push me away."

"You don't have a choice, Lex." The backs of my eyes burned with pain. I would love him until my dying breath. He was it for me. My first and last. No one else would take his place.

I could only pray that he'd let me go, and find someone who deserved him.

"How…how could you say that? This isn't you, *a ghrá*"

My heart clenched.

Please stop calling me that.

I had to tell him about the papers, and then he would see the truth.

"Lex, before I left Italy, I signed—"

At that moment, Chrystal came in.

"Mr. Duncan. Ms. Castra. I'm sorry to disturb you, but we must prepare the cabin for landing."

We nodded our agreement, and then Chrystal began readying for our arrival.

Lex released a frustrated breath. "This conversation isn't over," he said so only I could hear.

"Yes. It is," I retorted, then leaned my head back and closed my eyes, effectively shutting him out for the remainder of the flight.

* * *

Twenty minutes later, the wheels of the plane touched down at Logan International Airport. Immediately, a surge of happy giddiness entered my body.

I was home. Back to my work, my friends, my life, my hus—no, not anymore. The thought caused me to look at Lex, who was now ignoring me in return for what I'd done to him during the landing.

If I didn't say something, he would continue the silent treatment forever. He had the ability and stamina to wait as long as it took to make his point.

Cazzo! By shutting our conversation down, I'd reverted to the old Milla way of things.

How was he going to see I'd changed, if I kept reacting as I've always done?

Baby steps, Mil. Rome wasn't built in a day.

The doors on the plane opened, and we gathered our things. We continued our silence until we stepped onto the tarmac.

I touched Lex's sleeve. "I'm sorry."

He didn't look at me, but pulled his phone out. "For what exactly?"

"For shutting you out when I didn't want to talk anymore."

He shook his head and looked at me. "I'm not mad at you for that. I'm used to it by now." He tucked his cell back in his pocket and cupped my cheek.

I nuzzled without thinking, and a tremor shook my body.

"You're my wife. I feel lost at what to do for you. If we can't talk to each other, how are we going to fix whatever is wrong with us?"

Because I'm what's wrong with us.

"There's nothing we can do to fix it. The kidnapping made it crystal clear."

"Well, explain it to me because I don't understand any of the crap you're saying."

I pushed his hand away and stepped back a little, trying to put some distance between us, but he grasped my upper arm.

"I'm saying we can't be together. The old Milla only thought about herself. For the first time I'm putting you first. Please don't make it harder on me than it is."

"No." His grip tightened. "I won't make it easy. I know you want me."

I shoved out of his hold. "Wanting you isn't the issue. Doing the right thing is."

"God. You're so bloody frustrating. You keep talking in riddles. Give me a clear answer."

My temper flared. "You want answers, you deaf donkey? I'm saying we are over. I can't be your wife anymore. I can't be your submissive. I can't be anything to you." I wrapped my arms around myself. "I'm broken, and the only way to fix myself is to not make the same mistakes again."

"The hell we're over," he yelled.

"Excuse me, Mr. and Mrs. Duncan," James said from behind us.

I cringed at the address. *Merda*, I'd just told Lex we were finished, and James had to call us that, when he'd never done it before.

I bet Arya put him up to it.

Lex and I glared at James. He seemed unfazed by us.

"I suggest you continue this discussion out of public view." He gestured to his left, where a group of reporters stood, taking pictures and carrying large microphones.

I clenched my fists. I grew up with the paparazzi; I should have known better.

"*Cazzo*," I exclaimed as I moved past Lex and walked toward the waiting car. I was supposed to stay calm, to talk to Lex rationally. This was not supposed to be the way it happened.

I slipped into the limo and waited for Lex to enter, but the door closed and then moments later, James slipped into the driver's seat.

"Where's Lex?"

"He took another car."

Does this mean he accepted what I said?

I closed my eyes, letting the dread of what I'd set in motion hit me.

CHAPTER EIGHT

Forty minutes after leaving the airport and following a quick security search, I walked into my empty penthouse. Though my exhaustion from the trip and argument with Lex still lingered, a sense of relief washed over me the moment I crossed the apartment's threshold.

"Home sweet home." I sighed and scanned the room. I loved the eclectic style of my modern home with antique art scattered throughout the place. The smell of fresh flowers filled the foyer. A note sat under the vase sitting on the hallway table.

I'm so glad you're home, mera behna. I missed you. I've restocked the place so you won't have to survive on those yucky protein bars you love. Carmen also sent a case of your favorite Cabernet from her South African vineyard. Don't drink it all in one night.

x Arya

My heart warmed. Those girls loved me. The three musketeers always looked out for each other.

I walked into the living room, and the memories of the many years I'd spent in this penthouse with Lex hit me. The way he'd touch me and the tender way he'd attend to every one of my needs, always placing my pleasure before his. I glanced at the tear on the edge of the leather made after purchasing the oversized sectional.

I laughed to myself. We'd christened every available surface of this place.

How Arya never figured it out still amazed me. She was supposed to be the smart one of the group. The number of times she'd called to discuss something or came over unannounced and Lex was sleeping or working in the office were too numerous to count.

A little pang of guilt needled me. I'd lied to her and told her my Dom was here and he wanted to keep his identity private. Well, maybe not a complete lie, since Lex was my Dom, but the other part was a bold-faced fabrication. If Lex had any choice, he'd have shouted our relationship from the rooftops.

He deserves better than me.

Stop that, Milla. You deserve better, too.

I shook the melancholy from my head and strolled to my bathroom. I hoped that a hot shower would wash the funk from the flight, the guilt from my argument with Lex, and the sadness of my circumstances away.

Fifteen minutes later, I stepped out of the shower and slipped on my robe. Without a glance in the vanity mirror, I picked up the wine I'd left on the counter to breathe and moved to the balcony adjoining my bedroom. Staring into the night, I watched all of Boston come to life. Busy cars and high-rises everywhere, and in the distance the harbor and all the ships.

Music thumped from one of the units below me, making me smile. Oh, the parties the residents threw.

Hell, the parties Arya and I had thrown were memorable. Although the sneaky girl always orchestrated the chaos over here, instead of at her place, across the hall. There won't be any more of those. Especially not until the threat of Christof was gone.

No, I was using him as an excuse. The thought of Page Six capturing another picture of Lex throwing me over his shoulder after I decided to climb on a bar to dance held no appeal anymore.

As I told Lex, I wasn't the same girl anymore, and I didn't want to hear all the things my mother would call me when she learned about my escapades.

Shameful, slut, disgrace.

I closed my eyes against the names. Without thinking, I pulled out the phone in my robe pocket and dialed. Before I realized whom I'd called, Lex answered.

"Hello."

"Um. *Ciao.*"

"What can I do for you, Milla? Do you need assistance with something at ArMil?" His curt tone made my lips tremble. He still hadn't cooled off since we separated at the airport. "I just…just…I'm sorry I called." I shouldn't have dialed his number.

"Mil, it's okay. Sto—"

I hung up.

Depending on him for my comfort was wrong to both of us.

Why am I doing this to myself? I have to let him go.

I slid to the floor of my balcony and cried.

* * *

James picked me up for my short drive to ArMil's corporate offices around seven the next morning. A restless night and nightmares left me exhausted and a little bit on the grumpy side. Thankfully, my assistant, Rachel, sent a text informing me my favorite breakfast and coffee were waiting for me on my desk.

The gorgeous headquarters came into view, forty stories of steel and glass with clean lines and unique architecture. A grin touched my cheeks. The building belonged to Arya and me. Two girls from different worlds who created one of the top security software companies in the world.

See, Mamma, I didn't need your stinking money to make a success of myself.

"Mrs. Duncan, Are you ready for the day?"

I cringed as I glanced up from the window to James's refection in the rearview mirror.

He'd known me since the very weekend I'd married Lex. From the beginning, he used my formal name to address me, even when I told him to call me Milla. But until yesterday, he'd never called me by my married name.

"You're doing that on purpose," I stated.

"Doing what?" He feigned innocence, but the grumpy Russian wasn't going to get away with it.

"Why are you calling me that now and didn't before?"

"Because you need reminding. He isn't the same without you."

Guilt hit my gut.

"It's complicated, James."

"Take some advice from an old man. I was there the day you took your vows and saw the love between you. Even when I moved into my role of protecting Arya, I kept an eye on you. The love you shared hasn't diminished. Don't let it go so fast. What you think he deserves and what he truly deserves are two different things."

I cringed. "I guess you heard our argument?"

"Don't rush into anything." He glanced at me as he pulled into the parking garage.

I sighed. "I'll try not to."

James grunted in response and then said, "Getting back to work will be good for you."

"I couldn't agree with you more. I tried to keep up with all the finances in Italy, but our Arya has signed us up for so many new projects that my calendar is packed for the next month and a half."

James chuckled. "Bed rest has made her a little overzealous."

"That's an understatement. She thinks I'm Superwoman."

"I have complete confidence in your ability to multitask."

"Speaking of Arya. She's like a daughter to you; why didn't you tell her about Lex and me?"

"Because you're both mine. Protecting my family is what I do and that also means keeping the secrets they want me to keep."

"Oh." Tears prickled the back of my eyes. "Thank you for always being there for me."

"*Pozhaluysta*, Mrs. Duncan."

The car pulled to a stop at the private elevators to my office.

"Please allow me to escort you to your office."

"James, I can handle a little trip to my office. Remember, you're the one who taught me to shoot a gun."

He frowned, but remained silent, giving me that *I am a Russian enforcer and could give two shits what you want* look.

"Okay. Fine. Never too safe, right?"

Unaffected by my comment, he exited the car and opened my door.

My phone beeped, indicating a text.

I snuck out of the estate. Come see me in my office. Act casual and don't let James know or he'll tattle to Max.

Great, only two minutes in the building and Arya had already pulled me into another one of her schemes.

I stepped out into the garage and strolled to the private entrance. "James, I think I'll be okay going into the elevator alone."

He lifted a brow as if he suspected I was up to something. "I have strict instructions. Mr. Duncan informed me that you agreed to all of his terms, which include my accompanying you everywhere."

I had agreed to Lex's list, but what was going to happen to me here, in the headquarters of the largest security technology company in the world?

I sighed. "If I promise not to leave without calling you, will you give me some space? The elevator leads straight to my floor, and the impenetrable fort Arya created up there should keep me safe. Hell, I can't even access the elevators without a retina scan and a thumbprint. I don't believe there's anything to worry about."

James conceded. "As you wish, Mrs. Duncan." The slight smile on his lips told me he was testing me.

The sneaky old man wanted to see how far he could push me. I may have changed in the past six months, but I still wasn't a pushover.

I entered the elevator and responded to Arya's text.

I'm going to kick your pregnant ass if Max blames me for this. Give me a few minutes to drop off my stuff and I'll find you. I missed you so much.

I squealed a little inside at the thought of my best friend and me back together again. The doors opened, and a whiff of warm pastries greeted me. I loved Rachel so much. She deserved a raise.

Dropping my bag and purse on my desk, I picked up my coffee, gulped down half the mug, and refilled it with the giant thermos accompanying the cup.

Stacks of folders covered my desk, perfectly organized by level of priority. Thank goodness for my team. Even if I wasn't at the office to handle the day-to-day tasks, I had a crew to keep everything running while I recuperated.

I took a last sip of my liquid fuel and glanced at my waiting pastries and yogurt then shook my head.

Pastries versus Arya, Pastries versus Arya. Hmmm. Arya wins.

Her phone call before the gala and all the drama afterward left me in need of some one-on-one time with my sister. However, there was so much work requiring my attention, I had only a few minutes for socializing. With any luck, I'd sneak in a quick visit before Max arrived to collect his errant wife.

Errant wife… I'm one to talk.

I walked toward Arya's office and found Kerry, Arya's assistant, waving me into the office.

"Hurry, Mil. Max is on his way and he's furious."

"Don't tell me she has a tracker on him and knows his ETA?"

"You got it. Our girl genius wanted to keep tabs on her hubby so she could escape her luxurious prison."

I shook my head. "Max just wants to keep her safe. I don't think either of them is in a sane state of mind. At least until the twins arrive."

"Speaking of keeping one safe. How are you dealing with James? I told Lex you wouldn't go for it, but he just gave me that stare and walked out of the room."

Oh, I was familiar with the stare, but the effect it had on me was on a different level.

"James is just doing his job. He loves both me and Arya like his daughters. For at least a little while, I won't give him a hard time."

Kerry gaped at me, as if my words made no sense.

I shook my head, and I walked toward Arya's office door. "Is she in there?"

"No, she's in the tech lab. She snuck in through the service elevator and then hid in case James or Lex saw her."

I reached the vault room and worked my way through all the security doors. When I opened the last one, I found a very pregnant Arya sitting on a reclining sectional watching television.

"You can do this at home, woman."

Arya's eyes lit up, and she made her best attempt to sit up but failed. "Mil, stop laughing at me and help me get the fuck up so I can hug your stupid ass."

I rushed to her and held her tight. "I missed you, *bella*. By the way, I thought you were working on your potty mouth. If your kids' first words are 'fuck' or 'shit,' Aunt Elana is going to be pissed."

"Whatever. Stop saying that or you'll jinx me." Arya scanned me, and I turned away from her scrutiny. She captured my face and ran a thumb under my eyes. I guessed the concealer hadn't hidden the dark circles very well.

"You need to talk to him and fix whatever it is you fought about yesterday. I couldn't get anything but one-word answers out of him when he brought me my croissants today."

"It isn't as simple as talking about it, Ari."

"Don't be stupid like me and wait until you have no other choice, and then spill everything."

"I concur." A whiskey-smooth voice spoke from the doorway.

Arya cringed and tried to hide behind me.

"Sorry, *bella*. You're as big as a house and there's no way to camouflage you." I turned and hugged Max. "Hey, big brother, how's life treating you?"

"Nice try, Mil, but sweet talk isn't going to get her out of the crap she's in."

I shrugged and took a seat in the rolling chair near a computer console. "It was worth a try."

Max strolled over to Arya, picked her up, and then sat down with her on the sofa. He pushed her back to reclining and took her feet in his hands. "You do realize that I'm not letting you out of my sight from now on?"

"Ohhh," Arya moaned. "Right there. You have magic hands, babe."

"Gag." I pretended to stick my fingers in my mouth.

"You have nothing to say, Miss I Spent the Last Ten Years Having Foreplay in Public with My Secret Husband."

"Well, about that…oh, look at the time." I glanced at my watch. "I have to…"

"Stop right there. I want to hear all about it when you aren't distracted. You'll come spend the weekend at my place and we can discuss this over a bottle of wine that I cannot drink."

"Bossy as ever. Max, are you sure you aren't the submissive?"

"Fuck off, Milla." Max and Arya bellowed in unison.

I laughed and left the couple to sort out the escape from estate-gate.

CHAPTER NINE

I strode toward my office, laughing as I remembered the scowl on Arya's face. The girl was like an angry bear with a thorn in her paw. But I loved her. She radiated beauty, and pregnancy agreed with her.

Pain shot through my heart.

I'll never get a chance for my own.

I crossed the threshold of my office and watched the reflection of sunlight through the red-and-pink-crystal Pegasus that Lex had given me to celebrate the first anniversary of ArMil. I picked up the statue and traced the mythical being, holding it close to my heart. I stared out the window and gazed at the city below.

The last time we'd shared this space, he made love to me against the window while conducting a conference call on trade tariffs.

My core clenched, and an unfulfilled ache throbbed inside me. God, I missed him, not just as my lover but also as my confidante. I could share anything with him. He never judged and always allowed me to be me.

Was I making the right decision?

A buzz sounded. "Milla, your meeting will start in ten minutes. Lex and the team have just arrived."

"Thanks, Rachel. Let them know I'll be there shortly."

I grabbed a pastry, finished it quickly, and chugged my coffee. Breakfast on the go. I poured another cup, grabbed my papers, and headed for the conference room.

I walked into the room, and a storm of well-wishing and *welcome backs* greeted me. The only exception to the happy exchange was Lex. He scanned his phone, never glancing my way.

I approached the seat next to him, and he lifted his gaze. I inhaled sharply as our eyes clashed and my heart sped up.

Don't stare at me like that.

My lips trembled, and the urge to kneel overwhelmed me. He held my gaze as my Master, not my business partner or husband.

How long had it been since we'd played together? Six and a half months, to be exact. The dream on the plane didn't count.

Lex broke the trance by gesturing to the chair next to him. I shook the fog from my mind, took my seat, and waited for Rachel to dial into the conference call.

"How was your first night back?" Lex purred in the voice that sent a flood of sensation to my core.

"Fine," I said. "How was yours?"

"Not too eventful. I had to attend an opening for a gallery. I should have taken a shower on the jet. But then again, it might have been for the better since it holds too many memories. You remember, don't you, love?" he whispered and grazed a finger across my wrists.

The memory of him tying me to the handles of the shower and tormenting me flashed before my eyes. I squirmed, hoping to elevate the arousal now coursing through my body.

"Don't."

"Don't what? You seem a little flushed. Is something the matter?"

I fixed him with a glare, then turned back to Rachel as the conference started.

I spent the next hour and a half in complete frustration. Lex used "the voice" every time he addressed me, and my body reacted. The periodic quirk of his mouth told me he knew exactly what he was doing.

At this moment, the last thing I wanted to listen to was the detailed plans for ArMil's finances. My body was in such a state of arousal, I couldn't think straight. Thank goodness, Rachel ended the call. I had to get out of this room and away from any contact with Lex.

I gathered my papers and rushed toward my office. Shutting the door, I leaned against it. I closed my eyes and steadied my breath. How would I push aside ten years of training to respond to the slightest change in the inflection of his voice?

In the past, as soon as the meeting finished, Lex would've followed me to my office, locked the door, and then we'd have fucked like bunnies until we quenched our needs.

After a few more deep breaths, I walked over to my desk, poured another cup of coffee, and drank it down. Caffeine wasn't the best choice for my overstimulated nerves but it was my addiction. A knock echoed into the room. Why would Rachel knock?

I opened the door to find Lex waiting for me. He stalked forward as I retreated. His blazing blue eyes screamed angry Dom. A slight whimper escaped my lips.

I jumped as my back hit the front of my desk. Why was I retreating? This was my office. I stood straight, and my oversensitive body brushed against Lex's very aroused one.

At least I'm not the only one affected.

"What do you need?" I whispered.

Damn. I sounded breathless and desperate.

He leaned toward me and paused. His breath grazed my lips, and his eyes dilated. Without thought, my hand slipped to the front of his suit jacket.

"I know what you want. I know what you crave."

"L-Lex. I…"

He shushed me with a finger to my mouth. "You want me to push you onto this desk, part those luscious thighs, and fuck you until you can't see straight. Am I right?"

I bit my lips, hoping to keep myself from responding. The heat lingering on my face soaked into my whole body.

He rubbed a thumb over my chin, down my neck, and between the open collar of my blouse. "I know your body is burning"—he grazed his cheek against the side of my face—"with a fire so raw only I can quench it. Only I can tame the need making your breath shallow and your pussy wet."

I almost purred.

All of a sudden, he pulled back, stepped away, and handed me a folder.

"Wait. What?" I stared at him in confusion.

"You said we're over. Your body's reaction tells me we are far from it. But until you realize ending things is a mistake, I cannot relieve the frustration we both suffer from. Have these papers signed before you leave today. They rescind the power of attorney you transferred to me before you left for Italy."

With those words, he left me without a backward glance.

* * *

On Friday, after a busy week of playing catch-up and no time to do anything but work, eat, and sleep, I drove up to the gated entrance of Arya and Max's estate. As expected, a member of my security detail followed me and then left as soon as I passed through the gated entrance of the property.

Lush greenery surrounded the magnificent house, and flowers bloomed around every corner. The beautiful grounds remind me of the fun nights I'd spent laughing with my brothers during the balmy Italian summers of my youth.

I wasn't the wild child then. I was the spoiled but happy girl who thought no men were better than my papa and my brothers. I'd accepted that Mamma wasn't one to play or enjoy the little things in life.

I sighed. What could have turned Mamma into such an unhappy and cold mother? Papa insisted she wasn't always like this, but from all the rumors growing up, she was a royal bitch from the moment of her marriage. Guilt filled me. I shouldn't think of her like that; we all have our demons.

"Ms. Castra, welcome back." The security attendant approached my car. "So sorry I didn't recognize your car. Is it new?" He eyed the over-the-top Bugatti.

"Ciao, Robert. Yes. It was a gift from Mr. Duncan."

Lex loved his cars and telling by Robert's reaction, so did he. Boys and their toys. However, I couldn't lie to myself. I loved the car, too, especially the speed and the adrenaline rush I received whenever I took it to the track.

"Tell Mr. Duncan he has great taste." His eyes twinkled, and then he winked.

"I will."

Robert waved me through, and I drove toward the house. I shook my head. Why did I get the feeling he wasn't just referring to the car?

I parked behind a silver Viper and frowned as I noticed it had New York plates. Then it registered.

Carmen!

I jumped out of the car, and before I even shut the door, Arya and Carmen were running down the front of the steps. Well, Carmen ran; Arya waddled.

The girls wrapped me in hugs and kisses.

"God, I missed you, you Italian bitch." Carmen laughed.

I jokingly frowned. "Be nice. My delicate sensibilities can't take the swearing."

Both girls released me and led me up the stairs of the sprawling Dane mansion.

"Carmen, wouldn't you agree our nieces or nephews are going to come out with sailors' mouths?" I asked as Arya pinched me.

"Don't say that. Aunt Elana told me she's going to smack me every time one of my kids says 'shit.'"

"Well, then ixnay with the itshay."

I paused midstep. "Has hell frozen over or did Carmen come down with a case of pig Latin?"

"Hardy har, har. Didn't mean to upset your aristocratic Italian sensibilities. Let's get your ass inside so we can start our girls-only weekend."

I ignored her statement and looked around. "So what did you girls do with Max? He isn't the type not to hover while porky here is about to pop." I gestured to Arya.

"Hey, not nice. Bad *masi.*" Arya waddled her way to the first lounger as soon as we entered the pergola-covered terrace.

My heart warmed at the word, meaning "mom's sister."

"To answer your question, Max and Lex had to fly to Germany for some business negotiations. Max didn't want to leave, but the Japanese executives insisted he meet them. This would eliminate a trip to Japan in a few weeks, so he decided it was better to meet sooner rather than later." Carmen grabbed the lounger next to Arya, and I took the one opposite them.

"If I pop before he gets back, I'm going to kick his ass." Arya rubbed her belly but her lips trembled.

"Woo there, just lie back and calm down." I rushed to Arya and pushed her back against the chair.

"One of you bitches needs to start drinking. I can't but you can."

Who knew pregnancy cravings came in the form of champagne and sushi. Leave it to Arya to crave the two things she couldn't have.

Both Carmen and I grabbed our cocktails. I downed mine without a thought and then noticed Carmen's raised eyebrow and Arya's smirk.

I shrugged my shoulders. "What? I was thirsty." I rarely drank anymore, but with these girls, I was free to relax.

"So tell me what's been going on with you ladies while I've been under house arrest."

We filled each other in on our busy days, and Arya relayed her punishment for sneaking away from home.

"I can't believe he reprogrammed the door to your home computer lab. He does know you're a tech genius, right?"

The devilish grin Arya flashed me told me she'd had her revenge.

"Let me guess. You rigged the room to lock down on him."

Carmen cringed at my guess and then fell on the floor laughing.

"Not only was he locked in, he lost all cell and Internet connections. I stopped by on Wednesday and had the pleasure of dealing with Max until I could figure out a way to get him out. The cuss words coming from that room put the fat one over there to shame."

"Hey, don't mess with a pregnant woman and her technology."

We laughed and spent the next few hours enjoying ourselves. After dinner, we returned to our perch underneath the pergola.

"I need to discuss something with you." Arya picked up her drink, took a sip, and then stared at me.

Uh-oh, that tone meant I was in trouble.

"Milla, you need to fix Lex."

"What?" When did that become my duty?

From the moment you married him, idiot.

"The carefree Irishman we love hasn't made an appearance for most of the year. I'm tired of the over-the-top-serious, tell-everyone-what-to-do, grumpy-with-no-smile Lex."

"Arya's right, Mil. I've known Lex since we were kids. This isn't like him. Take him to the club, let him whip you to orgasm, and help him bring his mojo back."

I cringed at the thought of the club. My lips trembled, and I felt tears pool in my eyes.

Carmen jumped up and crouched in front of me. "Baby girl. What's wrong?"

"I can't…" Tears streamed down my cheeks. "You don't know what they did to me. I…I know Lex would never hurt me, but the thought of a whip…" I shook my head. "I…can't do it…I…can't."

Carmen held me as I cried. Soon Arya was holding both of us, and we cried together. Wanting Lex sexually was one thing, but the mere idea of a whip sent a wave of nausea into my stomach. Lex deserved someone who could enjoy all the kinks he loved. I wasn't that girl anymore, either.

After my emotions settled, I drank a glass of water Arya handed me, and then Carmen settled my head in her lap.

"I can't ask Lex to give up the lifestyle he loves. He deserves a woman who can fulfill his needs."

Carmen stroked my hair. "Love adapts to the needs of the couple. It's always evolving." She sighed. "Don't be stupid like me and push love away because of fear and then get pushed away in return."

"Speaking of…" I sat up. "What's going on with you and Mr. Thomas Regala?"

"Nice try." She quirked a brow. "Don't change the subject."

I shrugged my shoulders. "It was worth a shot."

"Carmen's right. I nearly lost Max with my stupidity. Give Lex the benefit of the doubt."

"Girls, I don't think you understand. I'm not good for him."

"That's an excuse." Arya crossed her arms and glared at me.

"No, you're wrong. Can't you see that I've caused him nothing but heartache over the last ten years? He doesn't need more of my baggage. The right thing to do is let him find someone who deserves him. I'm not doing this for me, it's for him."

"Mil, are you going to be okay with another woman touching your man?" Carmen asked with a disapproving tone in her voice.

It would kill me the day I saw it, but I'd learn to live with it.

"He won't be my man much longer."

"What the hell is that supposed to mean?" Arya pointed a finger at me. "Please tell me you didn't do what I think you did."

I flinched and then nodded. "I started the paperwork while I was in Italy."

Carmen ordered, "You stop it right now. If you sign the official decree, I will personally kick your ass."

"I'm trying to do right by him. Why can't you understand?"

Arya growled. "Because you're not. You're not only going to destroy your heart, you're going to tear his apart, too. The man loves you more than anything on earth."

"Staying with him would hurt him more."

"She's lost her mind," Arya said as she pushed herself to standing and then paced. "That's the only explanation."

"Calm down, Arya." Carmen helped her back to sitting. "Mil, please don't do anything rash. Don't make any final decisions until you've truly thought it through."

I sighed and rubbed my temples. Now I was second-guessing my decision more than ever. "I can't make any promises, but I'll think about it."

"That's all we ask," Arya whispered, taking a sip of her virgin cocktail. "Okay. No more serious talk. Time to enjoy our girls-only weekend with lots of chocolate and cakes."

"Says the land barge in a five-foot frame."

Arya scowled at Carmen, but her eyes twinkled with laughter. I should have been relieved by the change in subject, but all I could think about was Lex with another woman and how I was going to survive looking at a life I could have had from the outside in.

CHAPTER TEN

On Sunday, I returned from my girls' weekend to review some paperwork for a Monday morning meeting on shipping rights for a mine in South Africa.

After dropping my weekend bag on the floor, I charged straight for my coffeemaker. A little caffeine would do wonders for the task ahead. Lex had e-mailed me the overall legal logistics, but I wanted to make sure I entered the meeting with all the information at the tip of my tongue. The profits from the project would fund the foundation Arya and I created, to help women and girls across the world find access to education and health care.

I was apprehensive when Arya suggested the purchase. Who bought a ten-million-dollar deserted property without inspecting it? Arya, of course. She insisted the property was a gold mine since her computer analysis software had surveyed the area. Well, it turned out not to be gold but diamonds. Thank goodness for my brilliant best friend.

When it came to funding the purchase, we couldn't justify using company coffers for the land, so Arya and I split the cost fifty-fifty. Now I owned half of a diamond mine outside of Johannesburg. A mine no one knew existed.

After adding a spoonful of sugar to my espresso, I sighed.

Who would have thought the spoiled rebel child of the Castra dynasty would run the finances of two different billion-dollar companies and create a fortune surpassing her inheritance or the value of her entire family's estate?

I shook my head. "Eat your heart out, Mamma."

I finished my coffee, rinsed the cup in the sink, and strode into my bedroom for a change of clothes. Yoga pants and a T-shirt were on the agenda for the day.

As I entered my closet, I caught the glint of Lex's Rolex on my jewelry tray. My heart sank. He hadn't been in our apartment since I left six months earlier. All of his things still lined one side of my closet, from his designer suits to his favorite sneakers.

Why would he leave them here? He had access to the penthouse. Hell, he had access to everything in my life.

I picked up the phone and dialed his number. A sudden anxiety filled me. Would he be home or would he still be on his trip?

Lex answered on the second ring. "What can I do for you, Mil?"

I hesitated, and then spoke. "I…I wanted to return your things to you. Why didn't you come get them?"

"I've lived without them for the previous six months. I've gotten used to making do."

"What's that supposed to mean?"

"Exactly what I said. If you want to bring them by, it's up to you."

I ached at the emotionless tone of his voice. "I'll drop them off later this afternoon. I have to prepare for the meeting tomorrow. I'll stop by your condo on my way to the office."

"I don't live there anymore. I sold it."

What? When did that happen?

"Oh. Then where do you live? I'll drop it off there."

"Across the hall."

A ball formed in my stomach. He was only a door away. Had he bought it before or after the kidnapping?

"When did you buy the place?"

"Does it matter?"

"I…suppose not."

Lex sighed. "I bought Arya's place from her when she married Max. If you insist on returning my things, come over now. I leave in thirty minutes."

I'll chicken out if I don't go there now.

"I'll be there in a moment."

We hung up, and I gathered all of Lex's favorite things. With each piece of clothing or jewelry I placed in his travel bag, my heart ached more.

Am I making a mistake?

Shaking my doubts aside, I settled the strap of the bag over my shoulder and grasped Lex's suits with my other hand.

I exited my penthouse and crossed the hallway to Arya's—Lex's penthouse.

My finger reached to enter the access code, but I pulled back. It wasn't Arya's anymore, and I didn't have the right to enter without permission.

I grazed the keypad. Had he changed the code?

I closed my eyes and inhaled deep. Lex was my one safe place in the world, and now I was trying to let him go.

Maybe the girls were right.

I pushed the doorbell before I could wallow in the thought.

Lex opened the door, and my breath hitched. He wore jogging pants and a gray T-shirt that accentuated his muscular shoulders. Memories of half-naked workout sessions flashed before my eyes.

His brow lifted, and then he stepped back. "Come in. I was having a drink before heading to the gym."

He walked to the bar, poured a finger of Macallan, and drank deeply. "Set the stuff anywhere. It doesn't matter."

When did he start drinking before a workout?

It wasn't my problem anymore.

I set the suits over the back of his leather sofa. "Here." I handed him his travel bag and swiveled to leave, but he caught my wrist.

I turned back, and our eyes held. A tingle ran up my arm.

"You forgot something." His thumb rubbed the pulse on my wrist, and my heart sped up.

Don't do this, Lex.

"All of your favorite things are here. The rest you can get later."

He lifted my hand and grazed it against his whiskers. "There is something important you forgot."

I licked my lips. "What?" I questioned through a breathless whisper.

He leaned in, a hairbreadth from me. "You."

Then he fisted my hair and captured my lips, pushing me against the door and devouring my mouth.

God, I missed this. I have to stop this before we go any further.

But the taste of whiskey exploded across my tongue, making me crave more of him.

His free hand roamed up my waist to cup my breast. My nipples pebbled on contact.

"Oh, Lex," I moaned against his mouth as any lingering thought of leaving evaporated.

"I've waited so long," he murmured as he pulled back.

We stared at each other, not saying a word. My fingers trembled as I reached out and drew him back to me. But he resisted.

"Be sure, Mil."

"I was always sure of you. It's me I'm undecided on."

With those words, I sealed our lips together. He slanted his over mine in response.

Lex lifted me against the door and brought one of my legs around his waist. He ground his erection against my core, and wetness flooded me. My fingers flexed on his shoulders as I tilted my pelvis, trying to increase the sensation on my clit.

It has been so long. No one turns me on like he does.

Lex released my leg, clasped my wrists in one hand and pinned them above my head. I drowned in the sea of his eyes and the emotion staring at me.

Even though I never deserved it, he loved me.

He leaned his head against mine, breathing heavy. "I don't want to scare you, but I've been waiting over six months to claim you. Give me a second to catch my breath and gain some control."

My pussy contracted at his words. I smiled. "You'd never hurt me. Well, not unless I asked you to."

He chuckled and groaned. "Don't make me laugh. I'm a few seconds from tearing off your clothes and sinking into your heat."

A tremor quaked my body, and I rubbed my sensitized nipples against his chest. "Lex…please…I need you."

He tilted his head and grazed the side of my ear with his tongue. "As you wish, *a ghrá*. But promise you'll let me know if I'm too rough."

A tingle of worry crept in but then calmed. This wasn't a scene. We were going to make love like normal people.

My nod was all he needed. He licked and sucked my neck, biting down gently.

He released my arms for a mere second to remove my shirt before capturing them again. His fingers traced the chain with my wedding band, and then he sighed. He dropped it and moved lower.

I froze as his hand grazed down my stomach.

"What is it?"

The tenderness and concern in his voice melted my fear. "I don't have the perfect body that you loved. The scars are fading, but they cover most of my body."

"You'll always be exceptional to me." He kneeled down and allowed my arms to fall to my side. I remained pinned to the door and watched his face as he examined the light pinkish whip marks slashed across my breasts, stomach, and arms.

Will my body repulse him?

He cupped my breasts, pinching the peaks. "Still perfect. Still mine, always mine."

He skimmed his tongue down the middle of my body, over my belly button, to the waistband of my yoga pants. My skin heated under his touch. He tugged at the elastic, taking my pants and underwear down and pooling my clothes at my feet. I lifted my feet out of the garments, and he tossed them behind him.

He traced my bare flesh with his fingers. "Still waxed?" He nuzzled his face against my pussy.

"L-lasered," I whispered. "Remember?"

"Yes, how could I forget? What did you call it? Tit for tat." His tongue traced the seam of my lower lips.

A moan escaped my mouth. "Be happy it was only your chest and not your balls."

He smiled against me. "I think my balls were safe. My wife is a jealous creature and won't let anyone see the goods."

"Damn straight…" I tilted my head back against the door.

Lex parted my folds and sucked my clit into his mouth. My legs gave out, but his hands held me up.

"Yes, God yes." I loved his hot and hungry mouth. I parted my thighs to give him better access. He lapped at my aching nub, making me writhe against the door.

I drowned in the sensation coursing through my body. I shifted my hips to the rhythm of his tongue. He ate at me as if I were his last meal, sucking and savoring my taste. My heart thundered out of control, and a cry escaped my lips. "Lex, I need more."

The flick of his tongue and the squeeze on my waist told me he heard my request, but he wasn't ready to stop.

He lifted one hand from my hips up to my breast, pinching my nipple into a hard, aching bud. A sharp pleasure-pain shot through my body and increased the throbbing between my legs.

"More," he whispered as he pushed a finger into me.

I rode his fingers as he feasted at my aching, swollen nub. Just when I couldn't take any more, he bit lightly on my clit, and stars exploded behind my eyes. My orgasm roared through my body, lasting for longer than I could tell. He knew how to make my core sing.

"I could eat at your sweet pussy every day and never be satisfied."

I floated down with a final shudder. The urge to touch him overwhelmed me. With a last lick, he stood, capturing my lips. His tongue pushed into my mouth, and my essence flowed onto my taste buds, increasing my barely calmed arousal.

"Do you still like your taste?"

"Only from your lips," I murmured. I shifted my head to the side, trying to steady my breath. "Shirt now," I ordered between pants.

He quirked an eyebrow, smiled, and took a single step back. "Demanding, aren't we?"

He pulled his shirt off, and I nearly swallowed my tongue. He revealed a muscular chest and ropes of chiseled abs honed from years of Tai Chi. Then my heart clenched as I realized he'd lost weight. I wanted to apologize but kept my mouth shut.

He cupped my face. "Don't look so sad. I'll gain it back. Especially now that you're home."

I gave him a weary smile and nodded. Reaching out, I ran my fingers down the center of his chest, over his stomach, and to his cloth-covered cock. I squeezed, and a tremor traveled over his skin.

I can't believe this gorgeous man loves me.

Lex gripped my hair as I kneeled down. I tucked my fingers into his waistband and slid his pants to the floor. His beautiful cock sprung free and nudged against my lips. Out of instinct, I licked the tip.

"I don't think so." He pulled me up and lifted me against the door. "We'll save that talent of yours for another time. Right now I need your heat."

I wrapped my legs around his waist as his cock sat poised at my entrance. A drop of sweat slid down the side of his face, and his breath was ragged. My pussy throbbed with anticipation.

Why is he waiting?

I adjusted my hips, and his tip slipped in. I gasped then whimpered as the shock of pain and pleasure engulfed me.

Lex squeezed my hips, stopping my movement. "Baby, it's going to hurt. Not like the first time, but it will hurt. You aren't used to my size."

"Please, I'm dying here." I adjusted again, and he slid further in.

"Mil, give me a…Fuck." He slammed into me.

I arched my neck as white-hot pain shot through me. Holy shit, I forgot how big he was!

He instantly stilled. "I'm sorry, *a ghrá*."

My nails dug into his shoulder as my body adjusted and my muscles struggled to stretch around him. "How the hell could I forget you packed a monster cock?"

Lex grunted, breath heaving against my neck. "Don't make me laugh. I'm holding on by a thread."

I rubbed my face against his cheek. "I missed this. I'm sorry." My voice quivered.

He placed a finger across my lips. "Shh." Then he sealed our mouths together. He pulled out a fraction, and the bite of sweltering ecstasy pushed the melancholy away.

My clit throbbed, and a spasm fired in my pussy. "Lex. Move."

"As you wish, *a ghrá*." He pushed my knees up and wide and thrust deep. He pummeled my pussy, sending tremors back into my swollen core.

"Lex. Oh God." I dug my nails into his arms.

"That's it. Ride it out."

My body erupted, squeezing tight around his cock. Moments before I came down, he slid his fingers between us and strummed my strained clit.

"One more."

On command, my body convulsed again, sending him into his own release.

We remained against the door until our brain cells returned to functioning and our hearts calmed. Lex carried me to the sofa, keeping us connected. He sat down with me on top of him and tucked my head against his chest.

"I don't think I can move."

He rubbed the base of my neck. "Good. Then you can't run away."

"I was coming back home, Lex."

"I know, *a ghrá*." His other hand grazed the Pegasus tattoo above my right butt cheek.

My tattoo represented knowledge, glory, and inspiration, everything my mother accused me of lacking. I lifted my head and stared into his gorgeous passion-cooled eyes.

He cupped the back of my head and drew me in for a kiss as his cock stirred to life inside me.

"Am I going to be able to walk tomorrow?" I mumbled against his lips, allowing the reawakening sensation to fill me.

"I guess you'll just have to find out."

CHAPTER ELEVEN

A beep woke me from a deep sleep. As I turned over, the scent of soap and light cologne filled my senses.

I lifted my head and searched my surroundings. *I'm in Lex's room.* No wonder I slept so hard. He was my refuge.

Reality set in. *Oh, God. What have I done?* This was not good.

I dropped back onto the bed and covered my eyes with the back of my hand. Memories of the night before flooded my mind. After making love for the second time on the couch, Lex had carried me to the bedroom and made good on the promise of making it impossible to walk.

I stretched my legs, and the ache against the inside of my thighs sent a pleasurable sting through my body.

Don't get used to this, Mil. You're the one seeking a divorce.

My heart sank. How was he going to believe it was over when deep down I knew it would never be over for either of us?

I rolled over onto my stomach and covered my head with a pillow.

Last night, it was like old times but deeper, like he was trying to remind me of the connection we shared.

No matter how much I wished things were different, making love again didn't change anything. He deserved better than what I'd done to him.

My lips trembled.

Now I had to convince him of something I wasn't so sure I could live with anymore. Maybe, once the divorce was final, I'd move to another city. It would make it easier than seeing him with another woman. I didn't want to leave Arya, but the pain of seeing Lex and not being with him would tear me apart.

God, I am so messed up.

My phone beeped again. I ignored the alert. If it was Arya, I'd spill my guts, and I wasn't in the mood to talk to her. Especially when I didn't understand what was happening.

I tossed the pillow to the side, stretched one last time, and rolled off the bed. Heading straight for the closet, I grabbed one of Lex's T-shirts and slipped it over my naked body.

I walked into the bathroom and stared at myself in the mirror. The bags under my eyes were gone, but my irises still held the sadness of my attack and the decisions I planned to make.

Turning on the water in the sink, I freshened up and headed into the apartment in search of something to wake me up.

I entered the kitchen and found no sign of Lex, except the empty coffee mug in the sink. Pouring myself a cup, I drank deep and hummed to myself. He never skimped on the type of brew he kept at home.

How many mornings had I spent like this, searching for Lex and ending up in the kitchen with a cup of coffee?

I closed my eyes and inhaled deep. I had to talk to Lex about what happened yesterday. It was wrong to let him get his hopes up when nothing had changed. We weren't right for each other.

I glanced at the clock on the wall. Six fifteen. That meant he was in the gym practicing his Tai Chi.

Time to get this torture over with. I squared my shoulders and strode toward the gym. The place looked so different without Arya's feminine touches and knickknacks. Now dark wood furniture and masculine sculptures occupied every space.

I passed the door where Arya used to keep her prized artwork. *What did he do to this room?*

Opening the door, I froze in place. On the wall hung a picture of me lying on a hammock, eyes closed and smiling. I bit my lips as I approached the image and gently touched the glass.

I'd been so carefree and content then. Lex and I had finished making love, and I wanted to get some sun. All the hiking and swimming on Virgin Gorda had given my skin a deep golden hue.

We'd escaped to the beautiful British Virgin Island for our fifth anniversary. A time before the billion-dollar deals and the kidnapping, with only my rebellion against my mother to occupy my time.

I traced the wedding band I wore. I wasn't ashamed of it when we were alone.

How did we manage to keep it a secret for so long?

Especially from Arya. The girl genius was as naïve as they came when dealing with relationships. For years, she tried to turn Lex and me into a couple, not realizing our quiet chemistry was all foreplay for the nights we spent together.

Lex, for some reason, got off on the rebellious brat I loved to play. Why he'd put up with my shit for so long I'd never understand.

Because he loves you, Mil.

I shook that thought from my mind, glanced one last time at the picture, and walked out of the room.

I'd better talk to Lex before I change my mind.

I followed the hallway until I reached Arya's gym, er...Lex's gym. I pushed the door open and nearly drooled. Lex stood shirtless, facing away from me. The sunlight bounced off his sweat-sheened muscles. His loose pajama pants bunched in all the right places, highlighting his firm backside. I licked my lips, mesmerized by his gorgeous form. He slid his leg sideways, bending at the waist and crouching into a smooth stance, known as the snake creeps down in the grass. A series of poses I'd watched Lex perfect over the past ten years.

He rose and progressed through another succession of leg and arm movements. His muscles contracted and extended with graceful precision, reminding me of the control and power he held over me throughout the night.

I swallowed, trying to quench my parched throat. *Why does it never get old watching him like this?* My heart pounded as I shifted my legs back and forth in hopes of relieving the arousal rising in my body. One look at the man and I was ready to jump him.

"Stop staring at my ass and do your yoga. It will ease some of the arousal your shallow breath is giving away."

"Lex we need to...I need to...I..." Why couldn't I get it out?

He stopped his pose and stood, turning toward me. He gazed at me as if he could read my mind. "Mil, do your yoga. We'll talk after."

"How did you know?"

He picked up a towel and wiped the sweat from his brow. "Because I know you, and right now you can't decide if last night was a mistake or not."

I opened my mouth to deny his statement, but shut it when he raised his brow. Maybe he was right. A little yoga would give me the calm I needed to tell Lex about wanting a divorce.

"Lex, please, after we workout, we have to talk. I have to tell you about something I did." *I should just tell him now.* "Lex, when I was in Italy, I started..."

He placed a finger on my lips, silencing my next words.

"Yoga now, talking later."

I let out an exasperated breath. "Fine."

He scanned my clothing and gave me a smile that sent butterflies into my stomach. "Nice shirt."

"I wasn't planning on spending the night." I tugged at the white undershirt, pulling it lower down my hips, and then gave up. How was I going to do yoga with only this shirt on? "Let me go back and change."

I moved to leave, and he grabbed my hand.

"I'm not complaining." He rubbed my wrist where my pulse drummed under his thumb.

My skin began to tingle, and an unquenched need ignited again. "Lex, this isn't a good idea."

If I didn't leave, I was in so much trouble.

"Mil." His voice dropped into the timbre that made me urge to do his bidding.

"Yes."

His eyes dilated as I stared at him. "Yoga now. Then we'll talk."

If I stayed, I knew what would happen. It would end the way it had hundreds of other mornings, with me naked and sweat drenched and Lex trying to catch his breath after making love to me. There was no way I'd walk out of this room without making things worse.

"Lex…"

"Give me one more time, Mil."

My heart clenched.

How could I deny him something I wanted, too, something I knew I shouldn't do? The need in his voice ignited the desire brewing inside me.

"O…okay," I whispered, and moved to the mat, stretching my arms high above my head.

He let out a deep groan, and all doubts disappeared, replaced by thoughts of tormenting him for making me do this.

"Remember, you asked for it."

"This should be interesting." He took his spot behind me.

I bent to the side and circled back up. "I bet I can get through all the poses before you finish your next series."

"You're a wench." His Irish brogue sounded more pronounced.

Oh, this was going to be fun.

Lex stepped back giving me room in front of him. I started with sun salutation and then progressed through the warrior poses. I prolonged every stretch, making each move more provocative as I progressed.

I hadn't expected to become so stimulated. Being half-naked and trying to concentrate on each pose was wreaking havoc on my senses.

The final straw came when I moved to the camel stretch. I bent backward, and noticed the giant erection tenting the front of Lex's pants. I grinned to myself; the normal Zen state of Tai Chi wasn't working.

Our eyes connected, and he frowned, and a bead of sweat slid down his face. "You're in so much trouble when I finish this series."

"Hey. I'm not the one who wouldn't let me change." I shifted forward

"Milla, finish your poses. I plan to fuck you silly in about ten minutes."

My core contracted. Yeah, that was going to get me to finish faster.

I stood, raised my hands above my head, and bent at the waist into the spread-leg stretch. I closed my eyes, positioned my legs to their widest stance, and then relaxed, allowing my body to stretch to its fullest. After a few moments of concentration on my breathing, I peeked behind me.

Lex's wasn't there anymore.

Shit, where did he go?

This was not good, or maybe it was. Anticipation rose through me. I lifted my head, but felt the weight of Lex's hand pushing me back down.

"Stay just like that." His hand slid along my spine, up to where the shirt barely covered my ass, and between my soaked slit. "At least I'm not the only one affected by your sexy yoga moves."

"Lex, let me…"

"Oh, there's no getting out of this." His finger slid into my pussy and then back out. "I think I will have a taste of this while you hold that pose."

He walked around me, crouched down, and grinned at me from between my legs.

"I'm going to enjoy this." His tongue swiped at my folds, and a moan escaped my mouth. "No moving. I'm about to enjoy my breakfast."

He clutched my thighs tight and descended. I screamed as an unexpected orgasm erupted at the first contact of his lips. He sucked my clit into his mouth and then flicked his tongue into my dripping, aching center.

A hum vibrated from his mouth, and his tongue fucked me to another orgasm that had me losing balance. Lex held me in place, but I set my hands on the floor, just in case I fell forward from orgasm overload. When his fingers delved into me again, I knew I wouldn't be able to stay in the same position much longer.

"Lex, I can't hold on anymore."

With one last swipe, he pushed my ass down and helped me to kneel. He walked in front of me, allowing his tented pants to nudge my face. I peered up through desire-glazed eyes. With one hand, he gripped the back of my head and used the other to untie his pants. "I'm in need of your perfected oral skills."

My mouth watered. The few times he'd given me control was when his dick was in my mouth. His hard cock sprung free of its covering, and a drop of precum dripped from the tip. I licked the bead, moaning in delight. I loved his taste, clean and masculine.

Lex gripped the base. "Open up, baby."

I engulfed the flared head, bringing my lips around his engorged cock. I swallowed as he hit the back of my throat.

"That's it. Take me slowly. Get used to me again."

I lifted my head and sucked him back inside. My hand circled over his, and he helped me find the rhythm he needed. Releasing his grip on his cock, he cupped my face. I slid the fingers of my other hand behind his sac to the sensitive nerves at the base and stroked. I bobbed up and down, sliding my hands in conjunction with my mouth.

"God, I love your mouth."

He took over, setting a new pace as he thrust deep to the back of my mouth.

"Fuck, you feel so good. I have to stop or I'll come before I'm ready," he announced through a strained whisper.

I gazed up at him, cocked a brow, and tightened my lips in response.

"I don't think so."

He pulled out with a pop.

"I wasn't finished," I grumbled.

He ran his thumb over my swollen lips.

"I want to come inside your pussy, not your mouth." He motioned with his fingers for me to turn.

I rotated, but before I could get into a comfortable position, he slammed into me.

"Lex…" I fell forward onto my forearms. Oh, he was going to let me have it. I rested my head against the mat as he started his assault on my weeping pussy.

He rode me hard, fucking me like a man hell-bent on making me his. My heart pounded as my pussy spasmed around him. The sound of dirty, wet sex filled my ears. He trailed his hand down to my folds, slid my clit between his fingers, and pinched. "Come now."

I erupted on command. My vision filled with stars, and my body bowed.

"That's it, *a ghrá*. Let go."

"Your turn," I called, contracting my muscles.

He smacked my ass and came on a growl, and I knew leaving Lex was going to be the hardest thing I ever did in my life.

CHAPTER TWELVE

Let's go make breakfast."

I nodded and followed him out of the room. We remained silent as we walked down the hall. After making love, we dressed in silence, both of us lost in our thoughts.

The longer I waited to tell him about the divorce filing, the harder it would be. *Damn, damn, damn.* Sleeping with him not only once but multiple times over the night and this morning wasn't the way to see this was for the best.

Okay, once we sat down with a cup of coffee, I'd tell him in a calm, rational manner.

We passed the room Arya had used as her computer lab. I paused outside the area, causing Lex to stop.

"What's behind there?"

"A room you aren't ready to see."

My eyes collided with Lex's, and my heartbeat accelerated.

A dungeon.

An image of Jacob flashed before me. A tremor shook my body.

I hated that man so much. He took something beautiful and turned it into a nightmare.

"What if I'm never ready?"

"Then we'll turn it into an actual game room, with an Xbox and PS3."

He turned and without another word walked toward the kitchen with me trailing behind him.

Lex understood without my saying anything. He'd sacrifice an essential part of himself for me. I couldn't let him do it and then resent me years later.

Making Lex wait until I was ready for even the tamest things wasn't fair. Deep down I still craved the feel of the ropes and bindings. It brought me to a place nothing ever could or would again. Lex was the only man I'd experienced the unique pleasure with, and he would be the last.

Nevertheless, I couldn't do it. I couldn't give him hope and take it away. He was a Dom who'd enjoyed his games and lifestyle years before we met, and making him give up what he craved and desired was wrong. He'd put aside so much for me already.

It's his decision, Mil, not yours.

I pushed the thought back as I moved into the kitchen and pulled out everything I needed to make breakfast as Lex started a fresh batch of coffee.

For the next twenty minutes, we worked around and with each other as we'd done hundreds of times over the years. Lex chopped and prepped as I cooked. At the same time I reached over to place our omelets on our plates, Lex leaned over me to set the coffee mugs. His whiskers brushed my cheeks, and I leaned into him and inhaled his delicious scent and then pulled back just as fast.

No. I couldn't fall into our routine again.

"I'm sorry. I shouldn't have done that."

He caged me with his arms as I held myself stiff. "Why are you sorry? This is who we are, Mil. A well-oiled machine, working around each other and together without thought. Why are you so determined to end it?"

"Lex, please. I don't want to fight. Let's eat, and then I need to tell you something."

He released a deep sigh of resignation and moved away from me, taking a seat on the bar stool. I sat down next to him, and we ate in silence. A few times I glanced over at him, but he was lost in thought, staring out the windows that made up the back walls of the kitchen.

When we were both finished eating and I couldn't stand the quiet anymore, I spoke. "Are you ready to hear me?"

He kept his gaze out the window. "Say what you have to say, but if it has to do with ending what we share, save your breath. I won't accept it without a fight."

I pushed back from my stool, stood, and turned his seat to face me. "Why are you making this so hard? Why can't you understand that I'm doing this for you?"

"For me." His voice grew cold. "You're doing it because it's easier to give up on us than face whatever demons you're dealing with."

"I'm not giving up. I'm setting you free. Lex, all I do is hurt you. Why can't I get through to you? I'm making the best decision for us."

"Bullshit. You mean the best decision for you." He face was red with hurt and anger, and he clenched his fists at his sides.

I shook my head. "That's not true."

I was going to have to hurt him to get him to see the truth. God, I didn't want to do it this way, but I had no choice.

"I want a divorce," I gritted out as my heart collapsed inside.

He sat frozen for a split second, and then his shoulders dropped and he ran a hand over his face and gripped his hair.

"You don't mean that." He stood, moving toward me, but I retreated and lifted my hand.

Tears fogged my eyes. "I'm not good for you. I have too much baggage, and you deserve someone better."

"Do our vows mean nothing to you?" he shouted.

I swallowed. They meant the world to me, but this had to end. "You have to move on." Bile rose in my throat.

He stepped away and ran a frustrated hand through his hair. He grabbed the granite counter near the bar, dropped his head, and then slammed his fist down.

I jumped. "Lex—"

"No, don't say anything." He turned and walked over to me. "Answer a few questions for me, and I won't bother you again."

Oh, shit, this was his lawyer voice. I wasn't going to come out of this unscathed. I was already broken; what more could damage me?

"How will you feel when I touch another woman?"

I gasped but remained quiet.

"How about when I tie her to my bed, strip her naked, and pleasure her?" He touched my trembling lips with his thumb. "How about when I fuck her, the exact ways I've done to you. Would it bother you?"

"Don't…" My voice cracked.

"Do you want me to teach her how to satisfy me? How will you feel when I give her the same lessons in pleasure that I once gave you?"

It will kill me.

"I…I…can't stop you. I don't have any hold over you."

I had to get out of here. I turned to leave and he grabbed my arm.

"What the hell is wrong with you? Where's the Milla who fights? Am I not worth fighting for?"

I am fighting for you. For you to have a life you deserve.

The pain on his face was more than I could bear. Was I making a mistake? *Merda*, why did everything have to be so complicated?

"Lex. Please…," I pleaded as tears spilled down my cheeks.

"Was last night and this morning just some way to get a last fuck out of me before you destroyed what we have?"

My lips trembled, but before I could respond, the doorbell rang.

"Dammit. I forgot the courier was going to bring some documents for me to sign." Lex released my arm. "Go put on some clothes."

I rushed into the bedroom, grabbed my clothes from the night before, slipped them on, and walked back into the living room.

Lex paced back and forth, running a hand through his hair, and James's face relaxed as he saw me. Something was up, and I had a feeling I wasn't going to like it.

"What's going on, James?" I glanced at my watch. "I still have an hour before you have to pick me up.

"You gave me a scare, Mrs. Duncan."

I winced inside at his address. "I don't understand. What happened? Is Arya okay?"

"She's fine," Lex growled. "This has to do with you. Tell her."

"There was an unmarked package left in the lobby that contained photos of you."

The hairs on the back of my neck stood up. "What kind of photos?"

"They…" James hesitated, telling me it had to do with the ones Lex got. "They are from the time of your abduction."

"I want to see them." I moved toward James. "Where are they?"

I wasn't going to fall apart this time. I was home and safe. Whatever it was, I'd deal with it. I had the girls. I had L— *Fuck.* He wasn't mine anymore. I'd just set him free.

Keep it together, Mil.

"I don't think it is a good idea." James looked toward Lex.

"He saw them, but I'm not allowed to see them? Where are they?"

"Show them to her," Lex said, without looking at me.

James released a deep breath and opened the penthouse door, stepped outside, and then brought in two large frames.

Oh, God.

I braced myself for whatever they were.

I peeked at Lex. He had both hands against the wall and was doing the breathing exercise he used during Tai Chi.

"Turn them around."

James followed my orders, and the second I saw the pictures, bile rose in my throat.

One was a picture of me barely covered in my underwear, soaked in blood, and passed out on the floor of the warehouse where Jacob had taken me. The other was me blindfolded and bound to a pole with him behind me. I was still limp from the drug Christof had ordered him to give me so I wouldn't fight them anymore. Bruises covered my body, but there wasn't any blood, which meant they hadn't started my torture yet. The bottom of the picture read, *Wounds heal but the memories remain. Your debt to me is due. VC*

"Do you need to sit down?" James asked as he dropped the frames and rushed toward me.

Lex reached me first. I hadn't realized I was wobbling, and he steadied me with his hands on my hips.

I shook my head, pushing him away, and gripped the back of the sofa. "I'll be okay. I have to learn to handle this."

I closed my eyes and went through some of my own breathing techniques. Slowly my stomach settled, and I opened my eyes.

So maybe Arya was right; all those hours of therapy were worth it.

"From this point on, your every second will be accounted for. You don't move an inch without letting James know. Tony's clearance was approved on Friday, so he will tag team your security with James as soon as he arrives on Wednesday."

I kept my grip on the couch. "Okay."

"I'm calling in Thomas. His personal security company will work with our team to make sure no one can get to you."

Bringing in Thomas made sense. He knew more about protection than anyone I knew.

"Okay."

"All social engagements are canceled, and you will provide us with a list of all clients and appointments on your calendar."

This one would be tough; some of our clients liked their privacy. Plus, until Arya had the babies, I was for all intents and purposes the face of the company. I hoped that they'd make an exception for a few things we had to go to.

"Okay."

"The hell you're okay with it."

I flinched and turned to face him. "What do you want from me? I'm doing what you asked."

I saw James discreetly excuse himself from the penthouse and shut the door.

"That's what's wrong with you. Why aren't you upset?"

"I can't fall apart. I did that for six months."

"I need something more than this steady compliance. I need to see there is a pulse in there."

"You're impossible." I pushed my hair back from my forehead. "Why is it so hard to believe I've grown up?"

"This isn't growing up, it's shutting down. The moment anything to do with your attack comes up, you become docile and accept everything I throw at you. I'm taking away all your freedom, and you're accepting it. The old Milla would never restrict her independence without a fight. Why won't you fight?"

I couldn't win with him.

"Don't you see I was kidnapped because I ignored you? I ignored everyone, and by doing that, I became a target. Because of me they went after Arya."

If Jacob hadn't taken me, then Arya wouldn't have gone to the lab, and the whole ordeal would never have happened.

Lex sighed. "Is that what you've been thinking all these months? Mil, you were taken because of Arya."

I shook my head, but Lex continued, "She's the one who built the software. If you need someone to blame for the whole thing from the start, then it's my fault. I'm the one who got us involved in the project with MI6. I'm the reason Christof is after you."

He was wrong. The project was the reason behind Arya's success and mine. He introduced us to our first clients.

"I don't want to fight with you, Lex." My shoulders sagged, and I moved toward the door. "I'm trying to do right by everyone. I've fucked up so much. Let me do what I should."

"Then be yourself. Stop trying to fit into who you think you should be."

"When will you get that I'm not the Milla you married? That girl doesn't exist anymore."

"Then who are you?" he challenged.

"I…I don't know. I haven't figured it out."

"Do you love me?"

"What?" My fingers shook as I gripped the doorknob. Why would he ask me that in the middle of an argument about my security?

"You heard me. Do I even matter to you?"

You matter more to me than anything.

"Lex…I…"

He raised his hand. "Don't answer that. I already know the answer. You wouldn't have cried when you asked for a divorce. You wouldn't have tears in your eyes now."

His gaze burned into mine, and I looked away. No matter what I said, he wasn't going to accept it. I had to leave.

"Lex," I whispered as I faced the door. "I didn't come to you last night to give you the wrong impression. What we share…what we shared was beautiful—it always will be—but I…I'm not good for you. Let me go. I'll do whatever you ask of me when it comes to security, but I can't give you anything more."

With those last words, I left him.

CHAPTER THIRTEEN

I leaned against the island in the center of my kitchen and closed my eyes. I'd done it. I'd broken his heart and mine because it was for the best.

Step one in the Milla-grows-up plan was complete. Now I had to convince myself I could live without him.

After leaving Lex's penthouse, I went to mine, showered, and dressed for work in a haze of tears and pain. Nothing seemed to matter, not the new threats on my life or the piles of work I had on my plate. I'd spent so much time determined to do this that I hadn't truly thought about what it would feel like when it happened.

Lex's words kept echoing over and over in my head.

"Am I not worth fighting for?"

He was worth more than he would ever know. I'd loved him since I was a stupid teenager and would love him until the day I died, but he deserved better than what I'd given him. He'd put up with me for so long. Adding more of my crap to his world wasn't fair.

My fingers dug into the granite as I took a deep breath. I couldn't fall apart. *This was my choice; I'm the one doing the leaving.*

My eyes filled again.

Great, more tears.

It was time to move forward. I couldn't wallow in self-pity. I'd done that for six months and it had only caused me more problems. I'd set this in motion and I had to live with the consequences.

I placed my coffee mug under the espresso dispenser and poured myself another cup of the highly caffeinated brew. I swallowed the coffee in one gulp and went to look for my phone.

Merda, it was at Lex's place. I could do this, I could go over there get my phone and leave. If I were lucky, we wouldn't have to talk to each other.

That's what I'd do. Well, once I had another shot of espresso.

As I pushed the button for a refill, the doorbell rang. I checked my watch. I still had twenty minutes before I had to leave for work.

Please don't let it be Lex. I needed at least a few more cups before I composed myself to face him again.

I opened my door to find James there with a worried expression on this face.

Okay, there couldn't be two threats against me in the same day.

"What's going on?" I asked.

"We have to go, Mrs. Duncan. Mrs. Dane…" He sighed and tried to hide the emotion warring across his face. "Arya's in labor."

I swallowed the lump now forming in my throat and pulled James into the apartment. "But she isn't due for another six weeks."

The calm Russian I'd known for over a decade sat down on my couch and covered his face with his hands. "I don't know all the details, but she was in labor all day yesterday and kept quiet about it, thinking it would pass. By the time her water broke, she'd started bleeding. Max called me fifteen minutes ago to say MedFlight was helicoptering her from the estate."

"Oh God." I gripped the back of the sofa. My sister was in trouble.

Lord, please protect my sister and her babies. I don't know what I'd do without her.

No, I couldn't think like that. I had to be strong for her. *Cazzo*, Aunt Elana.

"James, does Aunt El know?"

He nodded. "Max sent the jet to get her. She won't be here for at least five hours."

This wasn't good. Time to go into boss mode. Arya's health took precedence over my personal life. She needed me, and I would do what I could to help her.

"Okay, I have a plan," I said as I paced. "You have to head to the hospital. Arya and Max need you there. I'm sure by now Carmen is already on her way from New York. I'll take my car and pick up the things Arya and Max need for the hospital. I'll be there within the next two hours. Once I get to the hospital, you leave to pick up Aunt El and do everything in your power to keep her calm."

"I can't let you go alone, Mrs. Duncan."

"Enough with the Mrs. Duncan already."

He ignored my reprimand and stood. "Arya's health does not trump your safety. I will take you, and we'll go together."

Oh, he was not thinking straight. His daughter for all intents and purposes was in trouble, and he was thinking about me.

"I'll be fine. What can happen to me in that short time?"

I winced. I'd spoken those exact words to him and Lex the day Jacob kidnapped me.

"Never mind. Forget I said that. Isn't there anyone who can cover for you?"

"No one I trust. Well with the exception of Mr. Duncan."

Lex. He had to know what was going on by now.

"Where is he?"

"Right here," Lex answered from behind me.

I glanced at him and moved to go to him without thought, but then held myself back. I couldn't rely on him for comfort anymore. It wasn't right to lead him on more than I already had.

"James, you need to leave for the hospital now. Max just called and said Arya is asking for you."

"Is she okay? Did he give you any details?" I asked.

"They're taking Arya in for a caesarean section. He tried to call you first, but you left your phone at my place." He pulled out my mobile and handed it to me.

Our fingers touched for a brief second, and a tremor shot through my spine. I hoped that he hadn't seen my reaction, but of course, he had; he noticed everything about me.

I scanned my phone. I had ten voice messages and twenty-five missed calls. The earliest one was from when I first woke up in Lex's bed. A pang of guilt hit my gut; while I was having sex with my soon-to-be-ex-husband, my best friend was calling me because she was in trouble.

I read the last of my texts and found a list of items Max needed for Arya. The least I could do was get what Arya needed to make her comfortable.

"James, why don't you go to the hospital. I'm sure Lex has already called Thomas. One of his men can take me to the estate to pick up the things Max and Arya want."

James hesitated but nodded and left me with Lex, who was scanning his own phone.

I didn't like the idea of having someone I didn't know carting me around. But I promised I'd let security stay with me at all times. I couldn't wait until Tony arrived; at least then I'd have someone I was used to taking me places when James wasn't. Hell, I couldn't wait until I was free to drive myself.

Lex was right. I hated losing my independence, but this wasn't the time for a temper tantrum.

"I'll take you."

I scrunched my eyes and tilted my head. "Why would you want to do that? I thought we'd said enough to each other."

"Because, despite our impending nuptial circumstances, I don't trust anyone, besides James and myself, with your safety. If you have a problem with it, then you can sit here and wait for any updates on your best friend." He crossed his arms and raised a brow in challenge.

Okay, Milla, count to three and let it go.

I knew what he was doing. He wanted to get a rise out of me. It all went back to the argument we'd had in his penthouse. Maybe he was right, that it was easier to comply than push back.

No. I couldn't go there right now.

I took a deep breath. I wasn't the old, *lose my temper at the drop of a hat* Milla anymore.

"Fine, but I get to drive." I turned, strolling toward my bedroom, before I said anything else.

"Where are you going?"

"To change into something more comfortable. It's going to be a long day, and my suit isn't going to cut it. I shouldn't be more than five minutes."

I returned in a little under three and went to the tray where I kept all the car keys. I scanned the contents and then glared at Lex.

"Where are they?"

"You're not driving. I want to get to the estate and then the hospital in one piece."

"Whatever," I muttered, grabbing my purse. "I'm not the one with four speeding tickets."

He grunted at my not-so-subtle comment and led the way to my car.

Our car.

Damn, we were going to have to separate everything we'd bought together. He could have it all. There were too many memories.

We drove the whole way to the estate in silence. Even when he took turns and curves that had my heart ready to jump out of my chest, I kept quiet. It seemed like the more I ignored his driving, the more he did things to get a rise out of me. He kept changing the radio, and then kept adjusting his mirror and seat.

For all intents and purposes, he was behaving like a child. This wasn't like him. He was the straitlaced one, but today he was channeling his inner two-year-old.

I crossed my legs and leaned my body toward the window, but as soon as I did, his hand landed on my thigh, pulling me back toward him.

My breath hitched.

"What are you doing?" I tried to push his hands away, but his grip tightened.

"You're still my wife, and I feel like touching you. So I will," he stated in his Dom voice.

A tingle went up my spine, making me bite my lip. I wanted to press my thighs together, but if did, then I'd confirm my body reacted the moment my Master appeared.

"Mas…L-Lex, don't."

"I'm not doing anything. But"—he hummed—"I will if you want me to. Or…"

"Or?" I asked, shifting uncomfortably in the seat.

"You can use your safe word."

I glared at him. "We aren't in a scene. I don't do scenes anymore."

"Yes, you do. But only with me." His tone deepened and I shook my head to keep it from clouding over.

I could do this; I could handle him touching me without begging him to fuck me.

"I'm going to take a nap." I closed my eyes and released a strained breath.

"Go right ahead, if you can," he said with a chuckle. "We still have a good thirty minutes until we get to the estate." One of his pinkies stroked the inside of my thigh.

I held back a groan and clenched my eyes tight.

He continued tormenting me with little movements, touching me but not touching me. My arousal soaked through my underwear and dampened my pants.

I knew why he was doing this. If I wasn't going to give him a reaction to his driving, he was going to get one out of me this way.

As soon as we pulled up the driveway, I opened the door and rushed out of the car. I ran to Arya's room, shutting the door and leaning my back against it.

A few seconds later, Lex entered through a door I'd forgotten was there.

I tried to run into the bathroom but found myself pushed back against the wall and his body pressing onto mine.

"Let me go," I ordered between pants.

I lifted my hands to shove him, but he anticipated my move and pinned my hands above my head.

A need I hadn't experienced in months awoke in my body. The desire for domination. The craving for my Master to tame me.

He positioned his cotton-covered erection along my folds. Without thought, I widened my stance, giving him a better position. My clit throbbed and swelled.

"I know you feel it."

"I have no idea what you're talking about." I turned my face so I wouldn't have to stare into his Dom eyes.

Merda, I was losing all willpower.

"Liar. Explain to me why you can't look me in the eyes. Explain why your nipples are hard and begging for attention. Why your pants are so damp that I can feel the heat of your pussy against my cock."

One of his hands slid to my waist and moved up, stopping at the lower curve of my breast.

"Tell me, Milla. Who's your Master?" He nuzzled my neck, and I tilted my chin to give him better access. "Who owns this body?"

A thumb swiped over my pebbled nipple.

"We…we can't do this."

"Why not?" He bit the sensitive skin at the juncture of my shoulder, my head rolled back, and goose bumps prickled my skin.

My hands slid into his hair, and I nibbled on his ear. "Because it doesn't change anything."

"The hell it doesn't." Lex released my hands and lifted my legs around him, sealing our lips together.

All thoughts of divorce and life afterward vanished. All I could think about was the taste of Lex's mouth, the feel of his tongue against mine, the need for him to fill my body.

My back hit the couch with Lex on top of me. He pulled at my shirt, lifting it over my head. I unbuttoned his and pushed it off his shoulders.

"I have to be inside you now, and then I'm going to spank you for making everything so difficult right before I fuck you again."

The thought of him spanking me made my core clench.

I nodded. "Yes, please."

I shoved at my yoga pants as Lex unbuttoned his slacks, and his cock sprang free. I grabbed it, rubbing up and down.

"Put me in, Mil."

I nodded and kissed him, pushing the head of his beautiful erection inside me.

At that moment, my phone beeped. I'd designated the tone for any calls or messages from Arya.

"We have to stop." My arousal immediately vanished, and I shoved Lex off me, trying to steady my heart. I leaned over and read my text.

"Oh, God, Arya started hemorrhaging during the C-section. They're taking her into emergency surgery."

CHAPTER FOURTEEN

Do you think we forgot anything?" I asked Lex as he drove out of the gates of Arya and Max's estate.

"We have everything, Mil." Lex shifted gears on the sports car and increased his speed.

I fidgeted with my fingers. The less-than-five-minute conversation with him was heartbreaking to hear. There was no hiding the worry in his words.

Please God, take care of my sister.

I sent my prayer up to heaven and then wiped a stray tear on my cheek. What was I going to do if anything happened to her? Who was going to keep me in line or get me into some wild and crazy project?

"It's going to be okay, *a ghrá*. Arya's strong." Lex took one of my hands in his and rubbed his thumb across my skin.

I glanced at him and saw worry lines etched around his eyes and mouth. Lex loved her as much as I did.

His fingers played with mine, sending a calmness to me that I hadn't expected.

"You're right. She's going to be okay. Someone doesn't go through all that she had to have those babies to give up now." My lips trembled. "Lex, I'm scared."

He brought our joined hands up and kissed the inside of my wrist. "I am, too, baby."

"Can we talk about something, anything, to keep our minds off the hospital?"

"Sure. I'm assuming our marriage is off the table."

I tried to tug my hand out of his, but he held tight.

"Just kidding. I'll tell you an Irish tale Ma used to tell me."

I smiled at him. "Okay."

Over the past ten years, he'd told me countless folktales. Every time I thought I'd heard all of them, he'd surprise me with a new one. A few times when I'd wondered if he'd made them up, I'd researched the story on the Internet, only to find out it was real.

He began weaving his story, and soon I found myself lost in the adventures of a boy who'd befriended a young water sprite.

He held on to me the whole time, only letting go to shift gears on the car before taking my hand again.

How many times had we driven like this, holding hands, while I was lost in the world he created with his words? I knew we shouldn't sink into the comfort of being together, but right now, it was panic with worry over Arya or take what we could offer each other.

We pulled up to the hospital valet, and I opened the door before Lex had put the car in park. We grabbed everything for Arya and Max and rushed toward the elevator.

"Hold the elevator," I called and thankfully, someone waited for us. "Thank you." I pushed the button for the surgery floor and waited.

"No problem," a deep voice responded.

I froze, and I heard an unsubtle groan from Lex.

Merda, just my luck. What were the odds that a famous tabloid reporter would be on the same elevator with Lex and me? Maybe if we ignored him, he'd leave us alone.

"Hello, Mr. and Mrs. Duncan. How are you today?"

The hairs on the back of my neck prickled. *Did he say what I think he said?*

I had to get off this elevator as soon as possible. This wasn't the time to confirm any rumors about us, especially since at this moment I wasn't sure what was happening.

I took a deep breath to calm my mind and smiled as I answered his question. "Um…good, given the circumstances."

"Oh yes, Mrs. Dane. She's about to deliver, right? I think I heard there were complications."

Neither Lex nor I responded to the question and statement. For all we knew, the reporter would splash the information across the cover of his magazine as an exclusive quote.

The bell rang indicating Arya's floor, and I sighed in relief.

We quickly stepped out of the elevator.

"Move fast before he asks another question," Lex murmured.

"Have a good day. Although, I hope the latest reports on your wife don't upset you, Mr. Duncan," the weasel called as the doors closed.

A lump formed in the pit of my stomach. Our marriage wasn't public knowledge. At least as far as I knew.

"Lex…"

"I heard. Let's get an update on Arya, then I'll see what's going on."

I stopped moving and glared at him. "Aren't you even a little bit fazed by what he called us? Doesn't it worry you that he knows?"

Because it sure as hell bothered me.

"No." He pinned me with a stare. "You are my wife. It's a fact."

I blew out a frustrated breath. I had to make him understand.

"Lex, what happened earlier doesn't change anything."

Hurt flashed across his face and then disappeared, replaced by a blank expression.

We approached the nurse's desk, but before we reached her, she pointed to the waiting area.

Wait a minute.

How would she know who we were?

Lex or I hadn't been in the tabloids in a while, and most people wouldn't recognize us outside of the business world and Europe. Arya was the face of ArMil. Oh hell, whatever was out there was going to cause me nothing but trouble.

I opened the waiting room door and strolled in. I set the bags I carried on a seat near the window and waited for Lex to drop his stuff.

"When do you think someone will come to give us an update?"

Lex didn't respond, and all of a sudden, what felt like an icy breeze assaulted me. Lex sat in a corner chair, refusing to look at me.

As I approached him, I glanced at the table. "*Che cazzo!*"

"Yes, 'what the fuck' would be an appropriate phrase."

I couldn't believe my eyes. The tabloid had a picture of Alberto and me at the ball in Milan. The image captured him running a finger down my cheek, and the headline read, TAMING OF THE REBEL HEIRESS.

"Lex, it isn't what you think."

"I don't want to hear it," he bit out and stared at the television.

"It isn't true."

"I don't want to hear it. Fucking hell, is this why you want out?" He gripped his hair and stood facing away from me. "Did you sleep with him?"

"I don't know what you're talking about. I've never been with anyone but you."

He whirled around. "Don't you lie to me. Don't fucking lie to me, Milla. I've put up with your shit for too long."

Was I in an alternate universe? He really believed I'd slept with Alberto.

"Are you kidding me right now? I've never slept with Alberto or anyone else."

"Then why won't you try? Ten years. Why are you throwing it away?" He paced back and forth, and the vein on the side of his face throbbed. He clenched his fists.

"I'm not throwing us away. I'm giving you a chance to be happy with someone who doesn't make you crazy or put you second."

My stomach burned from saying those words, but no matter how much it hurt, it was the truth.

"I can't do this anymore. You wanted it over, it's over. Send me the papers as soon as they're drafted." He pushed past me and I grabbed his arm.

"Lex, please, this isn't how I wanted it to end."

"What did you expect? That I'd be happy you're willing to throw away a decade of marriage, memories, and love?"

I cringed.

"Lex, please understand."

He jerked his arm out of my hand. "Going to someone else will destroy both of us, but since that's what you want, so be it."

He pushed past me and left the room, slamming the door on his way out.

I shook as the reality of what had happened hit me. I'd lost the man I loved. *This is what you wanted, Mil.*

I buried my face in my hands and wept.

What had I done? What was I going to do without him?

I didn't know how long I sat there crying until I felt two arms engulf me. "Mil, it's okay. It's going to be okay." Carmen pulled me against her shoulder. "Come here, *mia sorella*. Tell me what's wrong."

My grief kept me from talking and I continued to wail. Carmen held me until I had no more tears to cry. Finally, I felt the urge to say something. "He...he thinks I'm ending things because of someone else."

"No, he doesn't, Mil. He loves you."

"You don't understand. He thinks I slept with Alberto. But Carmen," I pleaded, "you have to believe me. I never slept with Alberto. I...I..."

"Mil, I believe you. Lex is just trying to make sense of why you're ending things. You told him, I presume." She tucked my head back against her shoulder.

I sniffed and wiped my nose on the tissue Carmen handed me. "What am I going to do? This isn't how I wanted it to be between us. I love him so much, and I thought he'd be better off without me. Now all I can think is how I'm going to handle not having him in my life."

"I need you to tell me everything from the beginning. I mean from when you two first got together. The only person you confide in is Arya, and I don't think even she has the whole story."

Arya barely knew anything. Hell, she only found out about us less than a year ago. "Carm, you know more than she does."

"That's hard to believe. You two are stuck at the hip; sometimes I feel like a third wheel."

"Without you our tricycle would fall apart," I joked, trying to lighten the underlying hurt she'd revealed and the pain tearing me apart.

"Nevertheless, I want you to start from the beginning."

Merda, we were back to me again.

I hiccuped, then nodded. For the next twenty minutes, I told her the backstory of my marriage to Lex, from the first time I'd met him to right before my kidnapping, when I'd agreed to come out in the open about our marriage. By the time I was finished, a surprising release washed over me, almost as if the weight on my shoulders eased. Carmen was the first person to know everything about my relationship with Lex.

"We'll figure this out, baby girl." She touched her head to mine. Carmen's unconditional support helped ease my tension. All of a sudden I realized my problems were nothing compared to what was happening in the operating room.

"My God, I never asked about Arya."

Carmen patted my hand, and a worry line crossed her forehead. "Nothing new. They took her into surgery over three hours ago. Max said he would come out and give us an update on the babies and Arya."

"I hope we don't have to wait much longer. I'm worried, Carm."

"Me, too."

The end of my marriage was going to devastate me, but losing

Arya would kill me. *Please, God, help my sister and her babies.*

Carmen and I held hands.

At that moment, Max opened the door. Both of us jumped up.

"Any news?"

Max's shadowed face showed signs of exhaustion but he smiled. "I'm happy to announce I'm the proud papa of two beautiful baby boys."

"What about Arya?" I asked, suspecting something was wrong.

Max's smile dropped. "She's in recovery."

"And?" Carmen interjected.

"She lost a lot of blood during delivery, and with the strain on her uterus from the pregnancy and her attack..." He sighed and looked down. "They had to do a partial hysterectomy."

"Oh God." Carmen covered her mouth, and a tear slipped down her face.

"Does she know?" I asked. Arya wanted a brood of children, and this was going to devastate her.

"I told her a few minutes after they wheeled her into recovery. She took the news better than I expected, but then again, maybe that was because she was still under the influence of the lingering anesthesia. All she wanted to talk about was the boys and when she can see them." The resignation in his voice told me there was more. "I think the two of you need to talk to her. I'm worried she's going to lose it. It isn't like her to be so calm, not one word of profanity." He half smirked but I knew it was forced.

I hugged Max. "Congratulations, Papa." He held me tight and then turned to hug his sister.

"I'm glad she has you two. This isn't going to be easy for her, but I'm just thankful she made it through." He paused as if trying to compose his thoughts and then regarded Carmen with wet eyes. "For the first time I understand some of what Dad must have felt when he lost Mom."

"But you're stronger than him," I said while squeezing his hand.

"Go talk to her before I embarrass myself and start blubbering." Max wiped his eyes.

"We'll handle her and make sure our stubborn mule is taken care of."

"It takes one to know one," Lex added as he entered the room.

Carmen pulled me out the door before I could respond. I looked back one last time. Lex's gaze bored into mine. He was hurting, and all because of me. *God, am I making a mistake?*

For the first time since I'd decided on this path, doubt settled in. Maybe if Lex was the one and only for me, then I was the same for him. What if my whole plan was wrong? What if growing up didn't mean letting him go but meant showing him and the world that he came first in my life?

Cazzo, what was I going to do?

All thoughts of my mangled love life disappeared the moment we entered Arya's room. The dark shadows from delivery had done nothing to hide the joy in her eyes.

"Come in, meet my boys."

I rushed to Arya's side, and then paused. "Is it okay for us to hold them?"

"Yes, they got the all clear from the NICU docs. My fellas are stronger than anyone expected." She handed one of her babies over to me. "This is Ashur Maxwell Dane." Then she lifted the other toward Carmen. "And this noisy fellow is Christopher Rey Dane."

"You named them after my mom and your dad." Carmen sniffled, and tears filled her eyes.

Carmen and I cooed and kissed our little fellas. My heart filled to exploding. I wasn't these kiddos' mother, but I loved them like my own. I hiccupped, thinking of the baby I'd never have with Lex.

Arya caught my reaction and whispered, "It will be okay, *mera behna*."

Not likely.

"By the way, both of your men just left." Arya gestured to Carmen and me with her chin.

"Who's my man?" asked Carmen.

"Thomas," Arya responded with a smirk.

"He isn't mine. Our tastes run to different cuisines."

"Yeah, right," I mumbled under my breath. My prim and proper best friend was a Domme, but somehow she fell in love with another Dom. How that situation worked, I'd never know. Well, I guess it didn't since Carmen insisted they weren't together.

"Thomas was his usual fun self, talking about spoiling the boys, but Lex. He's a different story altogether. What happened?"

Carmen sighed, and I didn't say anything and pinched the bridge of my nose. The headache from my waiting room breakdown intensified. I knew she directed the question toward me, but if I started again I'd fall apart, and I was here to talk to Arya so she could fall apart.

"Don't look so depressed. I know something bad happened. Tell me. Despite what Max thinks, I'm not going to lose my shit. See, I cussed; are you guys happy?"

"I'm sure that is going to relieve my brother. Not." Carmen tucked Christopher against her chest and closed her eyes.

"Let me clear this up so both of you can report to my overprotective husband that I'm not going to freak out on him. I'm fine. I wanted more children, but these boys are the chance I lost with my girls. I'm okay." She moaned as she adjusted herself in the bed. "My body hurts like a bitch, but I'm fine. Before the doctors rolled me into surgery, I prayed that if my boys made it out safely, I wouldn't ever complain about having more. I knew the risks. Yes, the testosterone in my house overthrows my estrogen, but one of you can produce the girls and give me my fill."

I cringed.

Fat chance of kids from me. If I wasn't having them with Lex, I wasn't going to have any.

"One of you needs to open up."

"Mil, tell her. I'm savoring my boy here. I can't tell your story for you."

"I'm waiting." I glared at Arya. She was enjoying this. "Remember when I predicted one day you would have more relationship drama than I do? Well, the day is here. Now spill it." Arya lifted a brow.

Okay, here goes. "I told Lex I wanted a divorce."

"What? Are you insane?"

My lips shook, and I got up to place the baby in the bassinet. I grabbed a tissue, feeling the tears resurfacing, and then sat on the chair near Arya's bed.

"He…he thinks the reason I'm leaving him is to be with someone else." I couldn't hold back my pain and started sobbing again.

"It's going to be okay, Mil." Carmen placed Christopher next to his brother and gathered me in her arms.

I cried and detailed all the events of the previous few months, including the tabloid article and the incident with Alberto at the ball. I sniffed into my tissue as I finished the story.

"The worst part of it is that I think I've made the biggest mistake of my life." I peered up at Arya through my wet eyes. "I'm so sorry you're hearing all the details now. That I didn't tell you about my marriage from the start. I fucked up. I…I…"

"Stop it. Stop it right there." Arya ordered. "You aren't to blame for the shit with Alberto and the tabloids. We've all had our share of issues with the papzz. God, I hate those vultures. As for Lex, deep down he knows there was nothing between you and Alberto. I'll talk to him. He's coming tonight to sneak me some real food."

"Um, Arya, are you supposed to eat outside food?" Carmen interjected.

"Shut up, Carm. I just delivered two seven-pound babies, lost my ability to have more kids, and my woo-hoo is bleeding like a mother. I can eat whatever the fuck I want. And if either of you tell Aunt El, I will cut you."

"Go right ahead and knock yourself out." Carmen raised her hands in surrender. "All conversations about food and torture aside, Mil, he loves you."

I never questioned that aspect of our relationship. What we felt was deep and consuming, but was it the right reason to stay together? "Maybe letting him go is the best thing for him. He can find someone else." I hiccupped. "But I don't think I'm strong enough to do it, no matter what I said to him."

"No one says you have to do this." Carmen stroked my hair.

"She's right, Mil. I saw you two. The love you shared after the windows darkened proved how deep you felt for each other. Behind the glass, you weren't putting on a show. I saw it. Lex would never want anyone but you."

I tilted my head and squinted my eyes. "Huh? What are you talking about?" All of a sudden it dawned on me. "*Mio Dio,* that night when you came with Max to the club for the first time, you saw us?"

Heat crept up my cheeks. That moment was supposed to have been private. It was the night Lex and I agreed to bring our relationship into the open. The night I'd told him I wanted to be his wife in public and his submissive in private. It was supposed to be our last public scene at the club, at any club.

"Wait a second, how did you see us if he darkened the viewing glass?"

Arya squirmed in her bed, and it wasn't from the discomfort of the surgery. "Well, you see, um, it was when Max took me to his private office. I didn't know it was you two. I didn't expect you guys to…um…you know." Arya blushed and bit her lip.

Instantly I knew what she saw.

I commit myself to you in public and private. I love you. I am yours.

I made those vows, and then I'd broken them. A tear rolled down my face.

"*Mera behna*, I didn't mention it to make you cry."

Carmen growled. "Mil, you need to stop being a scaredy-cat, grow some balls, and fight for your marriage. This need you have to prove you've grown up is bullshit. What's wrong with you? Growing up doesn't mean giving up or letting some other woman come in to take your place. It means taking responsibility for your past and making sure you don't repeat the same mistakes."

"But if it wasn't for the way I react to things and behave, Jacob wouldn't have captured Arya and me. The months in Italy taught me a valuable lesson, that there are consequences to my behavior."

"Bullshit. That's just bullshit." Carmen released me, got up, and paced. "The kidnapping wasn't your fault. Arya and I would have done the same thing, if it meant protecting our company. You're letting Jacob win?"

I stared at her in shock.

"This is what he wanted, you broken and afraid of your own shadow. Are you someone who's willing to give up the love of her life because she has no self-worth?"

"Carm, calm down," Arya said from the bed.

I'd never seen Carmen like this. She never raised her voice. She always had her shit together.

"You have so much at your fingertips and you're willing to throw it away. Do you know what I would give to have someone love me the way he loves you? The one man who I thought loved me died, and even he didn't accept all of me. And the other…" She ran a hand over her face, and then shook her head. "Never mind him. Lex accepts all of you. The good, the bad, the crazy. What man would put up with being a secret for ten years? You need to get your head out of your ass."

Still stunned from the outburst, I sat there for a moment and then glanced at Arya, who shrugged her shoulders. Apparently, she was as surprised by the reprimand as I was.

The sad part of everything she'd said was that Carmen spoke the truth. Ending things with Lex wasn't the answer. Maybe I was giving Jacob power from the grave. But could I be what Lex needed?

Carmen gasped. "I can't believe I spoke to you like that." She rushed to me and crouched down. "Mil, I'm so sorry." She took my hands in hers. "I…I didn't mean it. I'm so sorry."

I nodded. "You're right."

"What?" Her emerald eyes shone with sadness.

"Carmen, you didn't say anything that I didn't need to hear. I wouldn't be able to live with myself if I went through with the divorce." I shook my head. "What am I going to say to Lex? 'Hey, babe, forget everything I said about ending our marriage. I want to stay together and have lots of babies.' Yeah, I'm sure he's going to take me back with open arms."

"Yep. And a lot of groveling," Arya added.

I frowned. "I don't grovel." Well, for Lex, I would.

Carmen snorted. "Of course you do, you're a submissive. Begging is part of the role."

Both Arya and I glared at her.

Two identical cries pierced the mood, and the three of us laughed. At the same moment, Max walked into the room with a bunch of flowers.

"I guess I'm right on time. My boys are hungry."

"As if you have the goods to relieve that situation. I'm the milk factory."

"Yes, but I can hold them up to those gorgeous breasts."

"On that note I'm out of here." I smiled at Carmen. "Good luck with these two. They're a bit sickening."

"I'm on my way, too."

"No, don't leave. They won't let me out of this place for another week. I need some estrogen around me."

"It isn't my fault his sperm was of the male persuasion." I gestured to Max. "Besides, I have to run the business. My partner is slacking on the job by getting knocked up and having babies." I kissed Arya on the cheek and then Carmen.

"One day it's going to be you, Duncan."

I clenched my hand against my heart and used the other to open the door. "We can only hope."

CHAPTER FIFTEEN

"Get out of my way," I muttered as I maneuvered my Ferrari around lunchtime traffic.

Today was the first time I'd driven myself anywhere since the delivery of the photographs from Christof. In the past week, I'd gained back some of the confidence I hadn't realized I'd lost. Neither Christof's nor Jacob's name scared me anymore. Well, not as much.

Tony had officially taken over as my security lead, and Thomas's company of scary, but discreet, almost invisible operatives were active. Their unseen presence gave me a small increase in peace of mind.

After my discussion with the girls, I went to Lex's penthouse, hoping to explain what I was feeling and tell him I was sorry for putting him through this, but he wasn't there. He'd left to handle an emergency with contract negations for a project in England.

That was almost a week ago. I'd left him messages saying to call me, but he'd never responded. The brief conversations we'd had revolved around new projects and finance and were always over a conference call.

Oh well, I deserved the silent treatment. I hoped that I'd be able to fix this mess I created.

My phone rang and I pushed the button on the console to answer.

"Hello."

"So which one are you driving?" my cousin Adrian St. James's raspy aristocratic English voice asked.

"I have no idea what you're talking about."

"Which car? Lex says one of his babies is missing."

The hell it's his baby. I bought the car for myself. He just stole it from me.

"You can inform your friend that the title is in my name. Therefore, it belongs to me."

Ian chuckled. "So answer the question."

"The Ferrari F12berlinetta." I grinned to myself. I loved this car. I wove around another group of slower traffic with ease.

"Still have a little rebel left in you?"

"Of course. I have to keep up the image," I lied.

"If that was true, you've done a piss-poor job of it."

I sighed. "I know. Ian, things are different now. Hell, none of it was real in the first place. I only behaved like a brat to make Mamma angry."

"I know, *bella.*"

Besides Lex, Ian was the one person who understood my family's crazy dynamic as well as I did. Throughout the years, he'd taken the fall for many of the activities of my brothers and me. Mamma blamed anything to do with the lifestyle on Ian. She refused to believe that the taste was inherent in the family. *Per l'amor di Dio*! Papa owned a fetish club.

Lex was the true reason Mamma hated Ian. In her mind, if Ian hadn't introduced my brothers to Lex, then I wouldn't have become involved with him. What a crock. I pursued Lex. He tried to avoid me. I loved how she rewrote history.

"When are you coming to visit?"

"Well, that's the reason I called. I'm going to be in New York in a few hours."

"What? Why didn't you tell me? *Faccia di culo*!"

"We look a lot alike, so who's the assface?"

"Whatever," I said as I checked my speed. "*Merda*, you've got me going too fast."

"I see Arya has rubbed off on you."

"You'd cuss, too, if you were going ninety-five in a fifty-five and didn't realize it."

"Blame it on the car, if one of the bobbies pulls you over."

"Oh, I'm sure that'll go over well. 'Hello, Officer, it was the car that made me do it.'"

"Putting your reckless driving skills to the side, I need a date for tonight. I know it's last minute, but I'd consider it a favor."

"Okay, who do you want me to call?" There were more than enough girls I knew who'd jump at the chance of having a date with an English marquess.

"No, I mean you. I want you to be my date to the Met Gala."

"What? Are you crazy? That's like the fashion event of the season."

"I've got it covered. Just say you'll go."

I thought about it for a few seconds.

For years, I'd wanted to go to the gala. I loved all things fashion, and this was the event for it. Attendees planned their attire at least weeks if not months in advance.

"Ian, I'd love to help you, but I don't have anything to wear, and even with all my weight loss I'll never be a sample size. Why don't you go with Christina? She's the designer."

"The plan was for her to represent the European division of her C and C fashion house, but my dear sister has gotten herself knocked up. That leaves me to take her place."

"I don't know, Ian. I'm not sure I'm ready to be in the public eye yet."

"Come on, Mil. Say yes. You're the only person who can help my stodgy British self relax. I hate these PR things. Please."

"Are you using me as a way to avoid Caitlin?"

"No." The stoic change in his voice spoke volumes. Eight years earlier, he had a superhot romance with Christina's business partner. We all thought they'd marry, but mistakes on both their parts ended their affair.

"Ian, are you sure you want to go? You're bound to run into her."

"I'll be fine. We've both moved on. It's ancient history."

I highly doubted that, especially since both of them still wore the bracelets that symbolized they belonged to each other, but who was I to question him.

"Okay, I'll go."

"Thank you. I thought I'd have to beg."

"No begging necessary." I took the exit for ArMil headquarters. "Ian, Are you sure my dress is going to be ready in time?" I refused to go to a fashion gala in last year's discards. "You do realize it took C and C three months to finish my Salvatori gala gown?"

"Calm down. Christina sent a custom gown for you. Her assistants are finishing it at the New York studio. It will be waiting for you at the hotel when you arrive."

I pulled up to the driveway of the building and glanced at my watch. "Ian, I have to go. I'm about to be late for the family meeting. You know how much I love them."

He laughed. "Good luck and give auntie dearest my love since I'm her favorite nephew."

"Sure," I snorted. "She'll be so happy to hear that bit of welcome from her 'treasured' child. Love you. See you tonight." I jumped out of the car, handed my keys to the valet, and rushed to the executive elevators.

Less than a minute later, I dashed out of the elevator and rushed to my office. It surprised me how excited I was about my date with Ian. Too bad I couldn't say the same thing about the meeting ahead of me. Family gatherings were anything but enjoyable.

I saw Rachel as I approached the reception area, and she handed me my cherished espresso, the exact way I loved it.

"*Ciao*, Rach. Thanks. I can never get enough of this stuff." I swallowed a large gulp.

"You're welcome. Your lunch is on the heating tray near the bar. By the way, Mr. St. James just called to say his plane will be at the airport at five thirty to pick you up."

Wow, he worked fast. It was all of five minutes since I had hung up the phone with him. "Is everything ready for the meeting?"

She grimaced. "I've set up the video call and made preliminary introductions. The screen is set to off and the conversation is on mute."

"What are you leaving out?"

"Mrs. Castra was not pleased to be kept waiting."

I sighed. "That's my mother. Sorry you got the bite and not me."

"Don't worry about it. Your father settled her down."

I finished the last of my coffee, set the cup on the counter, and entered my office. Thankfully, the monitor was blank; wouldn't want my parents seeing me sneak in.

I grabbed a bottle of water and took a few bites of the sandwich I'd ordered. It would hold me over until after the conference.

I sat down at the desk and switched the screen on. "So sorry for the delay. I had to handle a few ArMil tasks. How is everyone?"

"We appreciate your taking the time to do your family duty and attend our board meeting. Punctuality was never your strong suit."

I clenched my jaw but refused to give Mamma the satisfaction of a response. "Hello, Papa. Where's the rest of the family?"

Dominic answered, "We're here, *bella*." He repositioned the screen to include the whole family. "Marcello's delayed but should be here shortly."

See, I wasn't the only one keeping everyone waiting. But of course, Mamma had to point out my flaws.

"How are you feeling, my beautiful sisters?"

Both Leena and Simona rubbed their bellies. "We're both fabulous," Simona answered. "We miss you."

My heart warmed. "I miss you too. How are the boys? Tell them I sent them the replicas of both Lex's and Arya's yachts."

"They'll love them. Let's hope they don't destroy them as soon as they get them."

I laughed and glanced at the clock. In three hours, I'd leave for the airport. I could make it until then.

As my attention turned back to the monitor, my phone beeped as did my brother's with an alert from the company, telling us a new fleet of ships was ready for loading in our South American ports.

"Is the new system working for everyone?"

Arya and I had implemented a new, streamlined, and more secure software to help all the assets of the shipping company. If I ran a technology company to help other organizations and the government, it made sense to use our software for my endeavors.

"It is a waste of our resources," my mother interjected.

Ignoring her words, Papa smiled. "It is a godsend. I never understood how inefficient we were until you integrated the program. We still have a learning curve, but with all the help you and Arya are giving us, I think everything will run smoother than ever."

Before I could respond, Marcello rushed in. "So sorry to keep you waiting, *bella*. I was in a meeting with your friends at the American Port Authorities." He blew me a kiss. "I don't know what we would do without your remarkable contract negotiations."

I grinned. "You're so welcome."

"We're wasting time." My mother's scowl told me our happy family chatter was at an end.

"You're right, Mamma. Let me go over some of the details of the new plans and contracts I'm working on."

For the next hour, we discussed and voted on various provisions and issues within the shipping company. A few minutes before I called the end to the meeting, my mother rose. "I have an announcement to make."

I figured that much out.

"I'm considering stepping down and selling my shares."

What the fuck! She had completely lost her mind. Those shares were part of my inheritance.

I remained quiet as my brothers jumped in. From the looks on their faces, this revelation was a surprise to everyone.

"Sorry, Mamma, but you can't sell anything without board approval," Dominic said.

"I will do as I feel. Your nonna gifted me the shares."

She had done no such thing. I'd spent the majority of my life waiting to inherit them. My head throbbed and I was ready to jump through the screen to strangle her. I took a few deep breaths to calm my nerves. Why did I let her get to me?

"I hate to inform you, but there is no selling of shares." Good, that came out without a quiver. "You can legally forfeit them, but no one outside of the family is allowed to own the shares." Thank goodness I listened in whenever anyone mentioned anything about the inheritance.

Mamma's face turned red and she smacked the table. "I would have transferred them to you years ago if you weren't such a slut and hadn't broken the marriage contract I'd arranged with Alberto's family."

"What the fuck are you talking about?" Marcello demanded. "Was once not enough? How dare…"

Leena stopped the angry outburst with the touch of her hand.

I bit the inside of my cheek. Lex could do that very thing to me.

"Yes, Maria. Explain yourself." Oh no, Papa was mad. He used the cold, emotionless tone only when he was about to bust a gasket.

"I had my reasons. We will discuss this in private."

"No, Mamma, tell us now. You've put Milla through too much not to explain yourself. Didn't you learn after what you put Marcello and Leena through? This isn't ancient Italy where you set arranged marriages."

"Dominic, you will not speak to me in that tone."

"Then start talking," Marcello commanded.

I tuned out the angry discussion. My headache intensified to an almost unbearable level. Tears clouded my eyes as I rubbed my temples, hoping to ease the pain.

Now it all made sense. Why Alberto was so determined to pursue me, even when it was obvious we never suited each other. He hadn't wanted me; he was after the family shares.

I picked up my laptop and moved to the window desk. With the way Papa and my brothers were arguing, I knew I wouldn't be able to get a word in. I almost felt sorry for Mamma. Almost.

I gazed out toward the city and the boats sailing the Charles River. A day out on the water would help alleviate all my stress. I'd have to ask Arya if I could borrow her yacht. With her house arrest and newborns, she wasn't going to be clear to sail anytime soon.

I could always ask Lex. No. Not until I knew if he wanted to stay married.

God. I'd made a mess of my relationship.

"Milla, are you listening? Why should the three of you care, if she doesn't?"

Mamma's rude comment pierced my thoughts. "I care," I responded. "But what is the point of saying anything? You made your decision about me years ago. Why can't you see I'm not the same girl anymore?"

"Don't you disrespect me. I am your mother and I have my rights. I know all about how that Irish *pezzo di merda* seduced you and tricked you into marriage."

He's not a piece of shit. He's the best thing that ever happened to me.

My lips trembled. It was time to accept that no matter how much I wished it, Mamma would never accept me.

"I see where we stand, Mamma. Don't worry. You won't have to see me anymore. I know I'm not welcome."

"*Bella*, no. The house belongs to you. It is part of your legacy. Nonna wanted it for you." Papa's plea broke my heart.

"Don't use tears to win over your papa and brothers' sympathy. Nonna left them to me to watch over, and I am entitled to do what I want with them."

"You should read the legal documents better, Maria. Wouldn't you agree, Lex?"

Lex's hand slid on my shoulder, and I froze where I sat. How long had he stood behind me? Relief and uncertainty flooded me. Why was he here? I glanced up and swallowed. He was in lawyer mode.

He smiled at me and at the monitor. "I wanted to, once again, apologize for keeping my relationship with Mil from you."

"As we said when we spoke, you are forgiven. We understand her stubborn streak well."

I frowned. "When…when did you speak to them?"

Lex kept his gaze on the monitor, ignoring my question. "I've read through the documents you sent me, and I now have a clear understanding of the details of the will and trust."

"How dare you involve an outsider in our family business? He is an American lawyer. What does he know about Italian laws?"

"Let me explain, Ma." He chuckled. "That's what we Irish *pezzo di merda* call our mothers."

Mamma gasped.

"I'm licensed to practice law in most of Europe and in the United States. Graduating university at seventeen allowed me enough time to learn the legal systems of many countries and acquire the licenses for those countries."

Pride filled me. I'd picked a seriously smart man.

"Now, back to the shares you are determined to sell. It's impossible for you to sell them as they no longer belong to you."

"What?" both my mother and I said in unison.

Lex squeezed my shoulder. "The trust left the shares for you to oversee until the first daughter in the Castra family turned thirty or married. One of the terms was met ten years ago, and the second will be met in nine months."

"How dare you dictate to this family? I will not stand for this." She pushed at Papa's arm. "Are you going to let him control us?"

"He is right. Until Lex pointed out the details, we assumed what Nonna told us was accurate."

She could no longer hold the shares over my head. I was free.

"I will not stand for this. Don't come to me when you all regret allowing this…this…foreign criminal into our family." She stormed out of the room.

A tear slipped down my face.

"Don't cry, my *piccola*."

"Papa, why does she hate me so much?"

He sighed. "There is a lot you do not know. We will sort everything out."

"I won't hold my breath."

He chuckled. "*Ciao, amore*."

"*Ciao*." I pushed the button to end the conference.

I sat without turning and giggled, and then fell into full-on laughter.

What had just happened? For years, I'd believed that to inherit the shares, I had to either turn thirty or marry a man the family chose. I'd kept Lex a secret for nothing. I endured years of my mother's demands and the threat of losing the shares. Why hadn't I questioned the will or even read the stupid thing? I never took anything for face value. If something wasn't in writing, it wasn't legal.

Lex swiveled my chair. "Care to share the joke?"

I shook my head, and I bit my lip. "The joke's on me. You were right. I'm an idiot. I've always been an idiot."

"What are you an idiot about?"

"Everything."

Last laugh is on me. I'm so stupid.

"I'm not following."

"You warned me that I'd regret keeping us a secret, but I didn't listen. I had to prove Mamma wrong."

I could have told the world about my relationship with Lex. I'd have been free from the time I was nineteen. I'd lost so many years and I'd hurt Lex so much. I laughed and cried at the same time. Wiping my eyes with the back of my hands, I ran my fingers through my hair and then pinched the bridge of my nose.

He smiled, grasped the armrest of my chair, and leaned in. "Too late for regrets, Mil. We can't change the past. Just so you know, I would have taken you without a penny to your name. All I ever wanted was for you to put me first, to tell your mother to fuck herself and the shares." His eyes grew cold. "But that day never came."

I grimaced. "When did you learn the truth about the trust?"

"I reviewed the will for the first time when I spoke with your father and brothers in Italy."

Huh? "When did you have time to read it? I thought you left after I fell asleep."

His gaze softened, and he rubbed his thumb against my lips. "I had to speak with your family and explain why I took you as my wife without asking permission."

I swallowed.

"I had to make things right with them. I'd expect nothing less if we'd had a daughter."

My heart clenched.

I want a baby, Mil. A little girl with your eyes and smile.

We can't, Lex. Not until I'm thirty and out from my mother's control.

My soul ached at the memory. I'd have been a mother by now if I'd told her to shove it.

"I'm sorry. I wish…"

Abruptly, he stood and moved to the door. "Sorry to cut you off but I have to leave."

"What? We were…"

"No time, I have to catch a flight."

"Where are you going?"

"I'll be out of town for a few days." He smiled. "Now if you were my wife in all aspects of the word, you'd have a right to know, but since you aren't, you'll just have to wonder."

I clenched my fists, trying to make sense of what was happening. "What the fuck does that mean? If it were me, you'd demand I tell you."

"Very well. I'll be on a weekend date with a friend."

He strolled out of my office.

CHAPTER SIXTEEN

I sat in a numb haze as his words soaked in and nausea filled my stomach. A weekend date? I couldn't have heard him correctly. We'd remained faithful to each other for ten years.

My heart plummeted.

You told him to move on. What did you expect?

I bit my lips and took a deep breath. This was for the best. If I lied to myself enough times, maybe I'd start believing it.

My phone beeped. I glanced at the message. I groaned.

Call me ASAP.

It was from Caitlin Stanfield. We'd become good friends during a gala for my cousin Christina's charities. The moment Christina introduced me to her new business partner, I knew anything they designed together would be something I'd want to wear to any event.

We'd talked less than a week ago; nothing could have happened in her life that couldn't wait until morning. My emotions were in too much turmoil for any fun, lighthearted conversation. Moreover, I didn't want to hurt her by bringing up the Met Gala or that Ian was my date. Her love life was as tangled as my own.

If only Ian wasn't such a bullhead, they'd be married and popping out babies, right and left.

I'm one to talk.

"Mil, I'm sorry to disturb you," Rachel's voice sounded though the intercom. "Your call will start soon. The team is waiting for you in the conference room."

"Thanks. Let them know I'll be there in a few minutes."

"One more thing. I took the liberty of organizing a weekend bag for your trip. Tony placed it in the trunk of your car. He also arranged your security while you're out."

"You're a godsend. That's why I keep you around," I joked.

"Is there anything else I can get you before I leave?"

"No, I'm set. Have a great weekend. Enjoy the time with your family."

"I will." The speaker went dead.

My computer beeped, signaling my five-minute warning for the meeting. I hoped the call wouldn't run over. I scanned at the agenda on my desk and groaned. The long-winded CFO of one of my subsidiaries was reporting on a new project.

I sighed. *Oh well.* At least the information overload would keep my mind away from Lex.

* * *

I arrived in New York a little after five thirty, which gave me enough time to reach the hotel and prepare for the gala. The glam squad arranged for me was another advantage.

According to Christina's text, my dress was hanging in the suite and a tailor was there in case I needed any minor adjustments. She gave strict instructions. First, I was to have my hair and makeup finished and then they'd help me into my dress.

I opened the door to my suite and gasped. The dress was breathtaking. The gown had a solid black jeweled high collar that clasped around the neck. Sheer silver lace made up the sleeves and top of the dress, giving the illusion of skin, but covering everything. Completing the dramatic work of art were black-and-silver ruffles that ran along the bottom of the floor-length skirt. The piece was something I'd expect an actress to wear during a theatrical performance.

"Mademoiselle Castra, we are so happy to see you." A willowy French woman approached me. I couldn't remember where I'd seen her, but I instantly knew I'd be in good hands.

"*Ciao*." I gave her my hand and allowed her to lead me to the bedroom.

"I am Collette. I believe you have lost weight since I saw you at Madame Christina's wedding, no?"

That's where I met her. "Yes, a lot's happened this last year."

Her eyes softened. "Let us not linger on those thoughts. Tonight is about fun with your family." She waved her arms. "Nicolas, Theodore, Mademoiselle Castra is ready for you to work your magic."

Two gorgeous, blond, model-like men rushed toward me. "Welcome, Ms. Castra. I am Nicolas, and that one is Theodore." He shook my hand.

Theodore took my hand and kissed the top. "Please follow us. We will have you ready in no time."

"Where do we start?" I asked as I entered the bedroom.

"First take a shower, and then we'll do hair and makeup."

They didn't have to tell me twice. I was desperate to wash the stress of the day away. I went straight to the giant master bathroom and turned the water to my desired temperature. Then I stripped, stepped under the scalding spray, and shut my eyes.

After today's revelations, I'd never take anything at face value again. I couldn't believe I allowed my mother to control me all these years, and for nothing. I wasn't a stupid teenager anymore. I had to face the fact I'd spent the last ten years playing a brat, for my parents, the public, and Lex. For Lex, at least, it was part of the kink in our relationship.

What relationship, Mil? He's on a date with someone else. A friend.

I clenched my fist and then finished my shower in an angry rampage of bottles and soap. I turned off the shower with a jerk and stepped into the cold air. I gasped at the sudden change in temperature, snapping me out of my self-pity.

"*Merda*, I hate the cold," I muttered, drying myself with a towel and sliding on a plush white terry cloth robe.

No point in worrying about something I couldn't change.

If I pretended long enough, then maybe I'd start believing it. Squaring my shoulders, I opened the door and prepared for my beautification ritual.

* * *

"Are you sure you don't want to spend the weekend in New York? You could use a break," Ian said as the limousine left my hotel and he passed me a glass of champagne. "We can call Carmen and keep her from working herself into an early grave too."

"I want to go home, but thank you for the offer." My emotions hadn't settled after my shower, and any hope of forgetting my worries was lost. Thoughts of what Lex was doing with his weekend date sent stabs of pain to my heart.

I smoothed my dress with one hand and smiled at Ian. He wore his brownish-blond hair longer than most English lords and had a golden tan year-round, thanks to my beautiful aunt. His eyes were an eerie shade of ice blue that, combined with his unique mix of genes, gave him a surfer-boy look but with tailored style.

A frown crossed his face, but he remained silent, and then he raised his glass. "Cheers to the mess we've made of our relationships."

"That's the understatement of the year."

We downed our drinks and grew quiet again. I placed my glass in the holder and stared out the window.

Who was Lex's date? Would she be beautiful? Probably someone who looked nothing like me. A tall, willowy blond-haired amazon, who complemented his coloring. Had he met her at the club or was she a vanilla date?

It is none of your business, Mil. You asked for a divorce. It doesn't matter that you changed your mind.

"We should arrive in fifteen minutes."

I shook the melancholy from my brain and refocused on Ian. "Sorry, I spaced out."

"Don't worry about it. We both have a lot on our minds." He chuckled. "Can I ask you something?"

His now somber tone had me concerned. "Sure, shoot."

"Why did you keep your marriage a secret?"

What the hell! When did my personal life become family news?

"How did you find out?" I pinched the bridge of my nose and

lifted my other hand, halting Ian as he began to speak. "Don't tell me. I bet it was a loving call from my adoring mother to her big sister."

Ever since I could remember, my mother had an animosity toward my aunt Isabella. Besides the scandalous way my uncle and aunt got married, there was nothing for my mother to be angry with her about.

Ian raised a brow in confirmation. "You haven't answered my original question."

There was no point in hiding the truth. "I did it out of stupidity and rebellion. I refused to allow Mamma to win. I'd planned to inherit the shares, cash them out, and start my life with Lex, but after my kidnapping, I didn't want them anymore."

"What are you going to do with them, now that they belong to you free and clear?"

"You heard about that too, huh? Nothing, they don't belong to me. I transferred my shares into my brothers' names a month before I left Italy."

Ian stared at me as if I'd lost my mind.

"Don't look at me like that. I don't need the money. I only wanted them to stick it to Mamma for holding it over my head since the time I was born."

"Does Lex know?"

"No." I closed my eyes and inhaled, then blinked at Ian as tears prickled my eyes. "I fucked up, and I lost him in the process. He's on a date with another woman."

"I need you to tell me everything, so I don't find him and kick his ass."

"Okay."

I gave him a quick rundown of the events of the last few weeks and the meeting this afternoon. Ian listened and waited until I'd finished to ask his questions.

"Do you love him?"

"Of course I do.

"Then fight for him. Tell him you don't want a divorce. Tell him you made a mistake. Grovel."

"You sound like Carmen and Arya."

"Well, they're smart like me."

I cocked my hand on my hip. "How do I talk to him when he's with someone else?"

"I've known him longer than you have. Believe me when I say he's not with anyone else. His vows mean the world to him."

My heart clenched, but a shard of hope ignited.

"Lex is a good man who's sacrificed everything for you. It's time to prove to him that you'd do the same."

Ian was right, but how was I going to do this? How would I get Lex to see that he was the most important person in my life?

"I'm scared he won't forgive me." I sighed. "But I guess I won't know unless I try."

"That's all I'm asking you to do. I destroyed my future because of my stubbornness. Don't repeat my mistakes." He looked out the window. "Put your game face on; we're pulling up to the Met."

I retouched my lipstick and grabbed my clutch. Ian stepped out of the car first and then I took his outstretched hand. I smoothed out my dress and smiled for the cameras.

For the first time in months, I felt beautiful. The risqué sheer silver ensemble emphasized every inch of the curves I was slowly gaining back. I turned with my back to the paparazzi and glanced over my shoulder. The closed back and pinched waist gave my body a more hourglass shape and covered the scars on my back. The Cs strategically placed everything on the dress to give the illusion of sexiness without revealing too much skin.

One day I'll strut around in my revealing dresses and not worry about old wounds.

I slipped my hand through Ian's elbow, and we proceeded into the gala.

"Christina and Cait did an amazing job on the dress." His voice grew grim.

I clutched his arm tighter. "Let's have fun and not think of our other halves for one night."

Ian grunted in response.

"Well, at least for as long as possible."

We entered the ballroom and mingled with designers and celebrities until Ian froze, scowling at someone behind me.

"What the fuck."

I turned in the direction of his stare and spotted Lex across the room with his arm around Caitlin's waist.

"My sentiments exactly."

* * *

Lex and Caitlin approach us, and my only thought was to throw the beautiful blond across the room. I could do it. She most likely weighed less than I did.

Lex's eyes connected with mine, and my breath hitched. His predatory glare ate me up and I licked my lips. He scanned me from head to toe and whispered something to Caitlin, who shrugged and wearily smiled. His hand squeezed her waist and I clenched my jaw.

"Hello, Milla." Caitlin stepped away from Lex, hugged me, and then kissed me on the cheek.

I stiffened at her touch but smiled. *Be nice, Milla. Be nice. She's your friend.*

"I've been trying to get in touch with you for a few days. I wished we could have spoken before the gala." I heard a hint of uncertainty in her voice.

"Mil, you look gorgeous as ever." Lex leaned in for a kiss on the cheek, and the scent of his cologne ignited a spark of arousal. I used all my willpower to keep from turning my face into his neck.

He pulled back before I gave in to the urge. "Hello, Ian." They shook hands but Ian's gaze remained on Caitlin.

Her cheeks flushed, and she scooted a little behind Lex, trying to hide from Ian.

Woo, she still wants him.

"Hello, Cait. It's nice to see you again."

"Likewise," she answered in a clipped tone.

Ian took her hand and brought it to his lips. He thumbed the bracelet on her wrist, and she snatched her hand back as if he'd burned her.

"Milla, would you mind joining me in the ladies' lounge? I need your help with something."

I shrugged. "Sure. Lead the way."

I followed Caitlin to the lounge in silence. She was perfect, everything Lex needed. Her white-blond hair was set in a sophisticated bun emphasizing her simple yet elegant one-shouldered black sequin gown. Her near six-foot frame gave her the regal appearance of a classic Hollywood starlet, but the sadness in her eyes as she turned to me reminded me of what I saw in the mirror most days.

"What's the matter, Cait? You look ready to cry."

"I'm so sorry, Mil. I tried to call you and tell you, but I never got ahold of you." She wiped the corner of her eyes with her fingers. "I called as soon as Lex told me he'd be my date for the gala. I swear. I'd never do anything to hurt you."

"Did you tell Lex I was going?"

"It was his plan to take you from the beginning. He stood in front of the dress I was working on for the gala, the one Christina designed for you, and told me how he couldn't wait to see you in it."

My heart sank. I'd talked about going for years, but something always came up. Now I was here, and we were with different dates. This wasn't how it was supposed to be.

Then it hit me.

Ian set me up! He planned to ask me the whole time. But why go to all this trouble?

"I'm going to kick my busybody cousin in the balls. Why would he tell Lex?"

"I can't speak for Ian. We haven't had contact in years." Her lip trembled for a moment before she bit it and continued, "I can only speak for myself. Lex and I have known each other since we were kids, so his coming to my studio to chat wasn't unusual. However, this time was different. He wasn't the Irish charmer I was used to."

"When did he come to see you?"

"A little over two months ago. He said he'd gotten tickets to the Met Gala and wanted to surprise you. He hoped the event would entice you to come home. Milla, it was like he'd lost hope that you'd ever return."

"I've made such a mess of my relationship. I don't know what to do to fix this." I wrung my hands together and sat on the sofa. "Did he tell you about the divorce?"

Caitlin nodded, took the seat next to me, and placed her fingers over my arm. "Talk to him. I know it isn't what you want. He's going back to Boston tonight and lives across the hall. You have no excuse."

"What if I've hurt him too much? What if he's done with us?"

Why did I ever think leaving Lex would make up for all that I'd put him through?

"It's a chance you have to take. If you don't try, you'll never know. I'm rooting for you. For you both."

"Same goes for you."

Caitlin's face fell. "There isn't any hope for me. He made his feelings clear. There's no redemption in his eyes, even if the love is still there. We've said too many things to hurt each other, especially me." She wiped a tear that slipped down her cheek. "Our childhood stupidity got us into the mess we're in today, but at least you have a hope of fixing the problem and the future."

I knew Ian loved her as much as she loved him. Maybe there was hope for them, too.

I squared my shoulders. It was time to go home and see if I could fix the mistakes I kept making.

"Are you sure about Ian? He cares for you more than you know."

Caitlin shook her head. "I can't hope. There've been too many women in his life since we broke up, and I've finally started to move on." She sniffed and then giggled. "Look at me. I brought you here to talk about your relationship with Lex, and now I'm a sniveling mess."

I squeezed her hand. "I think we both needed this talk. We

should do this more often; it's good for the soul."

"Yes, but next time, we need to be in pajamas, drinking alcohol, and watching a movie with a half-naked man," Caitlin added.

Our mood lightened, and I hugged her. "I promise not to wait too long to get together. We'll make it a girls' night with Arya and Carmen."

"I'll hold you to it."

I pulled my phone out of my clutch and glanced at the time. "I think I'm going to see if Ian and I can head out early, maybe after dinner. I love this event, but I've lost the mood to be here." I stood up but Caitlin remained seated. "Aren't you coming?"

"Not yet. I have to stay the night, so a few more minutes will give me a chance to put on my game face."

I leaned down and kissed her cheek. "Don't get into too much trouble."

"Who me? I'm a good girl."

I laughed and left the lounge to find Ian waiting for me a short distance away.

"Where's Cait?" He looked behind me.

I raised a brow at his question. "Touching up her makeup. Why? Did you have something to say to her?"

Something flashed in his eyes, but then he quickly masked it. "Shut up, brat."

We moved into the dining hall.

"Would you be okay with blowing this joint a little early?"

"That shouldn't be a problem. I was ready to leave five minutes ago," he responded as I tucked my hand around his elbow. "I'm only here for Christina."

I almost called him out on the lie, but kept my mouth shut. He'd endure being here for me, so I wouldn't miss my chance to come to the gala.

"I'll call Tony and tell him our change in plans. Hopefully, we won't encounter any more paparazzi."

Before I finished the statement, reporters rushed toward us. This was extreme. On a night when world-renowned celebrities were everywhere, we weren't noteworthy.

Ian stepped in front of me. "Gentlemen, we're about to have dinner. Please let us pass."

"We only have a few questions for Ms. Castra."

Ian clenched his fist, and I could tell he was itching for a fight. The last thing I needed was a front-page headline where an English lord and Italian heiress are arrested for punching a reporter.

I pushed Ian to the side. "Why would you need to ask me anything tonight? I'm no one special with all these movie stars, designers, and music industry elite around." I gestured toward an Oscar-winning actress only a few feet away from me. Then my eyes caught Lex and Caitlin walking toward said celebrity.

Lex smiled and quirked a brow, giving me the *I'm glad it's you and not me* grin. He hated the papzz as much as Ian did.

"But you're both aristocratic royalty."

"If you say so." I rolled my eyes in a playful way. I hated this fake-smile-for-the-camera act, but I had to maintain my calm or Ian might deck the snarky little man.

"Why don't you ask Milla your questions so we can proceed with our evening."

"Someone's in a bad mood tonight."

Ian opened his mouth to respond, but another reporter spoke. "Ms. Castra, is it true you're married to Alexander Duncan?"

I stood frozen for a split second. Had I heard him correctly? "Could you repeat that?"

I saw Lex stop his conversation and stare into my eyes, telling me he heard the reporter's question. My heartbeat echoed into my ears and I took a deep breath.

"Are you married to Alexander Duncan?"

"You don't need to answer that, Milla." Ian tried pulling me away.

I dug in my heels. "It's okay. I'll answer."

Here goes. Caitlin, I hope you're right.

"Yes, he is my husband."

Everyone around us gasped, including all the eavesdropping celebrities.

"When did this happen?"

"Mil…," Ian coaxed me to keep quiet.

I patted his hand.

This is it, I'm about to claim my man. I can only hope he still wants me.

"We were married over ten years ago in a private ceremony. Gentlemen, that's all I'm going to say on the subject." I turned. "Let's go, Ian."

We remained quiet until we entered the dining room, and as we passed the doorway, I glanced back at Lex. He smiled at me and raised his glass.

"I hope you know what you've just gotten yourself into. You can't take it back, Mil."

"I know."

CHAPTER EIGHTEEN

Ian and I parted ways at the airport. He decided to return to England instead of chancing another run-in with Caitlin, and I headed home to Boston. I was so nervous, I hadn't bothered changing out of my gown.

After my announcement, I hadn't seen Lex or Caitlin for the rest of the evening. I'd sent a text to Caitlin to see if she was okay. She'd responded, telling me that she and Lex decided to call it an early night and they were both heading home. She to her loft and Lex, back to Boston.

As my plane touched down, I received a text message from Lex.

Come straight to my place. Not yours. We have things to discuss.

My stomach clenched at the underlying Dom tone of his words.

I exhaled a deep breath.

It begins.

Forty-five minutes later, I made my way to the private elevator leading to Lex's apartment. I punched in his code and entered the elevator. Before I could sort through the anxiety coursing inside my body, the doors opened.

My heart stopped.

Lex stood by the bar with his shirt untucked, his tie hanging on his shoulders, and his tuxedo jacket thrown over the back of the sofa. The top three buttons of his crisp white shirt were undone.

Damn he's hot.

Lex watched me enter the living room as he drank his cognac. "So you have arrived."

"It looks that way."

Lex set his drink on the side table and strolled toward me. He smiled like a predator. I stepped back and hit the wall. He caged me and leaned in. "So you are my wife?"

"Yes," I said in a breathless whisper.

"Since when?"

My lips trembled. "Since I was nineteen."

"I see." He grazed his lips against mine, and I tried to hold back a moan. "Who do you belong to?"

"You."

"Who do I belong to?"

"Me." I licked my lips and exhaled in shallow pants.

"What about the divorce?"

His gaze was so intense, I lowered my eye, but he lifted my chin.

"I—I don't want one. I was wrong."

"Good, because I wasn't going to give you one, without a fight."

I swallowed.

"From this moment you are mine. In public and private. No more games. No more pretending. I want you to prove that I matter, that

I'm not your dirty little secret. You will wear my ring and your anklet at all times."

My lips quivered as I replied, "Okay."

"At work we are married but colleagues, equals. But as soon as you cross that door, you are my submissive and I am your Dom."

I swallowed to relieve my parched throat and nodded.

"Give me the words."

"Yes."

"Yes, what?"

"Yes, Master."

He bit my bottom lip, sucking it into his mouth, and then pulled away. The slight sting ignited my craving for more. I leaned into him, but he stopped me with a single finger.

"I won't take the past relationship anymore. I want it all. No more hiding or holding back. No more pretending we don't exist. It's all in, a real marriage, or nothing. You make the call."

Fear crept inside me. Could he accept the new Milla, the broken Milla? The girl who still had nightmares? "Lex, what if I can't…" A tear slipped down my cheek. "There are things I don't think I can ever do again."

"Shhh. I will push you only as far as I think you can go."

"No dungeons," I blurted out.

He closed his eyes and inhaled as a crease formed between his brows.

This was it, the deal breaker. If he couldn't handle the change, we were over. I held my breath, hoping for the best but expecting the inevitable truth.

He opened his eyes but remained silent. The emotions warring on his face crumpled my heart. My shoulders fell and I tried to turn, but he held me in place.

"It's okay, Lex. I...I..." If I left now, I'd make it to my penthouse before I fell apart. I could do this, at least I hoped I could.

"I agree."

I flinched. "What did you say?"

He tucked a strand of loose hair behind my ear. "I said, I agree. No dungeons."

Relief washed over me, but so did the uncertainty. "Are you sure? I don't think I'll ever change my mind. I won't survive if you decide later that I'm not enough."

"Mil, for better or for worse, marriage is about adapting. We'll move beyond the past and adjust for the future."

I gazed up at him and saw the truth in his eyes. He wanted me, even with the change in our relationship. He cupped the back of my head and sealed our lips. Any indecision evaporated, replaced by the intoxicating taste of his mouth. I moaned as he pulled back and smiled. "Are the negotiations finished?"

I smiled in return. This was the first time I'd ever negotiated anything personal with him. I'd stepped into our marriage without hesitation and navigated the following decade in the same way. I wasn't going to kid myself and think he wouldn't push my limits, but he'd never renege on his word.

"Well?"

"Yes, they're over."

"Good." He walked away from me and sat on his couch. "Strip and kneel."

My skin prickled, and my core clenched at his command.

I followed his directive without a second thought. I slipped off my shoes and then reached back for my zipper. That's when I realized I couldn't get out of the dress without assistance.

Lex raised a brow. "Is there a problem?"

A little embarrassed, I scowled. "I can't get this dress off without help. They stitched me in."

He chuckled and gestured with his finger to come toward him.

I stepped in front of him and he stood, skimming both hands over my hips, up my waist, settling under my breasts.

"Turn around."

I complied, and his thumbs grazed my lace-covered nipples, causing them to contract into tight buds. "Lex, don't tease."

"Now what would be the fun in that." His fingers traced the back of my dress and then outlined the curve of my ass. "I hope you aren't planning to wear this dress again."

Oh, I know what's coming.

"Do it. You had the dress made, anyway."

"I see Caitlin spilled the secret."

He gripped the top of my dress and tore it down the middle. It pooled at my hips and I peeked over my shoulder. "It's stuck."

"We can't have that. Hiding this body would be a crime." He pushed the gown down and allowed it to fall at my feet. The cool air from an open window sent goose bumps over my skin. "Now take off the rest. No wait. Leave the stockings."

How could I have forgotten? He loved thigh-highs.

I reached behind me, unhooked my bra, and stepped out of my underwear. I walked over to the end of the sofa and kneeled on the cushion Lex placed before him. I relaxed into the pose he liked, legs tucked under me, hands on my knees, my head tilted down, then I waited.

What would he want me to do first?

His growing erection caught my attention. It strained, outlining the seam of his right pant leg. My mouth watered for a taste.

"Now, before we play, I have a few rules for you."

I cocked my hand on my hip. "I thought negotiations were over."

He cleared his throat, and I quickly returned to my submissive pose and gave a little pout with my lips.

I've never been good at staying in character. I guess that's why he calls me his brat.

"This isn't a discussion of terms. These are rules you will follow from here on out. You're mine by your own admission. The rules come with the territory."

Oh boy, what could he be expecting of me?

"From this day forth, you will sleep with me every night, unless we're away on business. You will come to the penthouse every day, undress, and replace your clothes with what I have set on the bed for you."

I raised a brow. "Whose penthouse?"

"Tsk-tsk, brat. This is your home now. The other penthouse is your closet for all intents and purposes. Even when we fight or you want to get away from me, you will stay here. No more running away." His gaze peered into mine.

Shit, he's serious.

"Yes, Master."

"As before, you only call me 'Master' or 'Sir' during a scene. At all other times I'm Lex."

I inhaled deep. He said *scene*. I could do a scene as long as it wasn't in a dungeon.

"Yes, Master."

His eyes shifted to the ring pinned to my stocking. "Take it off and put it on. If it leaves your finger again, I'll know it's over between us."

I nodded and followed his command, unsnapping the ring from the lace on my thigh and placing it onto my finger. His ring never left his, and I owed him the same respect.

"Good. Now come here and relieve some of the tension you've put me through over the last few weeks."

And we begin.

I licked my lips and crawled over to him. Placing my hands on his suit pants, I leaned in and grabbed the buckle of his belt with my teeth. I moaned as my nose inhaled his scent, fresh, sharp, with just a hint of spice. Wetness pooled between my legs and I rubbed my thighs together. This man turned me on like no one else.

Lex's cock grew harder under my jaw. His hand crept under my chin and he grabbed the belt out of my mouth. "The only thing I want between those wet lips is my cock."

He finished unbuckling his belt, unzipped his pants, and released his long rod. He traced my lips with his flared purple head. "Open up."

I'd barely complied when he shoved in, rough and hard. I grabbed the base over his hand, so I wouldn't gag. I relaxed my jaw and took him further. After a few swallows, the back of my throat opened and allowed me to take him deeper.

"That's it, suck me in. I want every drop from my cock to trickle down your throat."

Lex arched up into me, and I moaned in response to his hoarse words. His taste consumed me, clean, masculine, all mine. I hummed at the smooth, silky feel of his cock against my tongue.

I bobbed up and down, and soon the salty essence of precum pooled in my mouth. I traced the throbbing vein on the underside of his beautiful shaft, and a groan escaped his lips.

He wasn't going to last long. My controlled Dom needed training of his own.

He threaded his fingers into my hair and pushed me down. I held my head still, stared up at him through my lashes, and shook my head no.

Smack!

I jumped and my pussy contracted as Lex's hand landed on my ass.

Good thing my hand kept me from choking on his monster cock.

"Suck me the way I want or I'll hold your orgasms for hours." The glint in his eyes told me he was serious. Moreover, my now aching pussy wouldn't handle the wait.

I nodded my agreement and bobbed to the pace he'd set. The longer he waited to come, the longer I'd have to wait, and I wasn't in the mood to prolong the pleasure. I slid my fingers around his balls, cupping them the way he liked and then stroking the sensitive skin underneath.

A moan escaped his lips and his hold on my head intensified. I contracted the back of my throat, sending a shudder through him.

"Swallow every last drop."

I prepared myself as he pumped his cock in and out and jets of semen released down my mouth. I sucked and licked until the last of his orgasm had left him.

His fingers remained in my hair but his hold loosened. I released his now softening cock from my mouth and rested my face against his thighs, trying to catch my own ragged breath.

"I should punish you for that little trick of yours."

I frowned up at him. He wouldn't, not after I just blew his mind.

"But I've missed my submissive, and I want to play." He sat up and tucked himself into his pants, and I returned to my kneeling position. He traced my swollen lips with his thumb and then drew me forward for a light kiss. "Come. It's time to play, Mrs. Duncan."

CHAPTER NINETEEN

My heart pounded out of control as Lex led me to his bedroom. This was it, our first scene after eight months. The room resembled the man: simple, dark, and completely masculine.

He guided me to the side of the bed. I sat on the edge but jumped up when a loud click echoed in the room and the ceiling above the bed opened, revealing a grid of bars.

My breath came in short and shallow pants, while a slow dizziness clouded my head. *Please, God, don't let me freak out.*

Sensing my fear, Lex walked over, kneeled in front of me, and gathered me in his arms. "Breathe, baby. I know your limit. I won't go back on my word." He gently kissed my lips until I relaxed and demanded more. "Focus on me and the pleasure." His voice dropped and his Irish brogue intensified on the last word, sending a shiver across my skin.

He placed me back on the sheets, stood, and moved to the front of the bed. "Crawl to the center and face me."

I climbed up and positioned myself.

"Good."

The opened ceiling was definitely an addition after Arya's time. What would she think if she knew of the upgrades?

She'd expect Max to follow Lex's example.

The clank of metal brought my attention back to Lex. He pulled two chains with leather cuffs from the grid above me and clasped them around each of my wrists. He tugged on the steel to make sure I had enough room to move, then he traced the peaks of my aching nipples. "So beautiful."

His soothing, seductive voice warmed my insides, and the earlier fear disappeared. He was mine and he'd never hurt me. He loved me. This was about pleasure, his pleasure by giving me pleasure.

He cupped my breasts and sucked one of the buds into his mouth. I cried out and arched into him. *Yes, just like that. I need the bite.*

As if reading my mind, he scraped his teeth on the tips, sending a wave of pleasure-pain over my body.

"Oh, Lex," I moaned.

He pulled away. "Tsk-tsk."

I immediately realized my mistake. "Sorry, Master."

He chuckled and returned to ministering to the other breast in the same way. I needed more bite. *I would give anything for a pair of clamps.*

In the next second, the exact sensation I craved shot into me. The pain was fire hot, but the awareness following sent me into the best place of euphoria. I closed my eyes, enjoying the delicious desire pouring into me.

"Did you think I'd forget your favorite jewelry?" He tightened the clasp of the nipple clamp. "I won't make it too snug."

I frowned, opened my eyes, and glared into Lex's ocean-blue depths.

"Don't scowl. I can still punish you. Remember I'm controlling the scene."

"Sorry, Master." The exquisite rapture engulfed my senses.

"We've barely begun, and I can see the start of subspace. I won't push you beyond what I think you can handle, even if you believe you can handle more."

I closed my eyes again and waited. Lex sucked the tip of my other breast, bit down, and then pinched with the nipple clamp.

"Please," I moaned but for what, I hadn't a clue.

"Look at me, Mil."

I followed his command and watched him move away from me, take a sip of his cognac, and strip out of his clothes. He lifted his undershirt over his head, revealing his muscled chest, covered in a sprinkling of light blond hair and ropes of honed abs leading to a V.

I swallowed and licked my lips. *Oh mio Dio, this hot-ass man is mine.*

My heartbeat accelerated, and I shifted my thighs back and forth. No matter how many times I'd seen him do this, I couldn't get enough.

His pants fell next, and his rock-hard shaft hit his abdomen.

"No underwear?"

"I forgot to pack it."

Thank God.

"Any objections?"

I bit my lip and smiled. "None whatsoever."

He strolled over to me and climbed onto the bed behind me. His hands skimmed my hips and settled on my waist. "You're every man's wet dream, lips swollen from sucking my cock, rubies dangling from your rosebud nipples, and luscious curves to hold."

"You're the only man who's seen me like this. With you I feel beautiful." With him, I wasn't a media spectacle or a shameful daughter.

He cupped my face. "You are. No thoughts of anything but us."

"Okay." My lips trembled.

"Now I want to taste your sweet honey." He reached up and pulled a lever, and the chain loosened. "Bend forward."

Oh, the voice.

I lowered to all fours and waited. The weight of the jewels tugged at my swaying nipples, lessening my focus. I needed release. I'd waited too long to play. If I was in this state, what was he feeling?

His finger glided between the cleft of my butt cheeks and through my soaked slit. He rimmed my pussy but refused to penetrate my aching core. I pushed back against his hand.

Smack!

"Hey, what was that for?"

"Mil, no brat tonight. You aren't ready for real punishment, and I want tonight to be about your pleasure. Besides, you love getting your ass spanked, and the flow of your pussy on my fingers proves it."

He had a point. My body had reacted at the moment of contact.

"Now to our first game. You're not allowed to orgasm until I say."

I frowned but kept my mouth shut.

Smack!

I breathed through the sting and hissed. *What did I do?*

"You don't need to speak for me to know you're being a brat. I won't hold you back too long. Neither of us is ready for a prolonged scene."

I glanced between my legs and saw the angry purple head of his engorged cock straining. At least I wasn't the only one ready to beg. Forget that thought; Lex never begged.

"Did you say something?"

"No, Master."

He grunted and reached over for something. I turned my head late and missed what he selected.

"No matter what I do, stay in this position. Don't come. The longer you hold back, the better it will be."

"Yes, Master."

"Close your eyes."

He tied a mask across my face. "You'll peek, and I can't have that." I sighed; he knew me well.

"Ready?"

"Yes." Or at least I hoped I was.

"Spread your legs and lift up a little."

Something cold touched my shoulder, slid down my back, and settled at the base of my spine. Soon he'd pleasure me. I hummed inside with anticipation.

The bed shifted, and I felt the first swipe of Lex's tongue at my clit. Thank goodness, I'd anticipated his touch. Otherwise, I'd have face planted on the bed. I wouldn't have appeared so sexy then.

"Good, you didn't move." He slipped the cold rod into me and clicked a button.

My body ignited as the dildo hummed to life, but I kept myself still. The urge to ride the vibrating cock rocked through me.

Dammit, in eight months, I've lost all self-control.

He was trying to kill me, which was the only explanation. How was I going to stay still with that thing in me?

A moan escaped but I stopped it before it came out too loud.

He chuckled as he slid underneath me. His breath grazed my pussy, and his shoulders nudged my thighs further apart. "Now sit back onto my chest so I can feast."

At that moment, I wished I could see him lying beneath me. The sight of his mouth on my pussy aroused me as much as the act itself.

An image of Jacob tying me to a post flashed before my eyes. *No.* I shook my head. I couldn't go there. *Lex is nothing like him.*

"Relax, *a ghrá.* This is for your pleasure." His lips sucked in my clit as the vibrator increased in speed. He strummed my nub with his tongue as one hand clenched my thigh and the other pumped the metal in and out of me.

I tossed my head back.

Yes, right there. Oh God, I'm in so much trouble.

I wasn't going to last without an orgasm. I shifted against his mouth.

"Please…"

Smack!

I convulsed around his mouth and the pulsating shaft as lights exploded behind my eyes. I tried to keep my hands up but I fell forward onto my elbows. Everything throbbed inside me. "Mmm…Master," I cried and tried to catch my breath.

Lex continued his ministrations and the pumping of his arm. "Naughty girl, you moved. Give me one more," he murmured. I felt him smile against my pussy, and then he flicked his tongue faster as his fingers bit into my leg.

He knew I'd come! Instead of being upset, I was grateful. My body was on fire, and that orgasm did nothing to alleviate the tension continuing to build in my body. I was ready for another eruption.

I resisted the instinct to contract around the vibrator. No coming unless he gave me permission. My training wasn't a complete loss. Scrunching my eyes behind the mask, I willed myself to focus on anything but the sensation pulsing over my skin and in my weeping pussy. My arms shook and I arched my head.

Lex, please.

"Now, *a ghrá*. Come now." His teeth nipped my clit and my body imploded. Lex pulled out the dildo and replaced it with his fingers. "That's it. I love the feel of your pussy milking its release."

I thrashed against my restraints and allowed ecstasy to flow over me. He fingers slid out of me, then he lifted me and moved from between my legs.

I shifted to lie down and rest my wobbly arms, but he held me in place. "Not yet. I still have plans for you." He cupped my tender rear. "God I love it when your skin gets that pink tinge. Next time I spank you it will be with a paddle."

A whip flashed into my mind, but I shook the thought away. "Are you sure I'm ready?"

"We'll take it slow, don't worry." He kissed the skin where his hand rested. Relief washed over me. He'd ease me into it.

After a few more caresses and kisses, a finger glided between my cheeks and rimmed my puckered entrance. "I'm going to fuck your ass."

I clenched my cheeks, remembering the many ways he'd taken my ass, with dildos, his cock, an inedible cucumber I was going to use in a salad.

I hoped that wasn't the plan tonight. His monster cock would tear me in half. The muscles had closed up from lack of use. "I don't think I'm prepared for you, Master."

"No, you're not, but I will stretch you, ready you."

"With what?"

He chuckled. "No vegetables tonight. Just my fingers. I'm going to fuck that sweet, hot pussy of yours while my fingers fuck your ass."

His words reignited a stream of new desire. "Oh."

A cap snapped open. "Oh fuck," I cried as a cool liquid slide down the crease between my butt and a finger pushed in. At the same time, he reinserted the vibrator, setting it to the highest level.

My ass burned from the invasion and my pussy spasmed.

"Breathe through it, Mil. Push back. Focus on the dildo."

I released the breath I hadn't known I held and focused on the dueling sensations. My body adjusted faster than I expected, and I rode both his hand and the vibrator. He inserted a second finger, scissoring as he pumped.

"Lex, I can't."

"Yes, you can."

I squeezed my eyes shut and allowed the pleasure-pain to engulf me.

Without warning, he pulled out his fingers, and my mind cleared. "No, please," I called.

"I've changed my mind. Stay right there."

I panted, trying to understand why he'd leave me hanging. I laid my head down and wiped at the tears in my eyes. My body screamed for release. "I'll let you take my ass if you'll just allow me to come," I begged.

He chuckled. "Not tonight, love, but something else is going up there. I'll give you two clues. They aren't grapes and you'll have to wear them every day as soon as you get home."

Anal beads.

He'd said the same thing when we'd first married. He'd made me wear them everywhere on our honeymoon. At night, when he removed them, I was so horny and ready that I'd orgasm with barely a touch.

At least I wouldn't have to wear them to work.

A round ball grazed my back entrance and pushed in, followed by another, then another. The sixth and last bead was the largest, and I had to breathe through the pressure and the discomfort, focusing on the burning pleasure. I shook my head, knowing that the giant bead wasn't even close to the girth of Lex's flared head.

I'd survived before, but at this moment, the thought was daunting.

"It will fit. It has many times."

I growled over my shoulder and he smacked my ass, jarring the beads forward. "Oh," I called as my original excitement returned.

"Now back to where we started." The electronic phallus pushed at my opening and I moaned. "That's it, take it in. I love how your beautiful pink pussy sucks in the cock. I can't wait to tunnel into that beautiful cunt."

His coarse words sent a flood to my aching clit. I wanted to rub it but my bound hands kept me on my elbows.

He rotated the dildo and I moaned again. "Ready?"

"Yes."

He rotated again. "Yes what?"

I pushed back onto his hand but he held me still. I resisted the urge to snap. "Yes...Master," I hissed.

"Good girl."

He began with slow, soft strokes and progressed to hard ones, rubbing the vibrator against the thin skin separating the beads. He ground back and forth, causing my back to bow and push into the addictive pleasure.

Yes, that's it. More.

He tortured me for another ten strokes, then increased the speed of the vibration and his hand.

"Please," I called. I had to come. It was almost upon me. "Don't stop, Master."

"I won't, baby; ride it through." He pumped faster. "Now, baby, now."

I came so hard that my nails tore the threads of the expensive duvet. Spots appeared behind my eyes.

"Let it go, love."

I milked the plastic cock until I was a shaking puddle.

He pulled out and threw the vibrator behind him, unlatched my wrists, then flipped me onto my back and climbed between my legs. The head of his cock drove in to the hilt. I arched in response to the sharp invasion.

"Lex!" I clutched his shoulders as he bit my shoulder and pounded into me. My body ignited again and moments later, Lex followed.

CHAPTER TWENTY

No!" I gasped for air as I woke from a nightmare. A chill ran over my body, prickling my skin, and my heart pounded in my ears. After a few deep breaths, my panic calmed and I glanced around the bed. Lex lay sleeping with the covers pooled around his waist. All I wanted was to crawl into his arms and forget the horrible memories.

Why tonight of all nights would I dream of Jacob? Would he ever stop haunting me?

Tucking my knees into my chest, I wrapped my arms around them and buried my face against my legs as tears covered my face.

Once this is over, I will fuck you the way Lex fucks you. Then I'll take a turn with your Indian friend. At least now, I'll forever know that the whip you loved will repulse you.

Bile filled my mouth. I rushed to the bathroom and vomited into the toilet. After my stomach emptied, I stumbled to standing, brushed my teeth, and washed my face. I scrubbed and scrubbed, but I couldn't shake the toxic feel and taste of Jacob from my skin.

A shower.

I had to wash this filth away. I turned on the water to the hottest setting I thought I could handle and stepped in. The shock of the blistering water snapped me out of my haze. I adjusted the temperature and leaned my head against the tile.

A sob escaped my lips. I was letting him win. What would Lex think if he saw me like this? He deserved someone who could give him all he needed.

The shower door opened and I jumped. Lex stood half-asleep and naked in front of me.

"Nightmare?"

My lips trembled, and I nodded.

He cupped the side of my face and walked under the spray of the six different showerheads. He ran his thumb along my lips. "Let me wash away the pain and give you brand-new memories."

He leaned down, planting a gentle kiss on my mouth. He slowly turned me, pulling my back against his chest. A hand slid across my stomach, holding me tight, as the other continued to rest on my shoulder.

I grasped his arm, relaxing into the comfort he gave without expectation. We remained quiet for what seemed hours, tears spilling from my eyes. "I don't know if I'll ever stop reliving the abduction. He did things to me, things I don't know if I'll ever get over. You deserve someone who isn't as fucked up as I am."

Lex grazed the back of my neck with his stubble. "I have all I ever wanted. I made the vows for better or worse. We'll make it through this, but I can't help you if you don't tell me what happened."

"He...he defiled everything we shared...he treated me like a whore." I sobbed. "He let others watch while he...he...used the whip to..." I wasn't sure I could finish. "I...I..."

"Shhh. You don't have to finish. Answer this one question, and I won't ask any more. Did he rape you?" His voice showed traces of anger.

Everyone assumed Jacob raped me, and my refusal to talk about the abduction must have confirmed their suspicions.

I nodded. "In every way but with his penis," I whispered. "They captured Arya before he got a chance." I rubbed my arms uncontrollably. "I can't get clean enough from what he did to me."

Lex grasped my arms, stopping my panicked movements. "Let me wash away his touch." He paused. "I need to wash away his touch."

I shook my head, ready to push him away but stopped myself and turned to face him. We stared at each other. I wasn't sure what I expected to see in his eyes, but all I found was love and pain, pain for me.

My lips trembled, and my vision blurred again.

"What if the memories never go away?"

He cupped my cheek, wiping away the stray tear on my cheek. "Then I'll do everything possible to give you new ones."

He kissed my forehead. "Please, Mil. Let me give you this."

"Okay."

Lex reached over, picked up the body wash, and poured it onto the loofah.

"Put your hands on the wall, close your eyes, and enjoy." He lathered the sponge as I complied with his request.

With slow strokes, he trailed the suds along my shoulders and back. He massaged as he progressed down my body and followed each rub with gentle kisses. His feathered touch glided along my spine, over the curve of my bottom, and then up and down the back of each leg.

Goose bumps prickled my skin, and by the time he had me turn, I was no longer focusing on my nightmare but on the slow arousal tingling throughout my core. He washed and kissed every scar on my legs, stomach, and breasts.

Once he was finished, I threaded my fingers through his hair and drew him to me. He came without resistance and sealed our lips. We savored each other's mouths, drowning in the passion flaring between us.

"I won't let anyone hurt you again," he murmured against my lips.

I knew it wasn't a promise he could possibly keep, especially with the blatant threats from Christof, but he needed to say it anyway. I deepened our kiss as his hand cupped my breast and the other drew one leg over his hip. He ground his erection against my swollen clitoris. "Lex," I moaned.

His lips nipped and licked down my neck and over my breast until he sucked one tip into his mouth. His tongue flicked and teased the bud to a hard point and then moved to the other. I arched my head back against the tile-covered wall, allowing the heat of the shower to massage my spine while Lex's mouth ministered to my breast.

"Please. I need more."

Without response, he released my leg and stooped between my thighs. He hoisted me up around his shoulders with only his body and my hands against the shower wall holding me up. He licked the seam of my sex and pushed his tongue between my folds. He glided from front to back, over and over, rimming my weeping pussy but not penetrating.

"God, I love the taste of you. You're like a drug."

He started fucking me with his mouth, and all coherent thought left my mind. I arched, forgetting about the wall, and gripped his head. I clenched my thighs and he smacked my bottom, sending me over unexpectedly. I screamed my release, begging and pleading for more.

Before I came down, Lex released my legs, stood, grabbed my hips, and entered me in one swift thrust.

We both groaned.

"Open your eyes, Mil." I followed his command. "No matter what happened in the past, you are mine." He pulled out and slammed back in. "No matter what happens, you remember my touch, your touch, us."

"I will. I promise," I cried.

"This." *Thrust.* "Body." *Thrust.* "Is." *Thrust.* "Mine."

"Yes," I responded.

"Forever. No matter what, we belong together."

"Yes."

His cock tunneled in and out at a pace I couldn't comprehend. "I love you, only you."

"I love you," I called and we both erupted.

* * *

"Open your e-mail now." Arya's voice blared into my ear.

"Well, good morning to you, too. It isn't even six in the morning, and I haven't had my espresso yet," I said into my cell phone as I walked into my kitchen. "Why are you bothering me? Lex is still sleeping. Call him and get his ass out of bed. Let me have my coffee in peace, then I'll call you back to discuss the new harbor agreements."

My heart contracted. For five weeks, we'd lived as a married couple. Things were so smooth that I worried I was dreaming. He never pushed me to go further than I wanted, and he accepted my limits. Sadly, that was a blessing and a curse in our relationship. Every time I walked past the dungeon, I regretted putting the restriction on what we did with each other. I wanted to feel like I was still myself, and I knew going in there would help me do that.

Maybe in time, Lex and I would enjoy that room again. Hopefully sooner rather than later.

I smiled to myself as I switched on my coffee press.

"Mil, this isn't a happy call. We've got a problem." She paused. "Actually, you've got a problem. The sick fucker cc'd me on your message."

Immediately sleep cleared from my mind, and I grabbed my laptop, logging into ArMil's secured server and opening my e-mail program.

"What am I supposed to look f…" I stopped my question as I saw an e-mail sent from one of Christof's shipping subsidiaries.

All the hairs on the back of my neck stood up. For almost two months, I hadn't received any communications or threats from Christof. I knew hoping things would die down was too good to be true.

"*Merda*, there goes my freedom to drive. Once Lex finds out, he's going to be my shadow." I clicked on the e-mail and read.

My dearest Mrs. Duncan,

I request your presence for a package pickup. It contains a proposal that will compensate me for the damage you and your

*friends have done to my enterprises. If my instructions are fol-
lowed, your debt to me will be paid in full.*

*Meet my representative at Caffè Bella, in exactly two weeks
from today at eleven a.m. Do not mention this to your husband
or your security team. If you do, I will know and I will release
details on Duncan's activities during the time you spent in the
company of Mr. Brady and myself. What would the authorities
think if they learned that your husband stepped over the legal
lines to rescue you?*

VC

   PS

   *I recently learned of your new harbor contracts. We'll discuss
the usefulness of those soon.*

"Oh, *Dio*, Arya, what am I going to do?" I set the computer away
from me with shaky hands and went to the espresso machine, placed
a cup inside, and pushed the start button. Hopefully, a little caffeine
would help settle my nerves.

I braced one hand on the kitchen island. He knew about the harbor contracts. No one outside of ArMil and the Port Authority was
aware of those negotiations. He also knew the name of my favorite
coffee shop. Oh, God, he'd probably researched me as he'd done
with Arya. Nausea filled my stomach.

All these threats meant only one thing: No matter what I did or
how I complied with his demands, he'd never let me off the hook.

I took a few deep breaths, trying to push the panic down.

"Ari, I'm scared. He knows about the shipping agreements. What
if he wants to use my ships for something?" My gut told me that us-

ing contracts and access to the port were exactly his plans.

"Mil, why would he cc me on the e-mail?"

"To let you know that he hasn't forgotten about you. *Cazzo.*" I pinched the bridge of my nose as a tremor shot up my spine.

I will not fall apart. I will not fall apart.

"We can't go through this again."

"I know *mera behna.*" In the background, I heard the sound of little whimpers. "Hold on a sec. Let me put the boys down."

As I waited for Arya to return, I grabbed a pen and paper and wrote down all the people who knew about the negotiations. There was a leak on one of the sides, and I planned to find out who it was. I eliminated most of ArMil personnel. They'd lose too much if they backstabbed the company. That left six people on the Port Authority side and two new employees from our side.

I opened my laptop and typed all the names into the background search program that I helped Arya develop. It would look into everything from childhood activities to spending habits and debts. I may not have Arya's superhuman knowledge of computers and development, but I was far from a novice.

I took a picture of my list with my phone and sent it to Arya.

"Hey, I'm back."

"Check your text. These are the people I suspect of leaking the information about the contracts. I've already started a background investigation. You can log in and scan the results as they come in."

A flag appeared on a name from the government side. It was someone who'd lived and worked in Saint Petersburg for a few years before he took the position with the Port Authority. He'd also served as an expert witness for a case Lex pursued against a computer parts wholesaler in Germany. There was also a two-million-dollar deposit from one of Christof's companies into a Swiss bank account under the man's name.

"Fuck, fuck, fuck. Are you seeing what I'm seeing?" Arya asked me.

"Yep." Dread engulfed me.

"Fucking hell. If this leaks, it could put any of the cases Lex worked on with him into question. Mil, whatever we decide, we can't let Lex know."

I pinched the bridge of my nose.

Lex was the grandson of a former Irish gangster. His family had spent years trying to move past the taint of their history. Integrity meant everything to them and in turn to Lex. Whenever he took a case, he made sure every *i* was dotted and every *t* was crossed. I could only imagine what this news about the witness would do to him.

"Don't you think I know this? He can't get in any more trouble. His license to practice law is already at stake because of the underground channels he used to find us during our kidnapping."

"Oh, shit. Who told you about that?"

"No one. Last week, while working in our home office, I found the affidavit open on the desk."

"And you didn't confront him about it? That's not like you, Mil."

"I was trying to think things through before I jumped all over his ass."

"Did you come to any conclusions?"

"Yep." I sighed. "That Lex didn't want to worry me. He knew I'd think it was my fault."

"Why would it be your fault?" Arya asked in her Aunt Elana voice, which told me she was on the verge of getting angry.

"Ari! I'm the reason the whole mess this past year happened in the first place."

"Bullshit. And you know it. I developed the software, I negotiated the deal for Arcane. It is not your fault that Jacob kidnapped either one of us."

Why couldn't she understand?

"Never mind that. I want to know why you kept Lex's legal issue from me," I growled into the phone.

"I know you're stressed, but don't take it out on me. Besides, I only learned about it a few days ago, and that was all because Max let it slip when we were discussing protecting our friends. His lame excuse was that he didn't want anything to affect our recoveries."

"Sorry." I shifted the phone so I could grab my coffee and chug it down. "I wish Lex hadn't kept it from me. I'm stronger than he thinks."

"Um, Mil? I know I'm that one that suggested this, but aren't you about to withhold something from Lex for his own good?"

"Shut up." Nevertheless, she had a point. "Ari, we have to come up with a plan. I can't go without protection. I'm not stupid enough to believe I'm safe." I checked my watch and paced.

I still had twenty minutes before I woke Lex.

"I'm already working on something. The first thing we have to do is make sure to take the Port Authority rep off the project. Damn, he seemed like such a nice guy. I guess anyone can be bought for the right price."

"I really hope he's the right guy. It would suck if Christof was framing him."

"Mil, we can't take any chances. This is something that could affect your family's entire company."

"I agree. There's something else you have to do. I need you to put a protection detail on Lex."

"Um, Mil. That's going to piss him off. He's pretty good at spotting them."

"You and I aren't the only targets anymore. Christof wants Lex to suffer too. Please, Ari."

She sighed. "Fine. Let me make a few calls and see if Thomas has a team he can send. I'll give you the details for our next steps when I come to the office later today."

"Okay, I trust you. I'll see you in a few hours."

"Love you. *Ciao*." I hung up the phone and closed my eyes.

How was I going to keep this from Lex? At this moment, all I wanted to do was crawl into bed next to him and hide. Maybe that wasn't such a bad idea. I could skip yoga for one day. I rushed down the hall and stopped. The door to the dungeon was open. Taking a deep breath, I grabbed the handle and shut it tight.

You're mine. I've waited years to have a piece of Lex's bitch. Before we're done, you'll be begging to suck my cock. First, I'm going to fuck you with this whip. Boys, get ready for some entertainment.

Nausea filled me. I ran toward the master bedroom and slammed into Lex.

"Mil, what's the matter?"

"I can't. I can't," I cried.

"Baby, calm down. What can't you do?" I struggled to get out of Lex's hold, but he held me tight against him.

"The door was open. I thought…"

He pushed my hair out of my eyes and held my face in his palms. "We don't have to go in there yet. Not yet."

"Why was the door open?"

"I went to get something." He kissed my forehead. "Calm down."

I pulled back. "What did you get?"

"Just a few items for tonight. Nothing to worry about."

My insides settled at his words, but sadness and anger also filled me. Sadness that I'd given up one of my favorite things about my lifestyle. And anger for allowing myself to be paralyzed by the past. All because of a sick fucker.

Cazzo! I'm letting Jacob win again.

I had to get over this. I was a strong woman. The best way to get over this fear was to go in there.

"I'm okay, Lex." I stepped out of his arms and grabbed his hand, bringing it to my lips. "I promise. I'm okay."

"I know, *a ghrá*." He tucked a strand of my hair behind my ear. "I'll never force you to go in there before you're ready."

"Sometimes I wish you would." I had fear but never of Lex.

He frowned at my comment. "That's my call."

Oh, that's my Dom talking. I conceded with a nod as my skin prickled.

"I won't let you top me from the bottom, no matter how much I enjoy your brat side."

I licked my lips, and his eyes dilated as they followed my movement.

A smile hinted at the corner of his lips. "Come. I have plans to replace yoga, then a quick shower before work."

CHAPTER TWENTY-ONE

I changed my mind. I don't think you should do this alone," Arya said over the intercom of my car. "Why did you ever listen to me?"

My stomach jumped in somersaults at her question. I shifted gears and switched lanes as I made my way onto Interstate 90. In twenty minutes, I'd pick up whatever package Christof sent me, and then I'd have to deal with whatever bargain the devil wanted me to agree to.

"Arya, you're the mastermind of this plan. Don't freak her out now," Carmen reprimanded.

"I'm worried. Give me a break. Do you know how hard it is to lie to Max? He knows I'm up to something."

"We're all worried, Ari." Carmen's voice softened.

"Ladies, stop talking about this until I'm closer to the bakery. Talk about something, anything other than what I'm about to walk into."

"Okay. Let's talk about the latest in the magazines."

Carmen groaned. "Someone kill me now."

"Shut up. It helps me relax and start my Mondays in a positive mood," Arya said, defending her not-so-secret guilty pleasure.

"Whatever," Carmen mumbled.

"You know you love hearing all the gossip as much as I do," I interjected.

"I suppose you're right. Well, as long as it isn't me in the news."

Arya squealed. "Okay, so the latest gossip is." She paused. "Nothing." She started laughing.

I shook my head as I took the exit onto Interstate 93 and the street that would lead to the bakery. "Arya, I think those kids are sucking your brain cells out through your nipples."

"Yes, what was the point of that?" asked Carmen.

"Just to say that none of us have been in the tabloids for over a month. Especially Milla."

"What is that supposed to mean?" I asked, even though I'd wondered about that, too. I'd been a fixture in European gossip magazines since I was a teenager. It was odd not to field calls from reporters trying to confirm any new tidbits of gossip.

"You know exactly what I mean. I don't understand why the tabloids are giving you a free pass."

"I wondered the same thing. Maybe I'm boring now that I'm married and not dancing on tables."

"We can hope, but I wouldn't hold my breath," Carmen said. "It's only been a few weeks since your marital status became public. Give them a few more days. They're vultures, circling fresh meat."

"Thanks for blowing my hopes," I grumbled as I turned onto one of the streets leading to Boston's North End, also known as Little Italy.

"That's why I'm here. Don't get too comfy, Mil. They're going to wait until you're least expecting it and then strike." There was a hint of amusement in Carmen's voice.

"Or capture Lex giving you a strike." Arya laughed.

An image of me this morning, lying across a spanking bench and a flogger in Lex's hand flashed before my eyes. My core spasmed in response and I shifted in my seat. The bite of the movement sent a flood of wetness between my legs.

I tried to shake the thought from my head, but all I kept thinking about was my desire to push Lex into taking me into the dungeon. I knew that by going back in the room, I'd gain back a piece of me that Jacob took away.

Maybe the girls would have an opinion on it. What was I thinking? Of course they'd have an opinion. They were overflowing with them.

"On that note, I have a question."

"Sure, shoot," both Arya and Carmen said at the same time.

"Not you, Arya. Every time I take your advice, I end up in deeper shit than I was in before. Carmen, this is for you."

"Fine. I see how it is. See if I bring you any fresh zeppole when you're stressed."

I rolled my eyes and pulled the car to a stop at a red light. "So here is my question. How do I get Lex to push me?"

"Um, Mil. Are you sure you're ready? Do you remember the breakdown you had at my place?" Arya reminded me.

"I am. If I don't go back in, I'm letting Jacob take something I love away from me, and he wins. The room isn't my demon, Jacob is. My problem is that I need Lex to see I'm ready." I bit my lip.

"I feel like you're leaving something out."

"I kind of freaked out two weeks ago. I saw the door to your former lab open."

"You guys turned my sacred computer lab into a sex dungeon?" Arya asked with a hint of panic.

"You're one to talk. The room you and Max use was once my homeschooling room," Carmen retorted.

"Anyway," I interjected. "I'm asking for advice. I saw the door open and assumed he was going to make me go in there. I started remembering everything Jacob did to me, and I lost it. Since then, Lex has kept the door locked."

"You want my opinion?" asked Carmen.

"Sure. Since you are the only Dominant on the line, maybe you'll have some insight I don't."

"I think you should talk to him, and if that doesn't work, do something super stupid. Something that will force him to take you in there."

"I'm not sure it'll work, but it's worth a try. All I do lately is give in whenever he says no." I hadn't played a true brat in so long, the thought of it almost felt foreign.

"Be careful how far you push him or you'll get more than you expect," Arya warned.

"He treats me like fragile glass. I won't break. I need my old Lex back, the man who doesn't put up with any of my antics. Although, I haven't given him any to punish."

"Then piss him off and suffer the consequences." Carmen chuckled.

"That's easy for you to say. You've never been in my position, Mistress Dane. I'm at a loss for what to do."

"I'm sure you'll think of something. Okay, ladies. Time to switch gears. Milla's GPS says she's a few blocks from the bakery. No more personal talk."

Carmen's change in subject snapped me out of my semi-relaxed mode to full alert. My heart pounded out of control, and my hands shook as I pulled into a parking space across from the bakery. I scanned the area, checking for my security detail. I spotted the familiar cars at various spots near the street of shops and restaurants.

"I don't know if I can do this. God, I wish Lex was here, or at least monitoring my meeting."

"He'd never have let you do this," Arya said as she typed. "Hell, if Lex knew, he'd lose his shit, and he's in enough trouble for his part in our rescue."

The inquiry into Lex's involvement now extended into his law practice, specifically old cases. He'd tried to hide the stress, but the more he worried, the more protective he became. Maintaining my driving privileges was the result of an argument where we'd not talked for two days. If he'd had one inkling of this plan, he'd have locked me in our penthouse.

"Thanks for the reminder." I pushed back the bad feeling and switched the conversation to my mobile phone. "I can do this," I said aloud to myself.

"Don't get doubts now. You know what to do. Act casual, order a cup of coffee, and wait for the package from Christof. Once you have it, wait five minutes, leave, and then come to my office immediately."

"Okay, Ari." I released a shaky breath.

"Get ready. In five, I'll bring the team online. They won't hear our end of the phone conversation, but will hear everything you say from the mic hidden in your necklace. I'm also going to hang up so

I can concentrate on jamming any tracking around you."

"Got it." Or at least I hoped I did.

"Nothing is going to happen. Stay calm. If Tony suspects you're scared, he'll make you abort the plan. I had to fight tooth and nail just to get him to agree," Carmen said. "He takes his loyalty to you and Lex seriously."

My stomach jumped again. "He's not with the group following me. Where is he?" I opened the car door, locked it, and scanned the street.

Slowly I made my way across to the bakery.

"Never mind." I spotted Tony in a corner drinking a cup of coffee. "Maybe getting him involved was a bad idea. He's as overprotective as James is with Arya."

"Stop worrying about it. I sent him so you wouldn't be alone inside," Carmen reassured me.

"Easy for you to say. You're sitting pretty in Arya's office while I'm out here."

"Mil, focus. You're on. Remember, you aren't alone."

I ignored Carmen's reprimand and walked to the counter, ordered my favorite coffee and pastry. "So did you ever look at the report I sent you on the new clubs we've started planning?"

"I'm reading through it right now," Carmen responded, realizing I was trying to keep a conversation going.

I looked to the back of the café and moved toward an empty table.

"So what do you think?"

"It looks good except for one thing."

"What?" I smiled at the server who approached me and placed my espresso and zeppole on the table.

"When did Thomas Regala become partners with us?"

I cringed. "For at least ten years. We own nine nightclubs together."

"That's not what I'm talking about and you know it. I'm talking about the fetish club deal."

"Carm, your personal relationship had nothing to do it. He wanted to move out of the nightclub circuit, and joining our private clubs was a perfect transition. Besides, I'd made the agreement before I found out you were bonking him."

Carmen snapped. "You could have told me."

"No, I couldn't, Carm. The deal was set two years ago."

"I don't like it." The underlying pain from the end of her affair lingered in her voice. No matter how tough she tried to act, anyone who knew her was aware she wore her heart on her sleeve. She just hid it under a cool-as-a-cucumber façade.

"Talk to your brother about it. He and Lex are the leads on the project, not me. I just got their financing together. All Max is going to say is, what happens in your personal life has nothing to do with the deal or the bottom line."

"I couldn't agree more."

TWENTY-TWO

All the hairs on the back of my neck stood up at the memory of the last time I'd heard that Russian-accented voice.

"Carm, I have to go. Let me eat my pastry, and I'll call you back."

"Got it. Stay calm. You're not alone."

"Ciao, bella."

I hung up the phone and took a deep breath.

"Christof," I whispered.

Why hadn't I seen him before?

Because he is a terrorist who's only seen when he wants to be seen.

I glanced toward Tony, who was reading a paper, but the slight twitch in his cheek told me he recognized who was behind me.

"Call me Vladimir." He scooted his chair out, sliding it until his back touched my chair.

"I thought I was coming to get a package with instructions."

"You are. But it's a message more effective if delivered in person."

The last time I'd encountered him, he'd looked me up and down, then told Jacob he'd captured the wrong woman and that he wasn't interested in his whores. It was as if I wasn't important enough to look at. By the time he'd realized who I was, Jacob had beaten me and assaulted me to a point where I thought I'd die.

I swallowed down the bile rising in my throat. He's seen the whip Jacob used on me and just shook his head but did nothing to help me.

"How is Mrs. Dane doing? I heard she had complications with her pregnancy."

Of course, he'd ask about Arya. The fucker's obsession with her and the software was the reason my whole life turned upside down.

"She's…she's fine." I picked up my cup and gulped down the scalding brew.

"Pity she wasn't interested in my proposal last year. It would have been a very mutually beneficial arrangement. I'm hoping you're more accommodating. Especially since now there are two debts owed to me. First, for the losses I incurred because of your work with MI6, and the second, for the damage done to my network as the result of the bugged Arcane software duplicate."

My heartbeat accelerated. "I don't know how I can help you. My skills are no match to Arya's."

"I've actually lost interest in software development. At least for now. I've thought of a different way for you to pay your debt to me."

"I owe you nothing. You owe me for what happened to me under your watch."

Good. I'd said that without my voice quivering.

"That isn't the way I see it. Your treatment by Jacob Brady was a sad situation. His tastes in sadism are more extreme than mine."

A dizziness entered my mind, and I gripped the table as I took a few deep breaths to keep down the anger flaring to life inside me.

"You knew who I was?"

"Not at first. Mr. Brady's interest was in keeping Mrs. Dane away from his friend, but later I'd heard his ramblings about this Italian submissive he planned to tame. So I told him if he brought me Mrs. Dane unharmed, he could take the submissive for himself. I never imagined he'd lust after you." Christof hummed. "By the time I was informed that Duncan was using his family's underground contacts to find you, it was too late, the damage was done. All we could do was redirect Mr. Brady's attention back to Mrs. Dane."

God, I'd blamed myself for this mess, and it wasn't my fault. I let guilt eat away at me for no reason. Arya and Lex were right. My hold on the table increased. Jacob planned to get me no matter what. Even if I'd listened and stayed, he would have found a way to capture me. I was his reward for helping abduct Arya.

Tears prickled behind my eyes, but I held them back. I would not give this man the satisfaction of seeing my pain.

Milla, keep it together. You have a job to do.

"I see the memories are still fresh." He tossed a white handkerchief over my left shoulder.

I refused to touch it, and let it drop to the floor.

I'd made one stupid decision after another, thinking I was doing right by Lex. And in the end, I was wrong. It wasn't my fault any of this happened. There was only one thing I could do right now. I'd listen to what this man wanted and figure out a way to make him pay for his part in my agony.

"Just tell me what you want from me so I can get on with my life."

Christof chuckled. "You are as feisty as your friend. Now, to answer your question, I need the use of your port."

"What port?" *Please don't say it.*

"The one you signed the agreement on yesterday. The one that gives Castra Enterprises exclusive right to two docks in the Port of Boston."

"H-how do you know about that?" *Merda*, I thought we'd gotten rid of our leak.

"Because I have someone on the inside in the Port Authority that keeps their eyes and ears on anything that would be of interest to me. You have to remember, if one man is eliminated, another is always willing to take his place."

"What do you need the ports for?"

"I need you to arrange for one of your ships to pick up a shipment in Venezuela and deliver it here. Once the freight clears customs, your debt to me is paid."

Was he crazy? I knew without a doubt I couldn't do it. He was a known arms dealer, and this would be only the first of many demands he'd place on me. Not only that, it would ruin the company generations of my family had created.

"Do we have an agreement?"

Of course we don't, but he doesn't need to know that.

"If I do this, I want any and all information on Lex, including all access codes to files and the names of people involved in the accusations. I know you're the one behind his investigation."

"I'm impressed. How did you figure it out?"

It dawned on me a few days after my e-mail from Christof, while I'd read through an investigator's report on Lex's case. Everything seemed too convenient. How could witnesses come out of nowhere? The man would go to any lengths to get what he wanted, and my ships were one of them.

"You're not going to deny it?"

"Why would I do that, *myshka*? There is no point. I'm a straight-forward man, and I will use any means necessary to achieve my goal, including using my connections to incite an investigation for impropriety."

"But he didn't do anything wrong." I wanted to turn around and smack him on the head, but I kept my body still.

"Well, that isn't for you to decide. The agents will deliver their findings soon enough. Do we have an agreement or not?"

This man had no fear. It was as if he lived in a world where he set the rules. The sad part was that, in a sense, it was true. He controlled a segment of the crime world.

I was in so much shit. God. I hoped Arya was getting all of this.

"I…I…" I swallowed to quench my dry throat. "Yes."

"Excellent." Christof stood as soon as I answered, and so did five other men and women with him.

He took my hand and kissed it, and for the first time I was able to get a good look at him.

Wearing a button-down linen shirt and dark khaki pants, his clothes were tailored to perfection. His face held the beauty of a fallen angel, white-blond hair with piercing pale gray eyes. If I weren't aware of his evil, I would have thought him as handsome as Lex.

"*Do svidaniya*, Mrs. Duncan."

I nodded, not moving from my spot. I waited five minutes like I'd discussed with Arya and for my heart to calm down. I wasn't sure I'd have had the ability to move anyway. There was no way to keep this from Lex. Just as I got up, Tony approached me.

"We have a situation, Signora Duncan." He handed me his phone.

I read the message. "That's an understatement."

You and my wife had better get back here now or you're fired.

* * *

Thirty minutes after leaving North Boston, Tony and I arrived at ArMil headquarters. Me in my Bugatti and him in his dark sedan. I'd spent half of the drive trying to figure out how Lex found out about the meeting, and the other half trying to come up with an explanation to tell Lex. Even when I parked the car at the front entrance, I hadn't a clue what I would say to him. At least my anxiety over Lex kept my mind off the deal I'd agreed to with Christof.

"I'll park your car for you, Signora Duncan."

"Thanks, Tony. Wish me luck." I handed him my keys and walked toward the doors leading to the executive elevators.

As soon as I reached my floor, I rushed across to the hallway leading to the legal offices.

As I approached, Lex's sixty-year-old Irish executive assistant stood. "Hello, Mrs. Duncan. He's waiting for you inside."

"*Ciao*, Fredrick. How is he?"

He cringed. "I can't give you any information. We weren't expecting him until after his lunch meeting. And as you know, when he has things on his mind, he ignores everyone and locks himself in his office."

"I'm in deep shit," I muttered under my breath. "Do me a favor. Call Rachel and tell her I'm in a meeting with Lex and she can go home whenever she's finished for the day."

He nodded as he lifted the phone. "No problem."

The door jerked open. "Is she here yet?"

Lex stared at me, and the vein on his head throbbed. This was bad. He was pissed. I should have stopped by Arya's office first.

"If I say come to my office as soon as you get here, that doesn't mean you chitchat with Fred. Get in here."

"Oookay." I strolled into his office.

He shut the door behind me and paced. "What the hell were you thinking?"

"Lex, I didn't have a choice."

"Do you know how I felt when I walked into Arya's office and found a group of government agents mixed in with our security team monitoring your conversation with Christof?"

I cringed and closed my eyes. "That's not how I wanted you to learn about this."

"When were you planning on telling me? How could you leave me out of this?"

"I'm sorry, Lex. I didn't know he'd be there. I was only supposed to wait for a delivery and then leave."

"From this moment your security is doubled. You will not go anywhere without Tony, one of his security detail, or me. No more driving. Your privileges are revoked."

"Are you out of your mind? You don't get to take away my privileges. I'm your wife, not your fucking daughter."

"The hell I don't. While you were out playing secret agent, I received this. It was the reason I went to Arya's office looking for you." He clicked on the television and pressed play on the remote.

An image of me bound to a pole, barely covered by my underwear, screaming in pain, flashed across the screen. Streaks of blood and sweat covered my arms, stomach, and chest.

My feet buckled, and I fell to my knees. Nausea filled my stomach.

No, you will not be sick. You will not let Jacob win.

Lex ran a hand through his blond hair. "It was sent to the office, to my attention."

"And?"

"There was a note. I won't put you in danger again."

"You never placed me in danger. I did that all by myself. No." I shook my head, pushing off the ground. I tried to steady my legs. "It wasn't anyone's fault but Jacob and Christof's." I moved to the couch and wrapped my arms around myself. "What did the note say?"

Lex stayed quiet, clenching his fists and watching the screen. I glanced behind me. I was spread eagle, held by two men as Jacob whipped me. Lex kept the volume on mute, but I didn't need it to remember Jacob's words. The memory would remain etched in my mind forever.

Soon my cock will be the only thing you taste. Do you think that bastard will touch you again?

I shivered, pushing the words out of my mind. "Lex. I want to see it."

"No."

I marched toward him "I want to see it! Do you see that?" I pointed to the TV. "They did it to me. Not to you. I want to know. Dammit!" I hit his chest.

He grabbed my wrist. "They told me to watch my wife punished for not following instructions," he bit out. His eyes glowed with anger and worry. "They told me if you didn't complete the task assigned to you, they'd finish the job Jacob couldn't."

"Oh, God." Christof had planned to send this to Lex whether I'd told him or not. God, I was in over my head.

Lex pulled me close and held me. "I will die before letting anything happen to you again. Why didn't you tell me they did this to you? Why didn't you tell me about the meeting?"

I had to protect you.

"It wouldn't have changed anything. I didn't want you seeing me like that." My tears soaked the front of his shirt. "I didn't want you to think of me like that. What we have is beautiful, that's what I hold on to."

He cradled my head and tilted it up. "Let me protect you, *a ghrá.*"

"Lex I can't be weak. I can't let him win. I can't let any of them win. Christof sent this to you as a way to warn me."

"What did you agree to?"

"You're not going to like it."

"Start from the beginning."

I nodded, pulling him to sit on the couch. Slowly I detailed everything from the e-mail and the threats against him to the plan Arya set up to pick up the package, including what Christof wanted me to do.

"I swear to you, Lex. I had no idea Christof would show up."

"I believe you, baby. Over my dead body will I let you go through with your deal."

I pushed back from him. "Of course I'm not going through with the agreement. I only said yes to get out of there in one piece."

"Let me talk to Thomas and Max. We'll figure out a strategy."

He had to be joking. When had I become the subservient little woman who allowed my man to take over my whole life?

Oh *cazzo*, that's what I'd been doing since I got back from Italy. I thought I was being mature and listening to advice, but in reality, I was pushing back my true nature to fit into a mold I'd created of the new Milla.

I couldn't do this anymore. Not after what I realized about my kidnapping. Yes, I had to grow up when it came to my childhood antics, but I didn't have to give up who I was.

The first thing I had to do was get my husband to see me as an equal again.

"Lex, I know you're worried about me, but I need you to reword what you said."

"I don't understand what you're talking about. I'm trying to create a plan for your protection. Are you upset that I'm involving Thomas? You're the one who hired him for the company."

"No, that's not it. Thomas is a great asset to us."

"Then what are you irritated about? It's my job to protect my wife."

I took in a deep breath. He hadn't a clue what he'd done. *Let me give it another try and then, if he still doesn't get it, I'm letting him have it.*

"Please take back what you just said before I call in my girls and kick your ass."

A crease formed between his eyes. "What did I say?"

Okay, this calm thing wasn't working.

"Are you kidding me right now? I am the CFO of a fucking security technology empire. I run the finances of an international shipping conglomerate, and I have an MBA from MIT."

"I know your résumé, Mil." He gave me an annoyed glare.

"What I'm trying to get through to that big thick skull of yours is that I'm not weak. I'm a smart, savvy businesswoman and strategist, and so are my best friends. And if you think for one minute we're going to sit by and let the men in our lives take over, you've got another think coming."

A fire flared in Lex's cobalt eyes. "Is that so?" He leaned in. "Then tell me where she's been for the past year."

I licked my lips. "I was trying to be something she wasn't, for reasons that weren't true."

"When did you learn this?" He crowded me against the back of the sofa and caged me with his hands.

"During my meeting with Christof."

The moment I said Christof's name, the arousal on Lex's face cooled, but he didn't move away.

"He's dangerous, Mil. I don't want you doing this alone."

"I won't. I'm willing to discuss the plan with you, but you can't decide for me."

"Your safety is my concern."

"I won't become a prisoner, Lex."

"I'm not trying to make you a prisoner. I wanted you to push back. Hell, I waited for you to push back, to show me the old Milla was still there."

"Well, you're getting it right now."

"It's about time." A smile touched his lips. "I'm never going to stop wanting to protect you."

I slid a stray hair from across his forehead. "I also have the right to keep you safe. I won't have you risk your reputation for me again. If Christof knows about what you did for me, there have to be plenty of others who do too."

"I have it under control."

"No, I have it under control. Arya recorded Christof admitting he orchestrated the case against you. We can use it to get the investigation dropped."

"Max and I have already discussed the situation and have a plan in place. Let me make this clear: If you want to be involved in my plan, you sure as hell better have me involved in yours."

"Do I need to remind you of what you said to me the night after the gala?"

"Go right ahead and enlighten me."

I glared at him. "You said 'At work, we're married but colleagues, equals.' Well, you aren't treating me like an equal."

"But let me finish the rest of what I said." He traced my bottom lip with a finger, and I swallowed. "As soon as we're alone, you are my submissive and I am your Dom." His voice dropped to one that affected me the second the sound touched my ears. I knew what he was doing. Those weren't the exact words he'd spoken, but it didn't matter at this moment.

Arousal sparked to life, and the desire to kneel before him pulled at me.

"Do you want your Dom?"

I stared into his stormy blue eyes. "Yes."

"First, whether you want it or not, your security is increased."

Before I could argue, he continued. "Second, I won't hold back any longer. You want all of me, then you will get it."

This Lex is the one I missed. He wouldn't take any of my shit. I held back the urge to kiss him. I licked my lips and I saw his eyes shift to them.

"Third, you will never try to fit into a mold of what you think you should be like. I fell in love with the wild, carefree girl who spoke her mind. Don't try to hide her again." He leaned down but didn't kiss me. "I believe you deserve to be punished."

A whimper escaped my mouth. If I moved the slightest, I'd taste him. The need for him pulsed through me.

"Go lock the door." He moved away from me and toward the floor-to-ceiling windows.

I rushed to follow his command and returned. "Now what?" I waited, twisting my hands together.

He glanced over his shoulder, smiled, and turned back to the window. "Take off your underwear, bend over, and put both hands on the desk."

My pussy spasmed.

I slid my thong over my hips, allowed it to pool at my feet, and then positioned myself as he directed. "I'm ready." I kept my gaze toward the door.

Sensing him behind me, I waited. His hand slid along the hem of my skirt, tugging it up. He cupped my bottom and kneaded. My breath quickened. I waited for whatever punishment he implemented.

"Don't think for one minute I don't know what game you're playing. I know you better than anyone else."

"Lex, what did I do wrong?"

His grip on my ass tightened. "Let me count the ways. First, you refuse to tell me what's going on in that mind of yours." He leaned in and grazed the back of my neck. "Second, you won't let me protect you." He bit my earlobe. "Third, you think you're the only one affected by the past eight months." He fisted my hair, jerking my head back. "Fourth, you thought to hide your little escapade from me."

I swallowed and bit my dry lips. My skin prickled as his finger slipped between my cheeks and grazed my puckered entrance.

"Open the drawer to your right and take out the paddle."

My excitement accelerated. Finally, he planned to do more than coddle me. However, something told me that I wasn't going to enjoy this as much as I hoped, but I was willing to take the chance. I reached to the side without him releasing my hair and followed his command.

"Place it in front of you."

I set it on the wood on the desk, examining it. "Are you planning to brand me?"

Etched in the cedar were cutouts of Lex's name, not Lex but Alexander. The last time he used it on me was after a vacation in Turks and Caicos where I wore a thong bikini to the beach. Lex hated the swimsuit and forbade me from wearing it, but I'd ignored him. When tabloids published pictures of my ass bent over to pick up my sunglasses, he marked me all over my bottom and thighs. After which, if I wore any bathing suit, everyone would see Lex's name tanned across my lower body. Although the orgasms included with the punishment made covering up worth the price.

"Yes. To remind you who you belong to."

I wiggled my ass. "Do your worst."

His grip intensified causing my scalp to sting. "Oh, I plan to, brat."

"Your brat," I breathed out.

"Yes, mine." He held out his hand. "Give me the handle."

My fingers trembled as I released the paddle, and my core spasmed.

"You will receive two for every item of your infractions. How many is that?"

"Eight," I responded

"Wrong." He glided the smooth wood against my raised bottom.

Yes, legal matters were his specialty, but basic math shouldn't be a problem for him. "Um, finance girl here. You listed four grievances, making a total of eight."

"I'm including an extra two for discussing our personal life with your girlfriends before talking to me."

"Oh, you heard that, huh?"

"Yep. I made Arya play the whole phone conversation you had with her and Carmen."

My face heated. "But the phone conversation wasn't recorded."

"Is that what you think? You're wearing a mic in your necklace. It's studio quality. It can pick up the sound of a flea farting."

"Great image, Lex."

"Shut up, Mil." His Irish brogue washed over me, causing my pussy to quiver.

"Sorry, Master."

"Now count."

Smack!

I cried out and jarred forward. The initial sting of the paddle scored my right cheek and settled into a dull ache. I loved it.

"One," I hissed.

Smack! Smack!

"Two. Three," I whispered, and breathed through the discomfort, focusing on the aching pleasure forming in my belly and pussy.

"Good girl. I love seeing my name across your beautiful ass." He caressed the raised, tender skin, causing me to squirm. "I think I need to make you more comfortable."

Oh no, If he does what I think he's planning, I'll have no way of holding myself still.

He repositioned my knees onto the desk, leaving my ass hanging over the edge. "Hold the edge tight. I don't want you falling off. Now count."

Before I adjusted my grip, the paddle landed.

Smack!

"Four," I moaned as my pussy wept onto his desk.

By the time I reached eight, I couldn't hold off my orgasm anymore. Every time I thought I had my body under control, he'd slap the board against my pussy, keeping me teetering on the edge of going over.

"I'm going to come, Master. Please let me come," I begged.

"No." He reached around my hips and rubbed his thumb over my straining clitoral nub. "You have two more left. Count."

Smack!

"Nine." I held my breath, in hopes of holding off my orgasm.

Only one more. My pussy throbbed, waiting for the last blow, the one that would send me over. My fingers gripped the edge of the desk, and my knees pressed deeper into the wooden panel. My essences dripped between my legs, and sweat tinged my skin.

"Please," I whispered and clenched my eyes tight.

"Are you ready for the last one?"

"Yes. Don't make me wait. I can't…"

Lex's cock slammed into me, and I called out his name. Pleasure-pain wrenched my body, but my orgasm remained out of reach.

He set a merciless pace and refused to let me adjust. I arched and pushed back. His hand on my back kept me from the one thing I craved more than anything else at the moment. Every time I adjusted to his pace, he would change it.

I wanted to cry. "Lex."

"Do you want to come?"

"Yes."

"Do you deserve it?"

"Yes. Please." I pushed back against his cock, but he held me still.

"No. I don't think so. Only I get release." He ground his girth into me and started a rhythm meant to make me crazy but not allow me to come.

"No, don't do this. I need…"

He jerked and hot cum ejected into my core. We both panted but for different reasons.

Anger flooded me as I gritted my teeth together. I kept quiet, knowing things would get worse for me if I spoke one word. My throbbing pussy begged for relief, and tears rimmed my eyes.

I couldn't believe he'd denied me release. The last time he'd done that was after I helped Arya steal his racing vessel; for almost two weeks, he'd refused to let me come.

Lex kissed the back of my head and caressed my sore ass as he pulled out. "Good girl."

A trickle of hot semen slid down the inside of my leg, increasing my frustration. Hopefully, this wouldn't be the day he knocked me up. I wanted to remember it with happiness, not with murderous thoughts.

I will get you back for this.

"I hope you aren't planning some form of revenge. That will only delay any pleasure I plan for you." His hands came around the sides of my waist.

I whimpered as he lifted me to standing. The indentation of the desk on my knees reminded me of my denied orgasm. My legs ached, but I refused to complain.

"Here." Lex handed me a tissue and then tucked himself back into his pants.

If I didn't get out of here, I'd kill him for what he'd just done. I dressed in silence, not trusting myself to say anything civil. After fastening the last button on my blouse, I rushed to the office door, but Lex caught my wrist.

"What do you want?" I bit out and tried to jerk my arm out of his grasp.

"Tsk-tsk. You've been naughty, *a ghrá*. You deserved that."

"Fuck you and fuck your orgasm. I'll find my own pleasure at home." I struggled against his hold.

Lex laughed. "I've stirred up a bloody hornet's nest, haven't I?"

I blew a stray hair out of my eyes. "*Vai a farti fottere.*"

"Now why would I screw myself, when fucking you is my greatest pleasure?"

"Stop laughing at me," I growled and lifted my knee but he blocked me.

"Stop struggling and listen."

"I'm not in the mood to listen. If you fucked me proper, then I might, but since you didn't, you will just have to wait."

He cupped my ass and brought me against him. "Is this what you want, *a ghrá*?" He tugged my skirt over my hips, and his fingers slid inside my soaked underwear.

"Don't tease me. I know you aren't going to give me what I want."

He grazed my neck as his digits found my aching clit, pinching it.

I cried out. "Don't fucking stop. Don't." I arched my pelvis against his hand, and he responded with a bite to my ear and an increase in his strumming.

Almost here. Yes, that is it.

All of a sudden, he shifted, breaking the trance he'd placed me under and moving to the door. My knees nearly gave out, but I held myself up.

He licked his fingers. "After the strategy meeting with Arya and our team to discuss this mess we're in with Christof, go straight home. Once you are there, take off all your clothes, using the key on the living room mantel, open the door to the dungeon, and wait for me by the swing, kneeling."

My brain couldn't focus on his words. My screaming body demanded a release I knew I wasn't going to get.

Did he say dungeon? Swing? Kneeling?

"You wanted to play, we're going to play."

CHAPTER TWENTY-THREE

I arrived at the penthouse with my heart pounding, pussy throbbing, and jitters like none I'd felt since my wedding day. My keys trembled as I placed them in the tray by the entrance.

Taking a deep breath, I scanned my reflection in the hallway mirror. Dilated hazel-green eyes stared back at me. My flushed cheeks and messy bun gave me a seductress look, but in truth, I thought of myself as anything but.

I'd asked for my Dom back, and now I was getting him.

The meeting in Arya's office was almost torture. By the time Lex and I arrived, Max and Arya were in a heated debate, Carmen and Thomas weren't even looking at each other, and security agents assigned to us looked like they were ready to escape our madness.

I wasn't in any better a mood. The last thing I wanted to be was anywhere near Lex. Of course, that meant Lex found every opportunity to touch me or sit next to me.

After two hours of discussions and arguments, the group came to a compromise. The plan was to use the tracer system fitted on all of the ships belonging to Castra Enterprises to track the shipments from Christof. If all went according to plan, the system would narrow down every person involved in the acquisition and sales of the freight being transported.

I was happy an agreement was reached, but honestly my focus during the session was on the ache in my core from my lack of orgasm, and the anxiety of what was to follow had me on edge.

It didn't help that Lex acted completely focused and unaffected. He smiled and casually discussed the logistics of the strategy.

That's because he got his rocks off and you didn't.

The only sign he'd perceived my anxiety was the slight upturn of his mouth every time I fidgeted with my necklace.

At one point, he leaned over and whispered, "Nothing to worry about, I will take care of you." Which resulted in a few raised eyebrows from Arya and Carmen, as well as intensifying my nervousness, especially when he followed it with a possessive caress of my backside.

My phone beeped, snapping me out of my daze, and I glanced down.

I'll be home in thirty minutes. Be ready. x Lex

I gulped, and a sheen of sweat prickled my face. *Here I go.*

As I strolled into the living room, I dropped my handbag on the couch and searched the room to see if the housekeeper was still in the apartment.

The place was spotless with no sign of her.

Finding out what her bosses were up to would send the fifty-year-old domestic goddess out the door, never to return.

"Amber?"

No response.

"All alone. Well, at least for now," I muttered.

I crossed through the hallway leading to the bedroom. A quick peek at the clock told me I had less than twenty-five minutes left to get ready.

I stripped at the entrance of the bathroom and rushed into the shower.

Ten minutes later, I was clean and ready. The no-clothing rule made things easier. I ran my fingers over the now barely visible scars on my breasts and stomach. In a few weeks, with luck and the cream Arya gave me, they would be invisible to the eye.

And hopefully invisible to the mind as well.

I took Arya's ointment and rubbed my skin, finishing with my hips. A slight smile tugged at my lips. *My ass is back! Thank God for Indian food and pasta.*

Last, I applied a light touch of makeup and walked into the kitchen. I filled a glass of water and drank deep. The cool liquid trickled down my throat, calming my overheated insides.

Now to find the key. I crossed to the mantel under the big-screen television. I searched the ledge but found nothing. Then I noticed a small box hidden behind a framed photo taken at my wedding to Lex. Ignoring the box, I picked up the picture and traced Lex's face, so young yet so commanding.

Christof wanted to hurt him through me by sending him the video. No one messed with my man.

The clock struck five, and I jumped.

Shit. He'll be home any second.

I set the frame back on the mantel, grabbed the box, and pulled out the key. I turned it in my palm. It was simple to look at, but it held the start of bringing my life back.

I'd hidden from my dark desires and made Lex suppress his need to dominate. Not that he'd admit it, but he held back too much. Punishments, until earlier today, were nothing but a few arousing spanks with his hands and the flogger, all tame in comparison to what we'd done over the years. I missed the crop, the cat, and the ropes. The thought sent my core into a spasm.

Ready or not, it was time.

I strode toward the dungeon door, slipped the key into the lock and, taking a deep breath, I pushed the wood door open.

Dark hues covered each of the walls, and large wood-trimmed cabinets filled one side of the room. A Saint Andrew's cross sat in the corner, and a swing hung in the center, next to the spanking bench. A grid of bars in rich mahogany covered the ceiling. Crops, floggers, and cats lined another wall.

I'd designed this room, years ago, for the house Lex and I planned to build together.

The only thing missing was a shelf of whips. The sole evidence they'd once been in the room was the empty space next to the cross.

I bit my lip. Damn Jacob for taking something special from us.

In our lifestyle, many considered Lex a master of the whip. Over the years, I'd watched women beg him to play, but I was the only one he'd indulge.

I sighed. Maybe soon I'd build up the courage again.

A double beep sounded, and my skin prickled. Lex was here.

I walked over to a crimson pillow sitting to the right of the swing. With as much grace as possible, I slid into position on the soft fabric. I winced as my tender, marked ass touched my heels, but I kept my head bowed and waited.

"*A ghrá*, you are beautiful." His velvety compliment was a soothing caress to my racing heart. "Stay just like that. I will change and return."

I almost sat back out of my pose as I heard the door open again, but for some reason I held myself still.

"Good girl, you didn't move."

Merda, he was still in the room. "Thank you, Master."

Lex stepped in front of me, threading his fingers through my hair. "Before I change, I want some relief. It's been a long day, and our little escapade in my office did nothing to reduce my need for you. I don't want to explode at the wrong time and end our scene. I want to prolong the experience as long as possible, with you breathless and begging for my cock."

His words send a gush of desire into my aching pussy.

He unzipped his pants, and his erection sprang free, a fraction from my lips. I stared at the angry purple head and the pearl-sized drop of precum beading on the tip. I stuck my tongue out and licked the fluid. His wild, unique essence burst in my mouth.

His grip tightened and the muscles in my pussy clenched. "Did I tell you to do that?"

"No." I smirked, and slight pain tickled my scalp, sending another wave of need to my pulsing clit.

"From the way you're panting, I can tell you want me to spank you again, but you aren't going to distract me with your brattiness. Now open up and suck my cock, Mil."

He guided my lips to his straining erection. I moved my hand to the base, but he pulled back. "No. Keep your hands in your lap. I will control the pace. I plan to fuck that mouth until you have an imprint of my cock at the back of your throat."

"Pretty confident, aren't you?"

"Mil," he growled.

"Sorry. I wa—" I mumbled, but before I could say any more, he pushed his cock past my lips.

He moaned. "Suck my cock, Mil. Show me how much you love it."

I purred, swirling my tongue around his width and bobbing my head up and down. Saliva pooled in my mouth, and I sucked harder, sliding down to the base and then swallowing.

"So good. I love that trick of yours. Thank goodness I taught it to you. Do you like it, baby? Do you like sucking my cock?"

I hummed in response. I stroked the vein on the underside of his monster erection with my tongue, flicking and rolling.

"Shite, if you keep that up, I'm going to blow."

I smiled around his rod and repeated the motion.

"Oh, no you don't. I control this, brat." He reached down and slapped my ass.

A sizzle of pain grazed my already inflamed ass and increased my arousal. I wiggled for more as I moved back and forth.

Five more landed, and I cried and moaned around the length of him. I wanted to move my hands and grab hold of him to keep from falling forward, but his grip in my hair kept me in place. He held me still with his hand and thrust deep until he hit the back of my throat. I moaned and felt his shudder.

"Fuck," he called. "I'm going to come. Swallow and lick every drop, Mil. Or I won't let you come."

I nodded and shifted back and forth on my legs, trying to ease the pressure building between my hips.

I was as desperate to come as he was. My lips tingled from their hard strokes on his cock.

"Now!" Lex shouted as he twitched and jerked. Warm wet cum shot to the back of my throat. I swallowed and licked until he finished his release. Years of practice kept me from choking. Some of his essences dripped from my mouth onto his pubic hair, and I released him with a pop.

"Clean me all up, Mil."

I raised a brow and glanced up at him. He cupped my jaw. "Do you want to come, brat?"

Of course I want to come.

I tongued the semen sprinkling his pubic hair and along his now softening cock until every drop was gone.

Afterward, he released my hair and allowed me to rest my head against his thigh. I tried to catch my breath, but my screaming need for release kept my body on full alert.

"Please," I murmured against his pant leg.

He traced a finger against my cheek. "Soon. Sit back and rest on your heels. I'll be back in a moment."

I followed his instructions and stared at the swing. Was I ready? In it, I'd have absolutely no control.

Lex will never hurt you.

It was time to allow my Master his rights over my body. I could trust him. I glanced at the empty wall that once held the whips, and sighed. He'd removed them without me asking. Hopefully, I'd be ready for them soon.

Baby steps, Mil.

"Stop thinking so hard."

I jumped and then settled back down. How long had he been watching me?

Lex crouched in front of me and cupped my face. I drank in the sight of him. He was shirtless with only a pair of low-riding workout pants. His abs bunched in his current position, and I wanted to bite his chiseled arms and shoulders.

"We don't have to do this, Mil." He ran a thumb over my bottom lip and gently kissed me. "I'll always want you."

His tenderness humbled me. My mouth quivered under his. "I trust you. I always have. I want all of you."

He searched my eyes, then nodded and stretched out his hand. I took it and stood by the swing. He picked up a remote, pushed a button, and the leather lowered. I swallowed and watched him adjust each stirrup and unhook the body harness.

"Come here." His Dom voice vibrated over me. My breath accelerated, and goose bumps prickled my skin.

This swing wasn't like any we'd ever used before. It hung suspended from a series of pulleys on the ceiling. From the way it swayed, I knew Lex would be able to rotate me in any direction he chose.

I stepped between the straps. Lex ran a hand down one of my thighs and then up the other. "Lean against the seat."

The soft buttery leather warmed against my back, and an unknown excitement awakened inside me. The slight sting from the earlier paddling added another level of awareness.

Lex closed the straps of the body harness around my waist and laced until it tied under my exposed breasts. He wrapped two velvety belts around the outside of my swollen labia and secured them to the back of the bodysuit. Out of instinct, I grabbed the leather-covered chain and held myself still.

"Good girl. I love how your pussy glistens, and we haven't even started."

His praise pleased me and I relaxed.

"Lift your leg." He slipped one stirrup over my ankle and settled it above my knee, securing it with a padded buckle. He traced his imprinted name on my inner thighs and then licked my now open slit, just barely grazing my swollen clit.

"More," I called and arched, pushing my pelvis up.

He pulled back. "Give me the other."

I hesitated.

The moment I lifted my leg, he would have me suspended. With one foot on the ground, I still had some control.

Can I do this?

"It's okay, love. I have you. Relax and sink your weight into the seat and raise your other leg. I promise to make it worth your while."

I followed his directions and soon found myself hanging from the ceiling.

My thighs were spread by the stirrups, and my pussy and ass were completely visible. I relaxed into the seat and allowed the gentle sway of the swing to soothe away my anxiety.

I lifted my head as Lex stepped back, and I noticed the raging hard-on tenting the front of his pants.

He chuckled. "That beautiful mouth of yours has done nothing to relieve this need."

"Want me to help the situation?"

He clicked the remote, and the contraption raised to Lex's hip level. "No. The next time I come, it will be in that sexy-as-hell ass."

"So romantic."

Lex spun the swing, forcing me onto my stomach. He lowered to eye level with me. "I don't plan to romance you. My goal is to fuck you stupid."

My throat dried up, and I gave him an unsteady smile. The pull of gravity had my full breasts bouncing and swaying to the movement of the swing.

Lex circled me three times, then stopped behind me. "I believe you deserve to be punished for your refusal to listen to your husband."

I shifted to argue but the restraints held me in place. "Wasn't the paddling enough?"

I wasn't sure my branded ass could take more. Then he cupped my bottom, and a shot of excitement coursed straight to my clit.

Never mind, I can handle it.

"Not really. I learned a few things during a conversation I had with Thomas after the meeting. Since when do you have me followed?"

Oh shit. Thomas was supposed to keep that a secret.

"I'm waiting." He released his grip and ran a gentle hand over my back.

"Well, you see—"

Smack!

I cried out as the sting of a flogger landed on my butt.

"Fuck! Lex. What the—"

Smack!

Fire burned across the other cheek. I breathed through the delicious pain and clenched my hands on the leather.

"Now, tell me, how long?"

"Since I got the e-mail from Christof."

A rain of four more smacks ran over my tingling skin.

"I'm sorry. I didn't think you'd get so mad. Besides, they weren't very good, no matter what Thomas believed. They couldn't keep track of you."

I expected another slap, but he moved toward my head and lilted my chin up. His eyes blazed blue. "Do you realize I knew someone was watching me? I thought it was someone from Christof's camp."

"I'm surrounded by constant security. Don't you deserve the same type of protection?"

"The difference is that I told you about yours."

He leaned down and bit my lower lip hard. I tried to bite him back, but he stood up too fast.

"Tsk-tsk, brat."

I blew out a frustrated breath. "Can we finish with my punishment so you can fuck me?"

"I don't think you're in any position to make demands."

He glided the soft leather tails of the flogger over my sensitized skin. Each gentle stroke sent tingles all over my body.

"Don't make me wait, Master."

"Now, that's a better response." He tilted me up and kissed my lips. "No more spankings, *a ghrá*. I think I made my point."

He walked away from me and opened a few drawers. I couldn't see what he pulled out, but I heard the distinctive sound of lube opening.

"When I tell you, relax your muscles."

I nodded, and cool liquid slid down the crack of my ass.

"Relax."

A hard object pushed in. My first thought was to resist; it was much larger than the beads I'd trained my body to accept but smaller than the plugs I now used.

"Breathe, baby. Open up to me."

I followed his request and loosened my muscles, allowing the flared head to ease past my contracted opening.

I felt full but not as when he'd used other plugs.

"I know what you're thinking. This is smaller than what you've worn. When I take you, I want you to feel the stretch and the sting of entry."

A lightheaded haze filled my mind.

"Now." He crawled under me. "Let's have a look at that soaked pussy."

His lips closed around my clit and sucked. He flicked and stroked until I was on the cusp of orgasm, and then he stopped.

"No, please, Master."

"I'm not going to stop." He continued his ministrations, fucking his tongue into my soaked pussy. "Now."

My release washed over me, and my body bowed in the harness. I couldn't comprehend anything but the thought of coming. All the frustration and tension of the day washed away.

He blew against my overstimulated nerves. "Hold your breath, Mil."

Oh shit, he wouldn't.

White-hot pain blazed into my core as a clamp pinned my labia and clit in a firm, tight squeeze. I thrashed against my restraints, and tears streamed down my face.

"Shhh." He licked the pinched bundle of nerves. "I told you to hold your breath, baby. Relax and let the endorphins take over."

I tried to follow his advice, but my body screamed from the overload of sensation. Pain, pleasure, ecstasy, and euphoria consumed my mind.

"Now to attach the chain to those sexy, large breasts of yours."

I spent the next moments in a haze. I barely felt the clips fasten to each of my nipples. Little by little, the throbbing from my screaming nerves lessened to a dull ache, but I knew the moment the swing shifted I'd feel the weight of the chain pull against my sensitized nerves and throughout my body.

"Is this my punishment?" I whimpered. Why didn't I remember it hurting so much?

Because this is the first time he's clamped both your nipples and your clit.

"No, baby, there's no more punishment. This is for your pleasure. I know you don't believe me, but you will."

He swung me forward and then back, the gentle movement intensifying the weight of the chain, but soon desire overtook the discomfort, and my pussy spasmed from the rocking of my metal.

"Oh."

"Yes, oh."

He continued the motion, allowing me to become accustomed, and then he positioned himself behind me. The tube opened again, and the wet sound of liquid gliding along his cock filled the air.

With a small tug, Lex dislodged the plug. "Now I want to hear you scream my name."

His erection traced the length of my pussy, nudging my pinched clit and causing me to flinch, and then slid into my dripping core for a fraction of a second before shifting to my puckered entrance.

"You're sopping, baby. I'm almost tempted to change my plans."

I whimpered. I wanted to shout for him to do something, but I knew he would hold off longer if the brat appeared.

"Maybe next time." He pushed into my ass.

A stinging burn singed my insides, until the head of his cock pressed through the tight ring of nerves. He slowly worked deeper, and my mind fogged further.

"More," I whispered.

The swing glided forward and inched back.

"Grab your knees."

"But…" My fingers clenched the straps harder.

"Now," he ordered.

I grasped my knees and pulled them toward my chest. At that same moment, Lex rammed to the hilt.

All thought left my mind, and sensation flowed over me. The clamps attached to my nipples and clit throbbed, and they jerked with the swing's flight, sending me to another world.

An orgasm loomed as Lex's pace increased, and the pressure on my nubs sent the first tremors into my aching core. I held my breath. Unless he gave me permission, I couldn't.

"Master," I gasped, "please, let me come."

"Go, baby, let it loose."

I exploded, my pussy convulsed, and my anus clenched Lex's pistoning cock.

I screamed his name, and moments later heard Lex call mine as his hot seed spurted inside me.

CHAPTER TWENTY-FOUR

W ake up, *a ghrá*."

I moaned and opened my eyes. Lex slowly came into focus. "I thought we were taking the day off. I'm up at four thirty every morning. Let me sleep." I rolled over and tried to cover my head with a pillow.

Lex snatched it and threw it on the floor.

"It's your fault I'm so tired."

His hand skimmed my naked ass. "I can't tell you how sexy it is to see my mark on you. You did well last night. I was surprised the brat didn't appear more than she did."

"I'm not the same anymore." A moment of worry crept in, and I turned to look at him. "Do you miss her?"

"You are her."

"You know what I mean. The old Milla. The girl who danced on tables and pushed your buttons."

"No."

Well, that didn't appease me. I wasn't expecting a one-word answer.

"Really?"

He sighed. "I love your tenacity, but sometimes the crazy, have-to-prove-yourself, fake party girl took its toll on me."

"Why didn't you say anything?"

"I did. You never listened. You were hell-bent on making your mother pay for your childhood. I allowed your antics, because I didn't want to restrain you, and I knew it was for show. But I hated that 'we' were second to your rebellion."

He'd sacrificed all these years to make me happy. I closed my eyes for a moment as my lips trembled.

"*A ghrá*, I didn't tell you the truth to make you sad." He leaned down and kissed my furrowed brow. "I wanted to give you a new perspective on where we are in life. I'm thrilled to have a more private Milla. You still have the spark of the old but with the common sense of a wiser woman."

"I guess you're right."

He tilted my chin, and I stared into his amused eyes. "Don't you like this new girl? The one I can't get enough of?"

I smiled up at him. "I like her a lot. But I'm still getting to know her. Maybe you can help me explore her likes and dislikes."

Lex's hand roamed up my ribs and cupped my aching breast. "I thought we did that last night." He pinched my nipple.

I arched up. "Let's research some more."

His other hand traced the seam of my now damp folds, then withdrew, sitting up and pulling me with him. "Not right now. I have plans for us today."

I scowled. My body was tingling, and he'd left me hanging. "I don't want to go anywhere."

"Stop the pouting, woman. I have the authority to take a certain extra-large yacht out for the weekend."

I jumped up with excitement. "Really?"

"Yes, now go get dressed so I can take advantage of my wife on our best friend's very expensive and ridiculously large ship." *Large* was an understatement for Arya's yacht. It was a small cruise liner. With everything going on, I never expected to indulge in a weekend getaway. Lex must be paying Thomas overtime to arrange all our security.

"I'll be ready in fifteen minutes. I have to take a shower."

"Just get dressed. You can shower on the ship."

I moaned. "But I smell like us from last night."

He quirked a brow. "I don't have a problem with it."

I shook my head, and headed to brush my teeth. "Well if it doesn't bother you, then why not?"

* * *

We reached Arya's yacht a little after ten in the morning. My excitement bubbled over at the thought of spending the weekend away from business and the family.

I strolled up the walkway with a little hop in my step and then turned to Lex. "Will you let me sail it?" I knew the answer, but I asked anyway.

After the last stunt Arya and I pulled with Lex's precious sailing vessel, there was no way he'd agree to allow anyone but him behind the wheel of Arya's ship.

The corners of his mouth turned up in the half grin I loved. "I could be convinced with the right incentive."

I blocked his way, stood on tiptoes, and wrapped my arms around him. "What do you have in mind?"

His hands slipped around my waist, and he leaned his forehead against mine while walking me backward. "Hmm. Let me think. I could want a new car."

I rolled my eyes. Between the both of us, we had more vehicles than a luxury car dealership.

"Or you naked, scrubbing the deck of the racing yacht you and Arya nearly destroyed."

"Never going to let me live that down are you?" I mumbled.

"Or a baby."

My heartbeat accelerated, and I pulled his glasses off to make sure he was serious. I wanted more than anything to have his baby, but I wasn't sure Lex still wanted one with me. Especially after the pain I'd caused him by leaving.

Before I could speak, we both caught the glint of light on the other end of the dock.

"Shite, those buggers are after us again," Lex muttered as he released my waist and took my hand, dragging me onto the boat.

"You go get changed. I'll talk to the captain and tell him we're ready to depart." He left me on the deck with all thoughts of a baby gone.

Shrugging my shoulders, I peered toward the now ten or so paparazzi standing on the waterfront. I guessed Arya was right; they were only going to leave me alone for so long. Now that they knew we were a couple, the previous years of privacy were long gone.

The ship started its sail into the sound, signaling my chance to freshen up and change into a bathing suit. Within twenty minutes, and after donning a robe to cover my marked bottom, I was ready and strolling along the palatial deck of Arya's ship *AlySas*, named after the twins she'd lost during her attack in Cape Town. Thank goodness, God gave her two beautiful boys to help ease the loss she still felt for her girls.

I lifted my face toward the sky.

Thank you, God, for giving both Arya and me do overs.

Shaking the melancholy thought from my head, I searched out Lex. He'd come into our cabin while I showered, changed his clothes, and told me to hurry so we could have breakfast.

I heard some muffled voices and peeked around the corner.

"Everything's ready, Mr. Duncan. I'll leave with the rest of the crew. Mr. and Mrs. Dane said the ship was in capable hands. Enjoy your time with the missus." The captain shook Lex's hand.

"Thank you. I'll contact you tomorrow so you can bring us back to port." Lex swiveled around and caught me staring at him. He grinned and inclined his head for me to come over.

I slipped my arm around his waist as the captain left.

"So we're all alone?"

"As soon as the speedboat leaves we are."

I watched the last of the crew board and they sped away. My stomach growled.

"I take it you're hungry."

"I did work up an appetite last night."

He cupped my cheek and drew me toward him. "I plan to do the same today and tonight, as a matter of fact."

A shiver ran up my spine, as another rumble erupted from my belly. "Feed me, and then tell me all the many ways you're going to ravish me."

"First, strip. We're too far out to sea for anyone to photograph us, and our security is anchored at a discreet distance. I want you naked for the rest of the day."

I took in his linen pants and white shirt. "What about you?"

He raised a brow.

Without another word, I loosened the belt of my cover-up and let it drop.

"Hold it right there."

I froze where I stood.

"On second thought, keep that on."

I glanced down at myself. Most of my curves were back, and the white bikini accentuated all my assets, from my ample breasts to my full hips.

"You like." I smiled at him, and my breath caught. Emotions swarmed his eyes. All of a sudden I remembered the swimsuit's significance.

"Yes."

"My husband bought it for me." I bit my lip. Without realizing it, I had worn the one thing that would move us onto a different course of our lives.

"I know." He stood still, clenching the tumbler in his hand.

"He gave it to me and told me to wear it only when I was ready to make him a father."

He settled his glass on a nearby table. "Mil, be sure."

"I am."

"You can't take it back once it's done."

"Lex, we haven't used protection since that first night in the penthouse." I cocked my hand on my hip, then moved over to him.

He gripped my waist as his other hand cradled the back of my head. "You've been on birth control for years."

I swallowed and told him what I wanted. "I want a baby with you, Lex. Only you. Plus…" I hadn't realized until a few minutes ago.

"Plus?"

"I haven't taken anything since before I left. I could already be pregnant." I leaned up and captured his lips.

Our tongues dueled, and my whole body hummed. Lex pulled back and kneeled in front of me. He kissed my belly, and my heart hitched. Tears rimmed my eyes. He gazed at me with so much love it was almost overwhelming.

"Thank you," he whispered against my flat stomach, then stood, taking my hand. "But just in case you aren't, I think we should practice a lot to increase the odds."

"Anything you say, Master."

* * *

Around one the following morning, I sat on the balcony of the yacht, drinking a cup of tea. For hours, I'd tried to sleep but to no avail.

As of yesterday, Lex and I officially wanted to become parents. I covered my stomach and stared into the night sky.

Would I make a good mother? My own wasn't the best of role models. Unlike the beautiful upbringing Lex had, I had years of hurt and manipulation to overcome.

Who would have thought the family of a former Irish gangster would foster such great love and devotion from their children.

I remembered asking Lex's grandfather what made him change his ways. His answer was etched in my mind forever.

My Ella accepted me, as the man I was, flaws and all. For her I wanted to be a better person. Therefore, I decided to leave my home-land and start fresh as a new man, no sordid history, just an honest laborer.

From the family account I knew, Lex's grandfather returned to Ireland twenty years later with three almost grown boys and a fortune far greater than the wealth he had left behind.

"What are you standing there thinking about?"

I glanced over my shoulder, smiled at Lex's nakedness, and turned back to the sea.

"Well?" He leaned against the railing next to me.

"Us. The future. Family."

He pulled my back to his front and caged me with his arms. "Any conclusions?" he said into my hair.

"*Sì*, I think you'll make a great papa."

He nuzzled my neck. "I plan to, but right now, I want to get the bambino's mamma pregnant with him."

"Don't you think the five times we've already practiced completed the deed?" My body hummed from the soreness of our lovemaking and the awareness of what was yet to come.

"Why take chances?" He jerked my robe off, trapping my hands by my sides. "You put on a nightgown," he mumbled against my hair.

"Yes."

"Shame." He pinched my nipples through the soft silk.

"Shame?" I asked as I arched into his hands.

"Now I have to ruin another of your gowns."

"I can't stay naked all the time."

"If I had a choice, you would." He pulled the belt of my robe from its loops. "Keep your hands right there."

I clutched the railing and waited; excitement and the cool breeze off the sound prickled my skin.

He looped the belt twice on the overhead beam of the balcony. "Give me your left hand."

I slipped my palm over his and he raised it, tying my wrist to the soft white terry fabric.

"Now the other."

After he secured me to the beam, I glanced to the side and saw his growing erection pointing toward me. "I think someone wants to visit his favorite place."

Lex smiled, pushing a chair under my spread legs. "What can I say? If he had a choice, he would stay snug in that beautiful pussy of yours for the rest of his life."

His words sent a shot of desire to my core.

One more time would increase our chances. Liar, you just want him to fuck you again.

"What are you waiting for? Fuck! Lex…," I cried as he pinched my nipples again, but this time harder.

"Tsk-tsk. Language." He slid his body between the railing and me, pulling the chair toward him, and sat. "Now I can feast on these." He positioned my legs on each side of his lap, cupped my breast in each hand, and bit a puckered nipple through my gown.

I arched and moaned, "More," then thrust my hips forward.

"Yes, *a ghrá*. More." He tugged my straps down against my shoulders to reveal my breasts. He laved, sucked, and bit until I was mindlessly pulling against the bonds of my belt. Each tug of his mouth made my clit throb.

One hand released my breast and slid up my gown, over my

thighs and between my slit. "Are you ready for me?" he murmured and pushed three digits into my swollen sheath.

I pushed down against his hand for some relief as he pumped his fingers inside of me. My orgasm rose, and I tugged my restraints harder. "Please, Master. I need to come."

All of a sudden, Lex stopped his pistoning.

"No," I cried and gasped.

"Yes. You won't come until I say." He pushed my gown up, exposing my bare pussy. "I love how you glisten in the moonlight."

He cupped my bottom and spread my legs wide, allowing the ocean air to cool my heated core.

He lifted and brought me toward his mouth. "Time for me to lick you clean." His lips descended on my pulsing nub, sucking it in. He lapped at my swollen folds, round and round, up and down, and when I couldn't take any more, he plunged his tongue into my pussy.

If he doesn't give me permission soon, I am going to die. "I can't hold on anymore, please let me come." I jolted my wrists, causing the beam to creak.

His hand slipped between us, and his fingers plunged into me. "Come."

I erupted, convulsing around him, crying and thrashing. My legs gave out, but he held me up with his arms, not stopping his ministrations. I continued to ride out my release.

My breath hadn't calmed when he pulled his mouth from my contracting pussy. He settled me on his lap, pushing his straining erection against my clit and then sliding between our stomachs.

I lifted my hips, trying to position myself over him. "Let me ride you."

He gripped my thighs. "No, I want to fuck you as we watch the morning." He lifted me to standing, slid out of the chair, and shoved it away from us.

He moved behind me and fisted my hair, wrenching my head back. "You're so fucking beautiful." He kissed me, plunging his tongue into my mouth. We dueled until we were both breathless.

Releasing my hair, he reached up and untied my wrist. "Grip the rail."

I followed his command and held on. Positioning his cock against me, his head nudged my weeping pussy. He rubbed it up and down, teasing me, and then drove in.

My body bowed and fell forward. Lex's hand came underneath my arm and cupped my shoulder and neck, and the other kneaded my hips and ass. "I've got you. Watch the sunrise while I fuck you."

He withdrew, plunged back in, and set an unyielding rhythm, driving me crazy. He rubbed against the perfect spot inside my clenching walls. He tilted my face up, and I stared into the rising glow of morning. The beauty of the sky dimmed as my desire overwhelmed me. Lex rocked in and out of me, increasing the pleasure strumming throughout my being.

"Faster, please."

He complied, and I busted, coming in intense waves. I clenched hard enough for Lex to follow. I milked the last of his release with my own orgasm.

We stood there for at least five minutes, trying to catch our breaths and building the energy to move back inside the cabin.

Finally, Lex spoke. "I think that did it." His hand curved against my stomach.

I giggled in response.

CHAPTER TWENTY-FIVE

The following night, I woke to the sound of my phone beeping. I glanced at the clock. Three thirty. I groaned and reached over to read the message.

Answer the bloody text. Your mother has lost her ever-loving mind.

What could she have done now that Ian would text me at this ungodly hour?

Ian, someone better be dead or in the hospital. I'm on a weekend getaway with my husband.

"Please tell me you aren't trading stocks this early in the morning? I don't care if Japan's exchange thinks it's Monday," Lex mumbled and covered his head with a pillow.

"No, something's up with the family. Ian's in a tizzy."

"Tell him to fuck off and call at a decent time."

"Yes, sir." I laughed.

"That's 'yes, Master' to you."

I rolled my eyes and another message came in.

Your mother is planning an intervention. She believes Lex's influ-

ence puts Castra Enterprises at risk. She's petitioned the whole family for a trustee meeting in England. Will you bloody well call me so I don't have to type this?

Fine, give me five minutes, I replied.

Great. All I needed was an intervention.

I slid out of bed, donned my robe, and stepped onto the balcony. I tied the belt and smiled as I remembered the antics of the night before. I'd never be able to look at Arya and tell her that Lex and I christened the balcony of her yacht.

She beat you to it, remember?

I forgot; she and Max put on a very loud display not so long ago during a group outing.

My phone beeped again.

Dial the fucking phone.

"Okay, okay. Keep your knickers on," I mumbled. I called Ian's number.

"It's about time."

"Well, *ciao* to you too."

"I should be out on my boat right now, not dealing with my upset mother and your crazy one."

Merda, he was mad. What could the old woman have said to make Aunt Isabella so upset?

"Okay, calm down and start from the beginning."

"Your mother threatened that if Mum didn't vote with her against you and Lex, she'd reveal the depravity of my parents' relationship and ruin her reputation with her peers. You know it's taken Mum years to be accepted in the aristocratic British circles."

"Oh, come on, Ian. They can't be into anything more than what you or I enjoy."

"That may be true, but once upon a time, my mum was caught in a sandwich between Lex's dad and mine."

"*Mio Dio*! I think I need to sit down." I collapsed on the lounger on the balcony. "So the shit my mom preached about Uncle Chris and Lex's dad was true?" I laughed.

"The thought of my mother in that kind of situation is disgusting, not funny."

"Sorry. I shouldn't enjoy this so much, but all I can think is 'go, Isabella.' Face it: The two dads are hot."

"I'm sure your husband would like hearing you say his dad is hot."

That wiped the smirk off my face. "Sorry, I see your point." Then a thought popped into my head. "Didn't you and Lex engage in the same behavior, once upon a time?"

"Yes, but that was before he hitched himself to my baby cousin. Since then, if he even thought to look at another girl, I'd cut his balls off."

"Now back to the story. What grounds does she have to call the meeting?" I pinched the bridge of my nose.

"On the grounds your marriage puts your family loyalties into question. She says your involvement in ArMil creates a conflict of interest with Castra Enterprises."

"Bullshit." I paced back and forth. "She enjoyed and reaped all the benefits of ArMil for the past six years. I even heard from Dominic saying Mamma would never admit it, but she loves the new software that keeps track of all cargo throughout the world at all times."

"Mil, you know why she's doing this?"

"Because I went public with my marriage."

"Bingo. I think she believes if the family votes to replace you in the company, then she can use it as a way to make you choose between them and Lex."

I want you to prove that I matter.

Lex's words echoed in my mind. I was never going to let him think he didn't matter again, and if it meant giving up my position in the company, I'd do it. Hell, I'd give up every cent of my inheritance.

"She actually believes I'd pick the family and the company over Lex? She's lost her mind."

"Well, you did keep your marriage a secret for ten years."

"Good point."

"What are you going to do?"

I peeked behind me to make sure Lex was still in bed.

Damn, no sign of him. I glanced to the bathroom door, and it was open with steam billowing out.

"Here's my plan. Tomorrow when I get in the office, I am going to contact Avvocato Gallo."

"And why would you call your family attorney? Are you planning on taking your mother to court?"

I smirked at the idea. It had merit. "No, I'm going to rescind all claims to Castra Enterprises and step down as CFO."

"Um, that isn't a good idea. Do you know how many contracts you negotiated? What if they fall through because you aren't there to oversee them?"

"Both Dominic and Marcello are more than capable of taking over. Ian, I have to do this. I don't ever want any doubt in Lex's mind that I'm not picking him."

"Are you going to tell him about this?"

"Not until everything is finalized. Besides, I want to have a family, and I can't run the finances of two companies and have a kiddo without losing my mind. I'm never going to put my family second, like Mamma did with us."

"Holy shit, you're serious?"

"What? Didn't I sound serious until now?"

"Well I was expecting you to say 'just kidding.' Give me a second to wrap my brain around this."

"Take all the time you need." I stared out toward the Atlantic and inhaled the salty air. My decision felt right. "On second thought, hurry up. Lex is awake."

"So what am I going to say at the meeting?"

"Nothing. As Lex says, let the paperwork speak for itself."

"Wow. Who are you and what have you done with my wild child, crazy cousin?"

"I'm still the same girl, just a little more grown up."

A whispered voice sounded on Ian's end. It was probably one of his submissives from the club. "Hey, I have to go. Love you."

"Love you, too."

I opened the door and entered the cabin. My hands shook as I set the phone on the counter. I was going to do it. I was going to give up the company that I'd kept my marriage a secret for. A sense of calm washed over me, and I knew I'd made the right decision. I closed my eyes and covered my stomach with my hand.

I'll never be a mother like her.

"What was that call about?"

I jumped as Lex walked out of the bathroom, wrapping a towel around his waist.

How long had he stood there?

"What time is it?"

"Just ten after four. Now answer the question. What's going on?"

"Nothing important. I've got it handled."

His brow furrowed, and he stepped in front of me. "Why don't I believe you?"

I lifted my chin. "I have no idea."

"Milla, you're hiding something. If this has to do with your mother, then it involves me. Now spill it."

"It isn't important. The situation is under control."

He ran a hand through his wet hair and examined me. "You don't seem upset, so it can't be that bad. Or at least you've got a solid handle on it. I'll find out sooner or later."

I smiled. "I expect you will."

He held out his hand. "Come."

I slid my palm over his. "Where are we going?"

"To watch the sunrise and have a little breakfast."

We walked to the hallway door.

"What's on the menu?" I asked.

He grinned at me as he tugged my robe off and threw it on a chair moments before the cabin door closed.

"You are."

* * *

"Here are your copies of the executed documents. The ones for Lex were delivered to him earlier today." Rachel placed a folder on my desk.

I picked them up and skimmed the file. "Oh, God, no."

My lungs contracted, and I couldn't breathe. A pain I couldn't describe clenched my heart.

"Rachel, you weren't supposed to file these. I left you three messages to stop the proceedings, one on your voice mail and two through e-mail."

What was Lex going to think? This couldn't be happening.

I looked up at Rachel, whose face had drained of all color. "What do you mean? I never received any messages."

"It was over five weeks ago, right after the Met Gala."

"Milla, I was on vacation that week, remember? We pulled in a temporary assistant from another floor to help. She was the one accessing all my e-mails and messages."

My hands shook. What was I going to do? I covered my face as tears overwhelmed me. I had to get to him. He had to know it was a mistake.

I stood up on unsteady legs. "I have to find him. This isn't what I want. Oh, God, what have I done?"

I rushed out my door and toward Lex's office.

Fredrick sat behind his desk, and the moment he saw me, I knew Lex had the papers.

I walked into his office and found his jacket on his chair and the remains of a broken glass tumbler scattered along the floor near the back wall. "Where is he? I have to talk to him."

"He left a little before lunch."

"Where did he go?" I ran a palm across my face. "Please, Fred. Tell me where he is. I have to fix this."

"I don't know, Milla. I've never seen him like this."

I walked back into Lex's office and collapsed on his sofa, wrapping my arms around my waist. Tears streamed down my face, and chills shook my body to the core.

Why didn't I follow up on my request? I'd just destroyed the marriage I'd worked so hard to restore.

Lex was never going to forgive me.

I let sobs overtake me until I had nothing left inside. Then I walked to the window to gaze out at the busy streets.

"Milla, dear."

I turned to look at Fred.

"I'm going to leave now. Is there anything I can get you?" Fred watched me with weary eyes.

I wiped the remaining dampness from my cheeks. "How long have I been in here?"

"For a little over an hour."

"I'm sorry. I didn't mean to hold you up." I picked up Lex's jacket, thinking I'd take it home but paused and placed it back on the chair.

"Do you need me to call Arya? She hasn't left the building yet. Her conference call went over."

I shook my head. What would I tell her? That I'd broken my heart and Lex's because of my stupidity?

"No. I think it's time I went home, too."

I walked in a numb haze from the office and to my car. I gripped the door handle, but I knew I wasn't in any condition to drive.

At that moment, Tony stepped out of his car.

"Is everything okay, Signora Duncan?"

My lips trembled. "C-could you take me home? I don't think I should drive right now."

He nodded and led me to his car.

Thirty minutes after leaving ArMil headquarters, I walked in the front foyer of the penthouse. I'd spent most of the drive trying to think of what I'd say to Lex. Every excuse I came up with sounded lame even to me.

I set my keys in the tray by the door and rested my hand against my chest as I steadied my breath.

Please, God, let him hear what I have to say.

The sound of ice filling a glass reached my ears, and dread washed over me. I squared my shoulders; whatever happened, I'd find a way to cope. I knew it was a lie, but I had to try to believe something.

"Lex?" I hesitated, but walked down the hall to the kitchen.

He closed the refrigerator and turned toward me. His eyes blazed with hurt and resignation.

"I see you're home. I didn't think you'd come here after what you sent me today."

"You weren't supposed to get those."

"Then tell me, when was I supposed to get them?" His voice grew cold. "Were you going to wait until our anniversary or was it going to be when we had our first child? I actually believed you were back. That you wanted this to work, but you had your foot out the door the whole time."

I took a step toward him. "It wasn't like that. Everything was real. Please listen to me. It was a mistake. I—"

"I don't want to hear it." He slammed his juice glass on the counter.

I jumped but remained where I was. I had to get him to hear me.

"I started the paperwork when I was in Italy. When I wasn't thinking straight."

"I said, I don't want to hear it." He walked out of the kitchen and to the front hallway.

I ran after him. "Lex, please stop. Give me a chance to explain. This isn't what I want." I wiped at the tears streaming down my cheeks.

He opened the coat closet and pulled out his leather bomber. "No. I'm tired of fighting for us. I've stood by you through everything. Why couldn't you give me the decency of telling me what you planned? Then I wouldn't have believed we had a future."

Panic filled me, and I clutched his arm. "No, please listen. Please understand."

He shook off my hand and moved toward the door. "I'm done with understanding."

"Lex, I love you."

He stopped midstep. "You have a great way of showing it."

I couldn't defend myself. Nothing I said would make any difference. He'd made his decision and I couldn't blame him.

"I'm so sorry. I'm so, so sorry," I sobbed.

He glanced over his shoulder and released a deep breath. "You want to know why I'm sorry? I'm sorry that I love a woman who will never put me first. Who loves her games. Who doesn't understand when things get hard you stick around and fight for each other. I can't do this anymore. You want a divorce? I'll give you a divorce. I'm done. I'll send someone to get my things."

"What?" A panic settled into my gut. "Please. I…beg you."

He pulled his wedding ring off and dropped it on the table by the door. My heart screamed 'NO'. He opened the penthouse door.

"Please don't do this. I can't…I…please." I sobbed, almost paralyzed by what was happening.

He ignored my pleas and slammed the door behind him.

Oh God, I've lost him

My body shook. I couldn't believe this was happening. I doubled over and collapsed on the floor.

CHAPTER TWENTY-SIX

Milla, where are you? Why aren't you at the office? It's nearly eleven o'clock."

I heard a commotion in my living room, but couldn't care less.

"Go away," I whispered. I didn't want to face the world, even if it was Arya.

I'd lost everything.

I covered my head with the comforter and buried my face in Lex's pillow. His scent filled my senses. Tears seeped out of my eyes.

"Where is she? Fuck, if she isn't answering, this is bad." Carmen's voice followed Arya's question.

I had eight meetings today, but I couldn't bother going to work.

I never should have thought about divorce in the first place. Now all I had was the ring I clutched in my palm.

"Milla?" Arya's worried voice blared over my head. "Get up. We have an emergency. You need to know what we found on the surveillance software."

"I don't care. I don't have the energy to deal with anything."

"Mil, are you sick? Shit, you never get sick." Carmen tugged the covers off my head. "Oh honey, you don't look so good."

I cried. "Go away. I can't…I just can't."

"Mil, it's going to be okay." Arya crawled onto the bed and gathered my head in her lap.

Carmen joined us on my other side and held my hand. "Talk to us. We can help you, whatever it is."

"I lost him," I mumbled, and another wave of tears let loose. I sobbed and sobbed while Arya cooed and petted my hair.

"*Mera behna*, Lex loves you with his complete heart. It can't be that bad. Tell me what happened," Arya said as she pushed the hair out of my eyes and wiped my face with a tissue.

I wiped at the tears streaming down my face. "I fucked up…he was served with divorce papers. I thought I stopped them, but somehow…it's my fault. I should have known better." I knew I wasn't making sense, but I just couldn't get it out.

"He…" I hiccupped. "He says it's over." I sniffed. "I'm so stupid."

"Did he say it was over?" Carmen asked.

I nodded. "He said he couldn't do it anymore." My body hurt remembering the determined clench of his jaw.

"Oh, Mil." She squeezed my hand. "We'll figure this out."

We sat in comforting silence for a few minutes until I could sit up without falling into a puddle of tears.

Carmen handed me a glass of water from the bedside table. "Drink this."

I followed her directions and then closed my eyes, leaning back against the headboard. Hours of crying followed by numerous calls and texts to Lex with no answer or response had taken its toll on me. My body ached everywhere.

"Mil, I know the timing couldn't be worse, but we have to tell you something," Carmen said as she took the glass from me and set it back on the table.

"Okay, I can take it. Nothing can be worse than losing Lex."

"You might think otherwise once you hear the news." Arya hesitated. "Christof's freight is on your ship, and it's left Venezuela."

"I'm not following. Why is that bad? That was the plan. To get his cargo here and then let the feds take over."

"Mil. The cargo is the problem." Carmen shivered, rubbing her arms.

Okay, that was dramatic.

"We already knew it could be guns or drugs. What could be worse?"

"It's people."

"What?" Did Carmen say what I thought she said?

Oh, God. We are involved in human trafficking.

"Arya, explain this to me. Carmen's freaking me out."

"It won't be any better once I tell you what we just found out."

I swallowed and adjusted myself on the bed. "Start from the beginning, Ari."

"So our team has been monitoring the ships in South America ever since your little chat with Christof. Well, yesterday one of your ships went offline for a few hours."

"We expected that," I interjected. "Christof wasn't going to tell us when he took one of our ships. My job was to accept delivery of the cargo when it reached port and transport it to one of our warehouses."

"Mil, our monitoring software for the ship detected people, not cargo. And a satellite scan showed heat signatures of at least a thousand people. That is eight hundred and fifty more people than they need to man the cargo ship."

This couldn't be happening. Christof was using me to take part in one of the worst crimes I could imagine.

My mind whirled.

"I think I'm going to be sick." I jumped off the bed and ran to the toilet.

I emptied my stomach and closed my eyes to steady my head and stomach. A memory from the warehouse where Jacob had taken me flashed in my mind.

"She's out, boss."

"Good. The drug should keep her from trying to escape. Leave her in the corner. We need to get the freight into the warehouse. What's the count this time?"

"Two hundred and sixteen women and one hundred twenty-four kids."

"Good. The buyers will be happy."

"Here, drink this." Arya handed me a glass of water as Carmen wiped my head with a cool washcloth.

After I finished drinking the water, the girls helped me up. I went to the sink and leaned against the counter.

"Mil, talk to us. What just happened?" Carmen rubbed my back.

I glanced at Arya. "I remembered a conversation Jacob had with one of his men when he thought I was passed out. They were selling people, specifically women and children." I gripped the counter. "We have to stop them."

I had to get dressed and find the warehouse. I turned to go into my closet but lost my balance.

"Woo." Carmen caught me. "Okay. Let's take a step back." She sat me on a bench I had in the middle of the bathroom. "When was the last time you ate?"

I glared at her. "My eating habits aren't important right now."

She frowned at me in return. "Let's go." She dragged me into the kitchen, pointed to the bar stool, and opened my refrigerator.

I conceded and followed her unsaid command and sat. "Carm, you don't understand. I know how to find the building where they're going to transfer the women and children."

"Mil, the building they held us in was destroyed by the blast during my rescue," Arya said as she took the seat next to me.

"I know, but I remember seeing a sign on the building with an eight-pointed star surrounded by barbed wire when I escaped. It was how I was able to describe the building to the agents." After my kidnapping, I learned it was the image used by mafia soldiers stating they'll never kneel to authority. "I want to go down to the port and see if I can find any building with that symbol. That way we can let our CIA contacts know what we learned."

"Do you know how many buildings line the port?" Carmen pulled a bowl out of the microwave.

"Yes, but we have to move before the ship docks."

"Okay, slow down for a second." Carmen placed the pasta she'd reheated in front of me.

I began eating without thinking and finished the bowl in a matter of minutes.

I looked up and saw both girls gawking at me.

"What? I guess I was hungry after all." I pushed the bowl away from me. "Okay, I ate. Now who's going with me to check out my hunch?"

"You're not going anywhere." Arya turned my stool to face her and then folded her arms. "Well, not alone, anyway. Right, Carm?"

Carmen rolled her eyes. "When do I say no to any of your schemes? But before either of you gets excited, we need to get our CIA contacts involved."

I knew my girl would help me.

"I'm fine with that. Let's get them here as soon as possible. On second thought." I paused and tried to push back tears that suddenly resurfaced. "Can we go to your place, Ari? I don't think I want to be here." If I stayed in the penthouse, I'd start thinking about the mess I'd made of my life with Lex, and I needed this to distract me.

"Of course, *mera behna*."

I jumped off the stool and hugged her.

Carm came around the counter and wrapped an arm around each of us. "You know if Max or Lex finds out about this, we're going to be in deep shit."

Arya and I ignored her comment.

"Let's do this, ladies." Arya stretched out her hand. Carmen and I stacked ours over hers. "All for one and one for all."

CHAPTER TWENTY-SEVEN

I can't believe I agreed to this. It doesn't matter how many people are monitoring us. I don't feel safe. Why the agents couldn't do this…"

I glanced at Carmen over my shoulder. She tucked a strand of her blond wig behind her ear. It surprised me how natural she looked with her disguise. No one would recognize her walking the streets along the pier. If my stomach weren't in knots, I'd laugh at the outfit I was wearing. My frumpy blouse, tailored peacoat, boots, and red hair made me look like an English professor at an elite boarding school.

"Because I'm the one who can attach and activate the tracer program Arya developed to monitor all cybertraffic and transmissions for Christof's building. It's the only way we can learn where they're transporting the women and children without breaking any security laws." I stepped over discarded lumber and moved toward another stretch of buildings. "It's not like I volunteered to go. The programming is complicated, and since there wasn't enough time to teach the commands, I was the only option."

The Port of Boston area was a maze of buildings and paths. We'd walked ten blocks in the guise of searching for a building to buy with our commercial real estate agent. Who happened to be Tony.

"I would have done it, but instead you left me at the estate, watching a bunch of monitors." Arya's voice came over our earpieces.

I winced. Arya still hadn't forgiven us for forcing her to stay and supervise the surveillance software. She wanted to be with us, but we weren't going to put her in danger when she had two small children at home. My stomach hurt just from the possibility of finding the building.

"Suck it up, Ari," Carmen and I said in unison.

"Besides, Max would kill us if we got you involved in anything. Hell, Lex and I are on the verge of divorce, and I know he'd lose his shit if he knew what we were doing."

"I hate you two," she mumbled, then added, "Shit, someone's coming toward you."

That was our cue. Well maybe not the "shit" part.

I pointed at something at the top of a building, and Carmen nodded.

"So do you think this area would be a good place to designate as a fashion warehouse for our stores?" I asked Carmen.

"I won't know until we take a look inside." Carmen scanned the roofline.

A man in jeans and a leather jacket walked in our direction and inspected us as he passed.

"If you are interested, I can call the seller's agent and arrange a time to view the interior," Tony said as he pretended to write the address on his phone.

"Let's keep it on our list, and we can decide later." I made sure I responded loud enough that the man could hear us.

"Okay, there aren't any more people near you." Arya typed in the background. "Tony, you can take them around the corner."

"*Sì*, signora."

Tony led us down a grim walkway, passing a few cars, and then turned down an alleyway. He looked around us, making sure we were alone, and then spoke. "I believe we should call it an evening after we walk the next street. Once it gets dark, it is harder to ensure your protection."

He had a point. No matter how much I wanted to stop Christof, I couldn't put us in further danger than I'd already done.

"Hey, this street is filled with shops and galleries." A crease formed between Carman's brows. "How did I grow up here and never know this existed?"

"That's because the Boston Danes were too hoity-toity to play on the pier," Arya said into our earpieces.

"Shut up, Ari. You're a Dane now, remember? And for the record, most people don't let their kids play along the docks. It's dangerous."

As we made our way to the last building, my breath hitched, making me stop abruptly. I'd spotted the symbol. The disappointment I felt a few seconds ago now turned to full-on anxiety.

"There it is. On that art gallery's sign." I tilted my chin in the direction of the building a few feet from us. On the top right corner above the name was the eight-pointed star with decorative barbed wire around it. To the passing person, it looked like the other stars on the sign. They wouldn't know the difference unless they looked for it. That's probably why they displayed it in plain sight.

A faint cry sounded from the side of the building, almost childlike. A shiver ran down my spine, reminding me to stay focused.

"Carm?"

"I heard."

"So did I," Arya said into our ears. "Mil, Carm, I think it's time to go. I have a really bad feeling about this. Forget about the plan and get out of there."

I couldn't agree with her more. Man, I should never have agreed to this. The agents wanted a bust, and our safety was important but came second to their mission.

"Tony, how far is the car from here?"

"Only a few blocks." He glanced along the side of the gallery building.

"Don't even think about it, Tony," I warned.

"Signora, I must. This will be our only chance. I'll go around the side, attach the transmitter to the building, and return in a few minutes. By that time the car arrives, I'll be back."

"I agree. I think you should stay with us out here, where the agents can see us. Said agents can figure this shit out on their own." Carmen glanced to the distant end of the pier.

"Carm, you know they heard you?"

"I'm aware of that, Arya."

"Fuck, Tony's gone down the alley. Neither of you girls follow him."

"Duh." I was impulsive but not a complete idiot.

Carm released a frustrated sigh. "Let's go check out the display until he gets back."

We walked to the windows of the gallery.

"*Zdravstvuyte.* Can I help you ladies with anything?" A well-dressed man with white-blond hair and almost transparent blue eyes stepped out of the shop and smiled at us.

Merda, he's Russian.

"Um. We were just looking at the photographs you have in your window." I pointed to a portrait of a girl sitting on a bench with her back to the photographer and her hair flowing loosely to her bottom. "She's beautiful."

"Yes, it's one of our prized pieces. Let me introduce myself. I am Abram Christi. I own this gallery." He shook both our hands as he surveyed us, but for some reason, I felt like he was studying me in detail. "I apologize if this seems forward, but do I know you from somewhere?"

I glanced at Carmen and then back at Abram. "I don't believe so."

With our getups, no one would be able to tell it was us, or at least I hoped.

"Shame, I could swear you look very familiar." He frowned and then gestured to the gallery. "Would you ladies like to come inside to browse?"

"Thank you very much, but no." Carmen pointed to her watch. "We're waiting for our sales agent to return from a call."

"I insist." Abram cupped my elbow and tried to guide me inside.

I jerked my arm and turned toward Carmen. That's when I realized a group of men surrounded us. A fear I hadn't felt since my kidnapping came full force to the surface.

Oh God, not again. Don't freak out, Mil.

"Girls, stay calm. I'm sending help." Arya tried to soothe us, but I knew we were in trouble. "I'm going to go silent now, but know I'm still here. I don't want to distract you and draw attention to the earpiece."

"Please let us pass," I said in the coolest voice I could conjure.

He tugged the wig off my head. "I can't do that, Mrs. Duncan.

I have orders from my brother, just in case this very scenario happened."

Cazzo. He'd recognized me. Hell, he said *brother*. Without a doubt, I knew he referred to Christof. Dammit, why hadn't I noticed before? Abram shared a family resemblance to Christof. This was not good.

"And what scenario is that?" Carmen asked, staring straight at him. Her boots and natural height had her at eye level with him, and if I wasn't mistaken, a small tremor passed over him as he glanced at the ground for a brief second.

Abram turned away from her and walked through the archway of the door. "The one where Mrs. Duncan's natural tendency to leap before she looks pushed her to investigate why Vlad was so interested in these specific piers."

I cringed inside. He was right. No matter how hard I tried to be the more mature Milla, I ended up making impulsive decisions.

No. I couldn't do that to myself. The agents helped us plan everything for today. They were the ones who suggested Carmen and I go in as property developers. We'd investigated every possible scenario we could think of and had a backup plan.

Well, except for this stupid situation we were in. None of the research we'd found mentioned anything about Christof having a living brother. Let alone one who owned a gallery in Boston. His known siblings, Ivan and Serge, died in childhood.

The men behind Carmen and I pushed us forward, forcing us to follow behind Abram.

I looked toward the alley, hoping for any sign of Tony, but saw nothing.

The moment we passed through the doorway, a loud screech

pierced my ears, making me cup them. Carmen had the same reaction.

Abram stretched out his hand with a grin. "We can't have our conversations monitored."

I pulled out the earpiece and placed it in his palm, as did Carman.

"Now you are free to browse the gallery."

I remained in my spot for a few minutes, scanning the room. I noticed a series of fetish-style portraits throughout the room. The pictures ranged in poses of basic submission on the floor to images capturing every type of intercourse.

"Do you like what you see?"

I wasn't sure whom he was asking, but I answered. "Some are very beautiful, but others look far from consensual." I referred to a picture where a knife was piercing a girl's skin, and fear and tears covered her duct-taped face.

"You are right in a sense. Vlad has a unique taste in art."

Vlad? I supposed even international terrorist went by nicknames too.

"Like the piece over here? It is Vlad's favorite." He pointed to a frame on the back wall.

I swallowed to help my dry throat as I took in the picture.

It's me.

I stared at my photograph. There was a drug-induced, glazed sheen to my eyes. I couldn't remember when they took the picture, but I knew it was somewhere in the middle of my torture. I still had part of my top on, and only a few welts covered my skin.

Breathe, Mil. Don't you dare faint.

I shook the haze from my mind. I refused to fall apart as I'd done the last time I'd seen images of my captivity. I'd come a long way since then.

"How much is it?" I asked, without letting my voice crack. Then I noticed at least five more, and my heart sunk as nausea threatened to override my will to stay calm. The poses showed me at various stages during my captivity. The last one was an image I tried to forget every day. Jacob had the handle of the whip pushed up against me, and my head was thrown back as I screamed.

"How much are all of them?" Carmen countered from behind me. She placed a hand on my shoulder and turned me away from the pictures. "I'll buy them from you right now. Name your price, but I want all the negatives, too."

"Ms. Dane, I have to say I commend your loyalty to your friend, but I'm not at liberty to sell these portraits. They don't belong to me." He wouldn't look Carmen in the eyes. He moved around her, as if he wanted to avoid direct contact with her.

"Then whose are they?"

The slight change in her tone brought Abram's gaze to hers, and he shifted uncomfortably.

Then it hit me. He was a submissive, and Carmen was using her Domme tactics to unnerve him.

"Ms. Dane." Abram hesitated. "Th-they're only here until Vlad decides to find a permanent home for them. We display them so our clients have an idea of the work we can procure."

The thoughts about what was happening between Carmen and Abram disappeared. I couldn't believe what he'd said. Christof was using my pain as art.

I could have lived my whole life without seeing those portraits.

I closed my eyes for a moment, and a slow anger filled me. If my pain was on display as art, then what was going to happen to the women and children on the ship?

If I could somehow save them from any more terror than they'd already endured, I'd do whatever I needed to help them. I knew Carmen would agree.

My stomach continued to churn, and I pushed the growing burn down. I had to stay focused. Arya and the team knew where we were. I wasn't going anywhere without them far behind.

I had to find a way to get my cell phone out without them noticing. This was the only way I'd know if Tony succeeded in planting the transmitter or if Arya had sent any messages.

"Mr. Christi, could I use your restroom?"

His attention snapped toward me, breaking the spell Carmen held over him.

"Of course." He motioned to one of his men. "Lev, escort Mrs. Duncan to the restroom."

Lev approached me and tried to unbutton my coat.

I smacked his hands away. "What the hell are you doing?"

"Place your purse on the table, take off your coat, and empty your pockets. Then I will take you to the toilet."

Damn. I had to think of another way. But what?

I followed his directions, pulling my work and personal phones out of my pockets.

Cazzo, I didn't want to go alone.

As if reading my mind, Carmon echoed my thoughts. "Milla, I don't think you should go alone."

Abram chuckled. "I assure you. No harm will come to her. None of us share Mr. Brady's preferences in kink."

A shiver ran up my spine at the mention of Jacob's name.

I walked toward the restroom and closed the door behind me, pressing back against it. I inhaled a few deep breaths. *There has to be a way out of here.* I scanned the room. The only way out was a window, and it was too small to crawl through.

Merda. Think, Milla.

I paced back and forth, until a hard knock on the window caused me to jump.

A large shadow covered the glass, followed by another rap. I gingerly approached the window and cracked it open. Tony peeked down at me from the opening, and a wave of relief flooded my body.

"You have to get us out of here."

"Signora, we are working on it. First, put this in your ear. It transmits a signal using Wi-Fi, not radio frequency. The signal can't be jammed." I followed his instructions and tucked the bud inside my ear.

"How did you know I was back here?'

"We've watched you through the gallery windows and were waiting for an opportunity to contact you." He handed me a phone. "Now, take this. We need you to activate the transmitter."

"Even if I trigger the software"—I clutched the cell—"there's no way of getting us out of here without you storming in. Abram is acting as if we are there to view the artwork, but I know he is keeping us there until Christof arrives."

"That's exactly what we plan to do, *a ghrá*." Lex's Irish brogue sounded in my ear.

"How did you…why are you…you said…" I couldn't get the words out. He wasn't involved in the plan. Oh no, if he knew, that meant Max knew. We were in so much shit when this was over.

"Mil, stay focused. Right now, you need to activate the program. You don't have much time."

I glanced up at Tony, who crouched outside the window. "Is Arya okay?"

"I'm fine, *mera behna*. Get to work."

"Okay."

I opened the app that allowed contact with ArMil's server. After signing into three safeguard firewalls, I gained access to a small section of the network. I logged into the transmitter software and defined the programming parameters.

A trickle of sweat slid down the side of my face, and I wiped it with the back of my hand.

"How much longer, Mil?" Arya asked. "You need to get out there. I don't want Carmen left alone too long with them."

"Almost done. God, you know how much I hate coding, and somehow you always get me roped into doing it." I typed in a few more lines of code. "Okay, here goes. Let me know if I'm online." I pushed the key that would activate the transmitter.

I handed the phone back to Tony and leaned against the wall, inhaling a sigh of relief.

"We're in. The data is coming in like a flood. Fuck, Mil, it's worse than we thought. Lex, look at this."

"Milla, you need to get to the front this minute." A tinge of panic underlined his command.

My heartbeat accelerated and I pressed my hand against my stomach.

"Guys, you're freaking me out. What's going on?"

"Move now. The women and children on the boat aren't the only people Christof plans to sell. There is a bidding war going on for you and Carmen."

"Oh God, this can't be happening. I wouldn't survive it a second time." A wave of dizziness hit me, and visions of my attack filled my mind. My knees gave out and I dropped to the floor.

"Signora, you must get up. You have to go to the front."

I couldn't respond to Tony. I wrapped my arms around myself and rocked back and forth.

"Mil, baby. Please. You have to get up. Don't think about what might happen. Don't let Jacob win. Go out there. The agents will take care of the rest."

I allowed Lex's words to soak in. He was right.

I will never let that monster win again.

I took a few deep breaths and, slowly, my panic eased. On shaky feet, I stood and walked to the door.

Lev knocked on the door just as I turned the handle. "Took you long enough."

I didn't respond and stepped out of the restroom. I returned to the gallery but Carmen wasn't there. My lungs contracted.

"Where is she?" I demanded.

"She is in the office with Mr. Christi."

"Why?"

Lev pushed me forward, making me stumble, but I caught myself on a nearby table. "That is not your business. Sit."

"She's fine, Mil," Arya said into my ear. "She's using her Domme skills. Can you guys guess who her highest bidder is?"

"Not funny," I mumbled.

"What did you say?" Lev glared at me.

"Nothing."

"Get ready," Arya's voice warned.

I closed my eyes and braced myself. A series of popping sounds echoed around me, and everything in the next few minutes seemed to happen in slow motion. The windows shattered, and a group of men burst in from all sides. I jumped off the chair and crouched under a table.

Smoke filled the room, making it hard to breathe, and I buried my face in my shirt to keep from choking. Seconds later, a pair of hands pulled me out from my hiding spot.

"It's okay, Mrs. Duncan. Let's get you out to safety."

I followed the agent's request but stopped when I didn't see Carmen. "You have to get Carmen."

"Mr. Regala is bringing her out now. We need to get you checked out by the paramedics."

"I'll be fine. I just need some fresh air. Nothing to worry about." I'd barely finished my words when an upsurge of queasiness filled my stomach, and my mind clouded.

The last thing I heard was, "Oh shit. Mrs. Duncan is down."

CHAPTER TWENTY-EIGHT

You need to get some rest, Mil. I don't want you passing out again. I'm not let you leave the estate until I know you're going to be okay."

I glared at Arya over the top of my laptop as I finished a glass of water and set it on my bedside table. "That was a fluke. The doctor checked me out. I'm completely fine. She said it was probably from dehydration and all the excitement."

Arya shifted from the foot of my bed to the pillow next to me. "I still think you need to lie down. I don't care if you're used to surviving on only three hours of sleep."

"Not until the boat docks. I'm going to make sure every one of those women and children has a place to go." I was tired but I didn't want to go to bed. I knew the moment I closed my eyes the nightmares would start.

"Watching the satellite image of the ship being seized by authorities isn't going to change anything."

"There has to be something we can do." I ran a palm over my tired face and pinched the touch screen to enlarge the ship's image.

"There's nothing to do. Interpol and the CIA have taken over. They've essentially cut us off from the operation. All they want is to collect any data we gathered at the debriefing and then send us on our merry way."

"I know, but what else am I supposed to do?" My lips trembled. "I don't want to go home."

Arya took the computer from me, setting it on the table and pulled my head against her shoulder. "You can stay with me for as long as you want. I have plenty of bedrooms."

A slight smile touched my lips. "Thirty-six, to be exact."

"You could change rooms every night of the week."

We both giggled, but then I sobered. "Ari."

"Yes."

"He didn't stay." I wiped a tear that slipped down my cheek.

After the rescue, Lex stopped by the estate to check with Max that Carmen and I were okay and then immediately left, saying he'd come back for the morning meeting.

"I know." She laced my fingers with hers. "I don't know what to say to you, *mera behna*. I know he loves you. He was going crazy when he found out what you were doing at the docks. And it took three men to hold him down and keep him from getting in his car when he read what Christof planned for you and Carmen."

"Speaking of." I lifted my head. "How did he discover we'd made an agreement with the agents?"

"One of Thomas's men followed us and reported it to him, and then it went up the chain to Max and Lex. Apparently, your security backup had backup."

"Have you talked to Max since all this happened?"

"Um...well...no."

I shook my head. "You're trying to avoid him, aren't you? That's why you're in here."

"Kind of." She cringed.

"Go talk to your man." I pointed to the bedroom door. "What's the worst he can do to you? Spank your ass and then fuck you silly?"

Arya perked up and slid off the bed. "When you put it that way. Okay. I'm going."

A yawn escaped my lips. "Go. I'm tired after all."

"See you in a few hours," she said as she closed the door.

I shifted in my bed and adjusted the covers around me. I took a few deep breaths and prayed I'd sleep through the night without any dreams.

* * *

I startled awake as a hand slipped over my mouth.

"Shh…it's me."

Lex!

"I'm going to remove my hand; don't bite it."

I nodded, and his palm slid from my lips. I grabbed his face. "Am I dreaming? What are you doing here?"

"I had to see for myself that you were okay."

I tried to focus on what he was saying. It didn't make sense. He'd said we were over.

I released my hold on him. "Why? You're divorcing me."

"Because no matter what happens between us…" He cupped the sides of my face and leaned his head against mine. "The thought of anything happening to you tears me apart."

"Please don't say things like that. I can't…" I tried to push him away, but he captured my hand in his.

"You stupid, beautiful woman. Why did you do it?"

"I had to protect those women and children. There was no way to know the plan would backfire."

"You make me so mad." He growled and covered my lips with his.

No, we couldn't do this, not until we talked.

He threaded his fingers through my hair, deepening our kiss and sending all my protests to the back of my mind. He pulled away for a moment and climbed on the bed, straddling my hips. "You're like a drug. I can't get enough." He took my wrists and pinned them to the mattress.

The darkness surrounding us kept me from seeing his eyes, but I knew they'd be glazed with angry desire. He held me in place as he pushed my covers down and my nightgown up, exposing my swollen breasts. His face grazed my neck, sighing as he moved the necklace holding his ring to the side, and then shifted his lips to my straining, pebbled nipples. Taking one in his mouth, he sucked and bit down.

"Ahaa," I cried and arched.

"So sensitive and ripe." He shifted to the other breast and then administered the same attention.

My core spasmed in response to every pull of his mouth. Wetness pooled between my legs, and I shifted my pelvis to feel even the slightest hint of the erection pulsing above me.

Lex lifted his hips, and I moaned.

"Not yet, not until I say you're ready."

Merda, I'm about to explode.

He released my wrists, but a tap told me to hold them in place. The position left me stretched out as he explored lower, down my stomach and to the edge of my underwear. His day-old whiskers tickled in the most exquisite way. My skin prickled, and a moan escaped my lips at the glorious sensation.

Fingers hooked in the edge of my G-string and snapped the sides. "I want nothing between me and the liquid gold hiding at the center of your beautiful pussy." He spread my lower lips and blew, but kept my legs locked straight under his weight.

"Master, please," I begged as spears of pleasure coursed through me.

"No 'Master.' This isn't a scene. This is only you and me, a husband and wife."

His words ignited a shard of hope. *Maybe he's forgiven me.*

Before my thoughts could linger too long, he pushed my thighs apart and pressed a single digit inside my soaked entrance, curling his finger up.

"More," I commanded, lifting my hips up and impaling myself on him again.

"No, you don't." He withdrew from my aching pussy and grabbed my hips. "You will receive your pleasure when I say."

If I argued, he'd stop. He couldn't stop. "Yes, Lex," I conceded. The more control I handed him, the faster he'd give my release.

Chuckling, he scraped a thick finger over the straining, sensitive bundle of nerves at the apex of my sex.

I gasped, and then almost broke down in tears when he stopped his strumming.

"No," I called, and my hands flew from their position and clutched his shoulders.

"It's okay, baby. Let me undress."

My grip eased, and he sat up, pulling his clothes off and throwing them on the ground. He climbed back onto the bed and pushed my knees apart, settling between my aching folds and teasing me with the engorged head of his cock.

He leaned down, his face a mere inch from mine. The glow of the moonlight shone across his face. "Do you know what I thought when I saw you sleeping?"

I shook my head as he prodded my entrance. Sweat beaded all over my body, and I lifted my hips.

"That I was the one lucky bastard who's had the privilege of losing himself between your legs." He pushed in further. "The only man who knows the beauty of your innocence. The only man who will love you with every fiber of his being." He thrust to the hilt, and we both cried out.

Tears rolled down the sides of my face. "Don't say things like that." He thrust again, and the throbbing intensified in my pussy. "I…I…can't have hope only for you to take it away. I'm not stro—"

He silenced me with his mouth and murmured, "No more talking." He repositioned my legs so they wrapped around his waist and slid out and back in, repeating the motion.

I gasped and arched, rubbing my face against his neck.

We threaded our fingers together, and his pace increased, long, fast strokes, drawing mewling cries from my lips. Our bodies collided in a rhythm so delicious, the only thoughts coursing through my mind were of release.

"Now," he ordered, and my pussy responded with powerful ripples, squeezing his pummeling cock. I screamed his name as I almost painfully rode through the orgasm.

A few moments later Lex stiffened. "Milla, my love," he groaned as jets of his essence shot into me, triggering another orgasm of my own. We both collapsed in exhaustion.

"I love you, Lex."

"I know, *a ghrá*." He tucked me into his arms, kissed the top of my head, and sighed. *If only it was enough* were the last words I heard before I drifted into sleep.

A few hours later, I awoke to the sound of my alarm. Happiness filled me. Lex was with me, sleeping beside me. I reached over for him and found an empty bed.

Huh? This can't be happening again.

I looked around the bed, and my heart sunk. Fantasizing about him wasn't going to make it a reality.

Don't be stupid, Mil. Stay strong.

I hiccupped as I pushed back tears. I slid off the bed, stretched, and then froze. The insides of my thighs were damp, and the distinct scent of Lex touched my nose. At the same moment, a small cloth caught my eye. Bending down, I picked it up and examined.

My torn underwear.

It wasn't a dream.

A knock sounded on the bedroom door. I went to open it and found Lex standing on the other side. His hair was damp, but he still wore the clothes from yesterday.

"Hey. Why did you knock?"

He didn't respond and stepped inside.

Okay, what the hell happened between earlier this morning and now? His mood seemed off.

I touched his arm. "Lex, what's…"

"It was a mistake, Milla."

I snatched my hand back and stared at him. "Say that again."

Oh God, this couldn't be happening.

"It was a mistake. I shouldn't have come to you last night. We aren't good for each other." He ran a hand through his wet hair. "You're an addiction I have to cut out of my life."

I sucked in an unsteady breath.

His words sounded so cold, but when I studied his face, I saw sadness, resignation, and determination.

"You don't mean that. We've been through so much." I grabbed his arm. "I petitioned to have the divorce papers withdrawn."

"It's too late, Milla. I can't fight for us anymore. I want a family and a wife who puts our family and me first. No matter what you say, it isn't possible for you. Even if we tried again, one day your mother will do something to come between us. And I'll be damned if I'll let there be a child in the middle of that."

I flinched, trying to hold in the pain erupting in my heart.

"Isn't there any possibility we could work this out? I…I…love…"

"Enough, Mil." He stepped away from me. "I'm going back to the penthouse to get my things. You can keep it or sell it. I don't care. Just know I won't be there."

My mind whirled as if the ground shifted from under me. I wrapped my arms around myself to ward off the chill now prickling my skin. Every drop of optimism I'd held evaporated.

I couldn't expect him to forgive me over and over again. Even if I was no longer the old selfish Milla, I still hurt him, and now I had to live with the consequences. This is what he wanted, so I had no choice but to give it to him.

"I'm sorry," I whispered as I moved away from him and went toward the bathroom. I paused before I closed the door and said, "I hope you find happiness one day."

CHAPTER TWENTY-NINE

In breaking business news, the rumors circulating for the past few weeks about Milla Castra Duncan are true. She is stepping down from her role as chief financial officer of shipping conglomerate Castra Enterprises.

Moments ago, we received a brief statement released by Mrs. Duncan's brother, Dominic Castra.

"It breaks our hearts to lose Milla, but it was time for her to focus exclusively on ArMil Innovations. Running one multinational organization is challenging, much less two. As of this morning, Marcello Castra stepped into the role of CFO of Castra Enterprises. Please note, business will function as usual, including all endeavors negotiated under Milla."

"You can turn the TV off now. The announcement makes it official," I said to Carmen as I took a sip of sparkling water.

She followed my request and then relaxed onto the chaise in the private dressing room of Trance, the New York fetish club she owned. She rubbed her baby bump and smiled. She was one gorgeous, pregnant amazon. Too bad Thomas wasn't part of her life to enjoy this with her.

"How does it feel to give up a piece of your inheritance?"

I sent her a halfhearted smile, set my glass down, and finished applying the last of my makeup. "I gave it all up over a month ago. Today's announcement is only a formality."

"Does Lex know what you did?"

My lips trembled for a second. "No. It's not going to make a difference, and I'm not sure it matters anymore. I've accepted that it's over, no matter how much it hurts."

For almost seven weeks, I hadn't seen or heard from Lex, except the formal e-mails detailing legal matters. True to his word, he'd moved out of our penthouse, leaving only a few items here and there. Items I could barely look at without crying, like our wedding pictures.

Arya kept me informed about things going on with Lex. No one knew where he was staying, and the few appearances he'd made at the office were when I was occupied or away. The only exception being the day he saw me with my head on my arms crying. Nausea had overwhelmed me, and he happened to walk by my office. I thought he was going to come inside, but he turned and strutted in the opposite direction, making his unspoken words clear.

He'd cut me out of his life completely.

Two weeks ago, I moved to New York and started working out of ArMil's Manhattan office. I missed Boston, but I couldn't stand the memories or the loneliness of living there without Lex.

"Have you told him about our mutual reproductive states? I'm positive it will matter a great deal."

I shook my head. "If he won't talk to me, how am I going to tell him? Besides, I've lost hope anything will change even if he knows. I received his notarized copies of the divorce papers a few weeks ago. All that's left to do is put my signature on it."

"Are you going to sign them?"

My shoulders dropped. "At first, I couldn't do it. I knew I should let him go, but I just couldn't. Now, I have to build the courage to sit down and finish the task. For ten years, it's been the two of us. Now it's time for both of us to move on."

"Whatever happens, you'll survive."

"It's not about survival, Carm. It's about living and counting my blessings." I placed a hand over my stomach. "This is a very important reason to live."

Carmen nodded and then gave me a weary smile.

My heart ached for her. At least she wasn't going to be a single mother alone. Although, she'd have a four-month head start before my bean came along. No matter what, I'd be there for her, just as she'd been there for me.

"Hey, what's all this moping going on?" Caitlin said as she walked in holding a corset and skirt. "Tonight's about having fun. No more thinking about the messes in our love lives."

"So says the most coveted fashion designer of the season. Aren't you the one who just rejected dates with two different oil billionaires and an Oscar-winning actor?"

"They don't share our lifestyle, and I can't commit to vanilla. It would never have worked with any of them. Plus, I'm not ready."

"It's been eight years, Cait." Dropping my robe on the chaise, I took the top from her, wrapped it around me, and then fastened the hooks down the front.

"It doesn't matter the time. I'm no longer looking for my happy ending. My only hope is to have some fun."

"I can definitely use some fun." I turned my back toward Caitlin. "Help me adjust this. It feels too tight across my abdomen."

Carmen snorted. "Filling out a bit, are we?"

I shot her a bird. "You told me I needed to fatten up, so Aunt Elana did just that when she came to help me settle into my Manhattan penthouse. You have no idea how much I miss coming home to the house smelling of yummy food."

"That reminds me, how is Arya doing?" Caitlin asked as she finished lacing the back of my corset and sat next to Carmen.

"She's in marital and maternal bliss," Carmen said.

I paused for a moment as I latched the necklace holding Lex's wedding ring around my neck and tucked it inside my top. Tonight would be the last time I'd wear it. Lex and I were over. No more hoping for something that wasn't going to happen.

I adjusted my corset and then walked to a row of shoes lining the side of the room.

"Wear the heeled boots. They'll accentuate your fabulous ass and tits," Carmen said from behind me.

"Yes, boss." I bent down to slip on the boots. As I laced up my boots to above my knee, a worry popped into my head. "Do you think people will talk, seeing me here alone?"

In the entire ten years of our marriage, I'd never entered a club without Lex. It felt almost wrong.

Mil, you're moving on. Remember?

"Yes," Carmen answered. "But who cares. It's not as if you're trolling for a new Dom. We're here to have fun, watch a few scenes, and hang out with each other."

"And if anyone says anything to you, Carmen will use her legendary Domme stare and make them pee in their pants," Caitlin joked.

I couldn't help but smirk. That was exactly what she'd done to Abram. Even as the agents burst into the office she'd taken him into, she'd stayed in Domme role.

"Let's hope it doesn't come to that." I stood. "How do I look?"

"Gorgeous." Carmen lifted a bottle of water in the air.

"Hot. I'm so glad I designed that for you." Caitlin applauded herself. "Let's go, ladies."

Nervous energy coursed through me as we entered the hallway leading into the social area of the club. Dark wood and soft lights decorated the hall, and soft jazz music played in the background. Floor lamps illuminated our path, guiding us to the end of the corridor. I pushed open a panel and entered the lounge.

The social area was lush and very intimate. Deep hues of green and blue with a hint of gold draped the walls. Rich mahogany woodwork lined the corners and ceiling. Two sets of stairs stood on either side of the opulent bar that carried every top-shelf liquor imaginable. Strategically positioned sofas, armchairs, and tables created individual seating areas.

"Follow me. I have a section reserved for us." Carmen inclined her head to an attendant, who opened up a roped-off area in the back of the lounge.

For the next thirty minutes, I did my best to enjoy the company of the girls, but my heart wasn't in it. Lack of alcohol and the fact it felt wrong being there kept me from delighting in the club's offerings. I'd come to the club too soon.

Cazzo. How was I going to move on if I kept thinking about him?

"Carm, I'm sorry to do this, but think I'm going to go back to my place. Next time, we should go to one of my dance clubs. I'm just not ready to be here without…" I closed my eyes and stopped myself before I said his name.

"I hope you're referring to me."

My heart contracted as I snapped my eyes open. Lex stood before me, sipping a drink. He wore a dark gray T-shirt and black leather pants, the same outfit he'd worn the last time we'd been in a club together.

"W-what are you doing here?" My voice came out raspy. I glanced behind me at the girls. They both looked as surprised as I was.

"I came for my wife, for my submissive." He traced a finger down my cheek.

I tried to push his hand way, but he captured mine.

"Don't do this. I'm finally functioning without you." My vision clouded.

"Please, *a ghrá*, don't cry. Let's go somewhere to talk."

Could I take the risk? Could I believe he was here for me? But why now?

"I know you have questions. Let me answer them." He thumbed the ring on my hand and sighed. "I never thought the day would come when you'd wear our wedding ring and I didn't."

I hiccupped, pushing the pain of his observation away. "We're still married."

"I know." A smile touched his lips. "I sent you those papers four weeks ago. Why didn't you sign them?"

I watched him for a few moments. Could I tell him the truth?

Milla, it can't make things worse.

"You said you wouldn't accept the end of our relationship without a fight. Well, that's what I was doing. Now I've decided to move on. That's why I'm here tonight."

His grip tightened on my wrist as I turned away from him.

"Please, fight for us. We can fix this."

I wasn't sure we could. No matter how much I wanted a future with him, if he couldn't trust me to put him first, then we'd never survive.

I kept my back to him as I asked, "Why now? I'm the same person from two months ago who you couldn't trust to make you or our family a priority. What changed?"

He released his hold on me and touched my lower back. "Let me answer your questions in private."

I released a deep sigh.

I guessed I could listen to him. Once I heard what he had to say, I'd go home.

"Fine. Follow me, but once we talk, I'm going back to my penthouse. Alone." I moved toward the hallway leading to Carmen's club office. I glanced at Carmen as she looked in Lex's direction and mouthed *good luck*.

"Traitor," I mumbled.

"Did you say something?"

"No, I was thinking aloud."

"Good to know," he said with a touch of humor in his tone.

The moment we entered the office, I moved to stand in front of Carmen's desk with my back to Lex. The door clicked closed, and I waited for him to tell me why he'd come, but he remained silent.

I turned to see what he was doing and discovered he was less than a foot from me. I tried to move backward but I was trapped between Lex and the desk.

I placed a hand on his chest to keep him from coming any closer. I stared into his beautiful blue eyes, seeing everything I'd lost.

"Why now, Lex?"

All of a sudden, it felt like we were back in Italy when I'd asked the same question.

"What if I say I came to my senses?"

"I wouldn't believe you."

A pang of sadness washed over his face. "I'm sorry, Mil. I'm sorry for not trusting you. For not having faith in your love for me. I was wrong. I should have given you a chance to explain. My only excuse is that I was so hurt I couldn't see straight."

His words pierced the shell I'd created around my heart. But I needed answers. I needed to know if I could trust him again.

"You didn't answer my question."

"Your father sent me copies of the inheritance transfer documents. He asked me to review them and to make sure it was what you really wanted." He lifted his hand to touch my face but then pulled back. "You gave up your entire claim to Castra Enterprises. Why?"

I pushed him out of my way and walked to the side of the office with the monitors. "It doesn't matter my reasons. It's done. As of today, I am no longer a shipping heiress or Castra's CFO."

"When did you decide to do it?"

I wanted to ask him why it mattered. It wasn't going to change anything. But I answered, "I decided to resign over two months ago. Papa's just having a hard time accepting it."

"Did you do it for me?"

I closed my eyes and gripped the back of the chair in front of the bay of monitors. I nodded. "Yes."

"Why?"

"I didn't want the company or my mother to come between us

again. I wanted you to see that I chose you. In the end, it didn't make a difference."

"It made all the difference in the world."

"No, it didn't." Rage ignited like it hadn't in so long. I turned to face him. "When I needed you to trust me, you couldn't. I know I made a mistake, but all I wanted was an opportunity to explain what happened, and you refused to give me a chance.

"For the first time in my life, I wasn't selfish. All I wanted was to make you happy. I can't live my life trying to atone for the stupidity of my youth. I'm sorry I hurt you, I'm sorry I wasn't the wife you wanted. I've accepted I'll never be the woman you deserve, and without trust, you'll never be the man for me."

I placed a hand on my chest, trying to steady my breath and calm the pain and hurt overwhelming me.

"Mil," he whispered. "I do trust you."

I shook my head. "If you did, then it wouldn't have taken Papa's document to get you to see how much you meant to me. I'm exhausted, Lex." I paused. "I'll sign and send you the papers on Monday."

"Please, Mil. I need you."

"I...can't. I..." My voice trailed off.

"I guess that's it, then." He lowered his head and sighed. "I'm not giving up, Mil. You're it for me."

With those last words, he walked toward the door.

Oh, God, this was really the end of us. My legs weakened, but I remained standing.

Could I do this? Could I let him go? He was it for me too.

I slid a hand over the slight bulge on my stomach. He'd picked me without knowing.

Merda, I was making the same mistake he'd made. I had to stop him. Reaching out, I took a step but then paused. This wasn't how I wanted to do it.

Slowly, I lowered to the floor and kneeled.

"*Master*. Don't go."

CHAPTER THIRTY

Master?" I repeated.

Lex stood by the door and remained quiet for what felt like an eternity and then spoke. "Mil, don't do this unless it's what you want."

"You're what I want. My husband and my Dom." Tears dripped from my eyes onto my thighs. "I was wrong. My heart can't endure living without you. I need you too much."

"Thank God." Lex turned, walked straight toward me, and crouched down, lifting my face up.

I hiccupped as I stared at the relief, hope, and love gazing at me.

"Shh. Don't cry, baby." He wiped the wetness from my cheeks with his thumb.

He slid his hands under my hair and to the back of my neck. "I don't think I want you to wear this necklace anymore."

He unclasped the chain and pulled the end holding his wedding band from the inside of my corset.

"Open your hand."

I followed his direction, and he dropped his ring in my palm. My breath accelerated.

Biting my lip, I closed my fingers around the ring. My lips trembled. We were giving each other a second chance.

His eyes shone with the same emotion I'd seen when we'd married ten years earlier. I brought his left hand up, sliding the ring onto his finger.

"For better or worse," I whispered.

"Till death do us part," he responded and cupped my face. "I love you."

I sniffed as more tears spilled down my cheeks. "I love you," I said, wrapping my arms around his neck. "God, I love you."

He held me close, burying his face in my hair. After a few minutes, Lex helped me to stand. "Come, time for me to play with my submissive."

His words sent goose bumps across my skin.

He strode out of the office, pulling me behind him.

We spoke no more words as he guided me along the hallways past the playrooms. He lifted his thumb to a reader panel, and a door opened in the wall.

"What's this?"

"The surveillance office. Carmen and Max built one in each of the clubs we partnered in."

"Wow," I exclaimed as we walked inside.

Glass made up the walls of the octagonal room, displaying all the large public playrooms. Each space had a couple or more in various stages of play, from bondage, wax play, and orgasm denial to ménage and full-on sex.

The room had a large desk in the back with monitors all around it. However, what surprised me was the spanking bench, Saint Andrew's cross, and the cabinets of equipment strategically placed in the room. For all intents and purposes, this was a voyeur's private playroom.

"I had no idea this was here." Then I remembered Arya mentioning seeing me and Lex performing a scene. "This is the type of room Max brought Arya to before they married."

Lex grinned. "The very kind where they watched me fuck you against the cross."

"You knew?"

"Yes." He smirked. "Max told me the day Arya ran away to South Africa."

"Oh." *Why did that turn me on?*

"My exhibitionist likes that idea."

My cheeks flushed. Why was I embarrassed? Lex had seen and done everything with me. The only difference was that I couldn't do it again. That was the old Milla.

He walked to where I stood. "No more public scenes. I enjoyed them in the past, but that phase of our lives is over. What we have isn't for spectators."

I nodded. "What we share is for us only."

"Now that we have an understanding"—he unbuttoned his shirt—"take everything off but your stockings, boots, and underwear. Then stand by the Saint Andrew's and wait for me."

"Wait." I moved to a wall containing a case of whips, opened the glass box, and selected a five-foot bullwhip made of soft, buttery leather. It was similar to the ones we'd used in the past. Then I walked back to Lex and offered the handle to him.

Lex kept his hands by his side. "Mil, I don't need it. I need you."

"But I give you permission." I offered the whip again.

"Baby, you don't have to prove anything to me. You're all I need."

My heart felt like it would explode. He'd willingly set aside something he loved if it meant my pain would ease.

"You don't understand. When I was in that gallery, staring at all those pictures of me, I realized that I'd spent the past year allowing my attackers to win. It wasn't the whip that scared me but the man wielding it." I lifted the coiled leather handle toward him. "I trust you with all of me. I won't let Jacob or Christof take away something beautiful we shared anymore."

"Are you sure?"

The change in his voice sent a shiver down my spine. "Yes."

He took the whip. "Follow the instructions I gave you, and then wait for me until I'm ready."

Adrenaline shot through me. From this moment on, he was no longer my husband. He was my Master.

My breath quickened and pussy throbbed as I unhooked my corset. My breasts spilled out and a groan echoed in the room. I glanced over my shoulder to find a hungry-eyed Lex watching every move I made while lounging on the sofa near the surveillance equipment.

"Do you want something to drink?"

"Yes. Water, please." I dropped the corset to the ground and slid the zipper of my short skirt down.

Lex raised a brow, then stood, walked over to the bar, and poured both of us a drink. He took a sip of his as he brought the glass to me.

Why was my request a surprise? 'Cause you love your wine, Mil.

No matter, I needed all my senses tonight, nothing to dull any of the sensations.

My skirt fell to the floor as he approached. I took the tumbler, swallowed deep, savoring the cool liquid as it quenched my parched throat and relaxed me.

"That's all you get."

I frowned, ready to object. It was only water, after all.

I handed him my glass and waited.

"Good girl. I half expected a smart remark."

When I didn't respond to his statement, he laughed. "Don't worry. I won't expect this to be a normal occurrence."

Smart-ass.

"Now to the cross." He trailed a finger over my naked breasts, along my shoulders, and then down my spine, guiding me to the Saint Andrew's.

My core spasmed as his heated touch marked me. Yes, this was my Master. Nothing would happen that I couldn't handle or didn't desire.

I positioned myself with my back against the wood.

Lex pulled a chain from the corner of the beam, then took one of my wrists and paused. "Are you sure?"

"Yes," I said without hesitation. If I wanted, he'd stop without any qualms. I was doing this for me, for us. "I trust you with everything. I…I love you."

Releasing the chain, he threaded his fingers through my hair and sealed our lips in an almost brutal kiss. Excitement filled me, and my skin tingled.

He'd awakened, my Dom. Even with all the things we'd done over the last few months, he'd held back. Now I'd given him permission to be himself.

"Lex," I murmured. "More."

He stepped away and *tsk*ed.

Merda, I was on fire. I couldn't get enough of him.

Taking my hands, he clamped one then the other. Then he kneeled in front of me. "Spread your legs."

I complied, and he shackled each to the cedar.

His breath grazed my thigh. "I can smell your arousal. I look forward to tasting that beautiful, bare pussy."

I hummed inside. We'd barely begun, and I was a panting mess. I expected some fear to petrify me, but all I felt was pure unadulterated desire for my Master.

"But not now."

I sagged against my bonds with disappointment.

"I think you will enjoy what I have planned just as much or possibly even more."

What could I enjoy more?

He stood and picked up the whip I hadn't seen him lay on the spanking bench and then placed it on the floor between my bound legs.

"Oh," I said without thinking.

He quirked a brow. "That's right. Oh."

With slow, precise movements, he finished unfastening his shirt. Every button he undid accelerated my heart rate.

I licked my lips. No matter how many times I'd seen him undress, I couldn't get enough of him. The wetness pooling between my legs increased. Thank goodness my underwear kept it in check, or my arousal would have dripped down my legs.

Lex pulled the shirt from his body and tossed it on the desk behind him. He approached me, his erection straining against his leather pants, then picked up the whip and touched the handle to my lips.

"Now we begin. Are you ready?"

I stared into pools of desire-clouded blue. "Yes, Master."

"Good, but one thing is missing."

I knew what it was, without him saying.

"I can't have you seeing what I do. I want you to anticipate and feel."

He covered my eyes with a mask, blocking my sight. Immediately my other senses fired. The woodsy aroma of the cedar tickled my nostrils, and I could almost taste the pleasure-pain awaiting me.

My skin prickled with both anxiety and excitement as I awaited his first touch. He cracked the whip in the distance, causing me to jump but igniting my already frantic body. I relaxed into the headspace my desire brought forth.

I was safe with Lex. I was loved.

"If only you could see how beautiful you look." The whip cracked again. "My sexy wife bound to the cross, skin flushed, lips swollen from my kiss."

"Master, please don't make me wait."

"As you wish."

A strike pierced the air, and at first, I felt nothing. Then a slow fire seared my hip and wrapped around, sending electricity to my throbbing pussy.

I gasped and arched. "More," I called.

He struck five more times, across the other thigh, over my breasts, against my arms, and around my hips. I waited for him to sear over my stomach, but he stopped.

The lingering sting flared my desire for more. *Not enough* was all I could think, but then I realized I'd actually spoken the words.

Lex ran a finger over my lace-covered cleft.

"Are you sure?" he teased, pulling the material to the side. He plunged two fingers into my pussy and pumped. My body bowed against the wood. My core spasmed as the hilt of the whip rubbed against my swollen clit.

Oh God, I have to come. Please don't stop.

"Now," he commanded, pumping faster, and I convulsed around him. He sealed our lips and pushed his straining erection against my body. "That's it, *a ghrá*. Ride it out."

The Irish in his voice thickened, and the arousal I hadn't come down from reignited. But before I erupted a second time, he pulled out and moved away from me. I heard his unsteady breath and smiled inside. He was affected as much as I was. The sound of the fridge opening and liquid filling a glass hit my ears.

"Tilt your head up." I obeyed and Lex poured cool water down my throat from his lips. I swallowed and moaned.

"I need you."

"I know, baby, but the next time you come will be from my whip."

My pussy quivered with excitement.

"No one will ever take away what we share again."

"Never again," I responded.

I wanted to see him, tell him how much I loved him, but he wouldn't remove the mask until he was ready.

"I'm going to go fast. Your skin will burn, but I won't leave any marks except the fading blush of the leather."

He didn't have to explain. I had no fear. This was my man. He'd protect me with his life, if necessary. "I trust you, Master. I love you."

Lex fisted my hair and yanked my head back. "Mine."

"Yes," I agreed as he poured his uncontrolled passion against my mouth. He bit my lip and pulled away.

"Fuck," I shouted. The strike surprised me. I hadn't anticipated he'd start so soon. The erotic sensation and the arousal of heat pulsed through me. Another landed on my breasts. I arched up with each strike.

More, I wanted to scream, but the haze filling my mind kept me from speaking.

He scored every part of my body except my abdomen and the one place I needed it most. My pussy throbbed and screamed for release.

Six stokes landed in succession, along my thighs, my arms, my chest, and my weeping center shuddered. I thrashed and tugged on the chain. I had to get closer to each strike.

"Please," I begged, tears soaking though the mask, but he ignored my plea. Another nine strikes landed. Like a lover's caress, not too hard, not too soft.

If he doesn't hit my clit or fuck me, I'm going to die.

"Are you ready?"

I pushed my pelvis out. "Yes, Master. I need…" Before I could finish, the whip landed across my aching center, and I detonated.

I screamed my release at the top of my lungs, arching and bucking against the Saint Andrew's.

Lex ripped my underwear from me and buried his cock deep inside me with one hard swoop.

We both groaned, and then he pounded into me.

"Master," I called.

He tore my mask from my eyes. "Lex," he demanded.

"Lex." I jerked against him, unable to meet each thrust. "My Lex, always."

He kissed me, and we erupted, milking each other's release until there was nothing left in us. I was free, no more Jacob, only Lex and me. I sighed as I came down from my orgasm and then rested my head on Lex's shoulder.

After a few more moments locked together, he pulled out of me with a reluctant groan. "Let me get you down."

He released me from my restraints and carried me to the sofa. I scanned the room and noticed all the glass walls blackened. He wanted privacy for us even if the others couldn't see us through the glass. I rested my head against his chest, and he rubbed my stomach. Hope bloomed at the possibility.

"Where do we go from here?"

"I would think it was obvious."

I lifted my head and frowned.

He laughed and tugged me back down. "Home. I don't care where that is, Boston or New York, as long as we're together. But first I have to ask you a question."

What could he want to know?

His palm slid over the bulge on my stomach. "How long have you known you were pregnant?"

Epilogue

Are you sure you'll be okay handling three? Maybe I should cancel the trip." I wrung my hands together and glanced at the bedroom behind me.

"I'm fine, Milla," Carmen insisted as she pulled me into the kitchen of her Hamptons waterfront estate. "One more isn't going to kill me. Besides, my two are the ones I have to worry about. Your princess is calm as a cucumber. And Caitlin's going to copilot this endeavor with me."

"I forgot she was coming into town today. I can't understand how you make it look so easy."

She shook her head at me and poured both of us a cup of coffee. "It's not easy, but I don't have a choice. No woman wants to be a single mom, especially to twins. Besides, once he finds out, my peace away from the city will end. I'll have no choice but to go back to New York."

"He needs to know. He has a right to know."

"Milla, I'm not discussing this, okay? All you need to know is that our families' histories will always come between us." She hiccupped. "I get it, but I won't put my boys in the middle of their issues." Her hand covered her stomach, and she peered away from me to look out the window.

God, Thomas is making the same mistakes I'd made.

"Sorry, Carm, I won't bring it up again."

She sniffed and turned back to me. "It's okay. I know you love me. Shit, I hate this. Even after six months, I'm still a hormonal mess."

"I'm in the same boat. Every time I think about being away for five days I get weepy."

"She's going to be fine. Go enjoy your time with your husband. This is your reward for pushing a twelve-pound baby out of your woo-hoo."

I winced. The memory of the sixteen-hour labor and fourth-degree episiotomy during the delivery sent a shudder down my spine. "Thank God Dr. Hardwick is a master with the needle and sewed up my goods nice and tight again."

"I told you she was a genius. Lex owes me."

The recovery from the delivery took longer than expected, but it gave us a chance to bond with our little Briana Violetta Duncan. Two and a half months post-delivery, we received the all clear from the doc to resume "marital relations," but with the exhaustion of a newborn, any sex time was vanilla at most.

"That he does. I just wish it were like before. You know?" I shook my head. "I know you don't want to hear about our sex life."

"It can't be any worse than hearing about my brother's from Arya."

"True, true. I won't get as graphic as her, but everything we do is tame. I need the kink."

"I'm not the girl for this advice. Remember, boy's family hates girl, boy threw away relationship with girl, left girl pregnant, now girl lives in self-imposed isolation with twin boys who never stop eating."

"Carmen, I'm being serious here." I cocked my hands on my hips and glared at her.

"Mil." She frowned back. "He's a Dom. He knows what he's doing. Do you think he went to all this trouble to arrange Briana's care if he planned to spend your vacation having vanilla sex? He can do that shit between feedings."

"I see your point." All of a sudden, nerves prickled my stomach. A murmured cry sounded from the baby monitor, and Lex's voice followed.

"Be good to your zia Carmen and zia Caitlin. Don't be like your mamma and give everyone a hard time."

Carmen busted out laughing, and I frowned.

"We'll see you in a week, princess. Let's hope your nosy mamma is ready as soon as I get downstairs."

His Dom voice vibrated over the last part of his statement.

"Merda." I hopped off the chair and raced to get my bag. "Stop laughing at me and help me get my shit together."

Carmen remained at the kitchen island, enjoying my panic. "No, I think you have it under control."

I glanced at the schedule I posted on the counter. "Do you think I forgot anything?"

"Mil, I have two kids of my own. If you forget anything, I've got it covered."

"I trust you. I'm just nervous."

Two hands crept around my waist, pulling me back. "Nothing to worry about, *a ghrá*. Bri's in good hands." He turned me in his arms and kissed the top of my head. "Time to go."

I peeked at Carmen, who waved. "I've got this. Go enjoy some monkey sex with your man."

"We plan to," Lex responded for me and led me out of the house and toward the waiting helicopter.

We remained quiet for most of the flight to the airport. I hadn't expected to feel so conflicted about leaving Bri. Lex tried to reassure me that it was normal, and my sisters-in-law were the same way with their babies.

After nearly twelve years together, we had our baby, and I was determined to be the mother I never had. Although, I had to admit my brothers and I weren't the easiest of kids to manage.

A giggled erupted as I remembered some of my childhood antics, and Lex raised a brow at me.

"Care to share what you find so funny?"

I smiled. "I was reminiscing about some of the chaos I caused my parents as a child."

Lex shuddered. "If Bri gets into even half the things your papa said you did, we are in trouble. And if she even thinks to dance on a table, I will send her to a convent until she turns twenty-five."

"You do remember, Arya and I met while I was at a convent school?"

"Never mind, I'm doomed." He drew my hand to his lips, helped me exit the helicopter, and led me toward our waiting plane.

I laughed. This was true happiness.

He stopped at the foot of the jet and tucked a strand of my hair behind my ear. "Ready?"

I nodded.

"Good. I have a few instructions for you."

Oh, the voice.

"The moment you climb onto the plane, you will go to our room, strip, and meet me in the lounge."

I licked my lips, and his eyes dilated as they followed my tongue's movement.

"The only clothing you will wear from this point forward will be your cover-up, and that is only to and from the plane when we land on the island. Is that understood?"

My core clenched in response to the thickening of his Irish brogue. I swallowed, and my arousal ignited. I'd waited over five months to play again, and now I would have a week of nothing but. "Yes, Master."

"Good."

I ascended the stairs and walked in a haze to the bedroom. I kicked off my heels as I shut the door, sat on the bed, and waited for liftoff. Fifteen minutes later, I stood, slid my jacket off my shoulders, and let it fall to the floor, followed by my dress and underwear. Reaching up, I loosened the knot holding my hair, and it tumbled down my back.

I strolled into the bathroom and freshened up my makeup. Surveying my body in the mirror, I smiled. My figure was back to my pre-baby form, with the added benefit of more pronounced curves. The ones I'd lost while in Italy. After a last touch of the perfume Lex loved, I was ready.

I opened the door and walked down the hall to the lounge. Lex sat on a loveseat, drinking a glass of cognac. His gaze locked with mine, and I nearly swallowed my tongue. The desire darkening his eyes gave me a boost of confidence.

I walked toward him with slow, precise steps, eating up everything about him. He'd removed his jacket, and the top two buttons of his shirt were undone. His face held the scruff of a day-old beard, giving him a rough, roguish appearance.

As I approached, he gestured to a pillow on the floor. "Kneel."

I followed his command and noticed both the leather whip on the arm of the chair and the growing erection lining the front of his designer pants.

"Do you want me to take care of that, Master?"

"Did I ask you to?"

Oh, he's really into Dom mode. I bit my lip. "No, sir."

"Keep your head down and spread those thighs. I want to see the pussy that belongs to me."

His coarse words excited me, and I complied.

"Good, now touch yourself."

I brought my fingers between my folds, caressing my swollen nub. I worked my clit until sweat sheened my forehead. Any moment now, he'd give me the command to come. Almost there, I tilted my head back.

"Stop."

My fingers stilled, and a whimper escaped my mouth, followed by a growl.

"Tsk-tsk."

"You suck." I pouted.

"No, soon, you'll suck."

I growled again.

A chuckle sounded over my head and he patted his thigh. "Remember I reward good behavior. Come here, brat."

I looked at him, and his gorgeous smile warmed me. I crawled over to where he sat, making sure I wiggled my ass the way he liked it. Once I reached him, I pushed his legs open, rubbed my face against his straining cock, and waited for him to give me further instructions.

He reached down, fisting my hair. "On second thought, I think I'll fuck you first."

"Anything you say, Master."

About the Author

Sienna Snow's love of reading started at a very young age with *Beezus and Ramona*. By the time she entered high school, a girlfriend had introduced her to Bertrice Small and Jude Deveraux, and an avid romance reader was born.

She writes sexy romance, some with a lot of heat and spice, and others with a bit of fantasy. Her characters represent strong women of different cultures and backgrounds who seek love through unique circumstances.

When she is not writing, traveling, or reading, she spends her time with her husband and two children.

You can learn more at:
SiennaSnow.com
Twitter @sienna_snow
Facebook.com/authorsiennasnow

CPSIA information can be obtained
at www.ICGtesting.com
Printed in the USA
LVOW12s1532191017
553030LV00001B/58/P